KISSI

Laura tilted her chin, her sm to speak with me again?"

Adam considered every aspect of her face and especially her lips, before coming to a mesmerized stop at those deep violet eyes.

"You are—"

The growl from deep within his throat was a new and fearful reaction. His mouth covered hers and he took a kiss without thinking. He swallowed her gasp and hitched her tight against him.

He waited for her shove, her push—her slap, but it didn't come. She kissed him back. Matching his need with equal fervor. She moaned into his mouth with a passion that sped his heart. Her hot tongue touched his.

Abruptly, she pulled back. Satisfaction, desire, and—dare he think it—need, stormed in the depths of her eyes. Her lashes, as dark as night, sparkled with tears that shone like diamonds.

Adam shook his head. "Who are you?"

She grinned and swiped her fingers under her eyes. "More woman than you could ever handle, Mr. Lacey."

She waved past him and disappeared into the darkness . . .

Books by Rachel Brimble

THE SEDUCTION OF EMILY

THE TEMPTATION OF LAURA

Published by Kensington Publishing Corporation

The Temptation
of Laura

RACHEL
BRIMBLE

KENSINGTON
Kensington Publishing Corp.
www. kensingtonbooks.com

KENSINGTON BOOKS are published by

Kensington Publishing Corp.
119 West 40th Street
New York, NY 10018

All Kensington titles, imprints, and distributed lines are available at special quantity discounts for bulk purchases for sales promotion, premiums, fund-raising, educational, or institutional use.

Special book excerpts or customized printings can also be created to fit specific needs. For details, write or phone the office of the Kensington Special Sales Manager: Kensington Publishing Corp., 119 West 40th Street, New York, NY 10018. Attn. Special Sales Department. Phone: 1-800-221-2647.

Kensington and the K logo Reg. U.S. Pat. & TM Off.

eISBN-13: 978-1-60183-088-3
eISBN-10: 1-60183-088-2

First Electronic Edition: February 2014

ISBN-13: 978-1-60183-221-4
ISBN-10: 1-60183-221-4

Printed in the United States of America

Chapter 1

Bath, England, 1896

Laura Robinson stared along the steep descent of Milson Street and fear for tomorrow skittered up her spine. The hazy October moon rose in the distance, announcing the end to another day of lost opportunity. The people of Bath milled around her. The gentry mixed with the poor and the marketers with the city's best tailors—an avalanche of profession and possibility. Would any of it ever be hers?

"Excuse me, love. Did you want one bag or two?"

She blinked and turned to the stallholder. The white-haired woman gripped a ladle of gleaming brown chestnuts.

"Two." Laura smiled. "If I can't take a bag for me and a bag for the most special person in my life, there isn't much point carrying on, is there?"

The woman returned her smile, revealing more gum than teeth before emptying the ladle full of nuts into a second paper bag. She twirled the ends and handed both bags to Laura with a flourish. Laura put some coins in the woman's outstretched hand. "Thank you."

"Enjoy." She turned to the gentleman waiting in line behind Laura. "Can I help you, sir?"

Duly dismissed, Laura put the bags into her basket along with the baking soda, flour, potatoes, and four measly carrots she'd managed to get for the lowest price possible as the shops closed for the day. She'd whip up some food for her and Bette for tonight and tomorrow. She exhaled a shaky breath. The day after would be dealt with soon enough.

Keeping her head bowed against the risk of recognition, Laura hurried on through the market, her skirts drifting atop the few puddles left after the early-evening downpour. The skies had opened on this unseasonably warm night, reminding her that fall would soon come to an end, leaving winter to stretch its gloom over the city. The next worry would be keeping her and Bette's "two-up, two-down" house warm enough so their fingers and toes weren't frozen upon waking.

She hurried along, fighting to clear her mind of the negative thoughts that had harangued her since the early hours. She passed Charlotte Square toward the theater, even though she and Bette lived on a much quicker route in the opposite direction. Guilt lingered as dreams of the impossible bloomed once more.

She should get back before Bette woke and found her gone. She didn't want her friend to worry a single moment in her current ailing state. Yet, Laura's dreams and aspirations burned like fire behind her ribcage and she continued ever closer to the theater.

If only she could . . . She silently berated herself. If only she could what? Be whisked away into a world so far from hers it was laughable? Heat pinched her cheeks. Lord knows, if she became an actress, she'd pay back every penny, every meal her friend had ever earned, stolen, and borrowed for her.

She'd take away their worries and have the money to pay the best physician in the whole of Bath to make Bette well again. She cursed the tears that stung her eyes. Her beloved friend had to get better. How would Laura go on without her most trusted mentor and protector by her side?

Irritation fanned her stupidity and she swiped her fingers beneath her eyes. Women like her didn't cry. They survived. They brought friends back from the brink of pneumonia to full-blown health. Crying was for people who'd lost everything. For people who thought their days were numbered. Not people like her and Bette.

She stopped at the steps of the Theater Royal. The lavish façade shone beneath the gas lanterns above the windowed doors, and the ruby red carpet of the foyer and the stairs glistened and sparkled with cleanliness and opportunity beyond. What promised excitement lay within those four walls!

The sepia fliers pasted to the billboards caught her eye. The current play featured Adam Lacey, a rising star and as handsome as they came.

Barely twenty-nine, with dark blond hair that curled at his collar and even darker chocolate brown eyes, he was an actor with the world at his feet. Tall, strong, and muscular, he wore an air of quiet confidence and possessed a flash of a smile that could curl a woman's toes.

She leaned forward to get a closer look and smiled. Darn, if the man didn't have the clear sparkle of a rogue in his sinfully dark eyes. Dragging her gaze from their careful, confident study, Laura sighed at the beauty of his costar's frock. She imagined it to be emerald green and made of the most luscious velvet. Monica Danes looked beautiful. What it would be to wear such a gown! They made an unfairly handsome pair—and she wished them all the future luck in the world.

Who was to say it wouldn't be her name on a billboard one day, starring opposite someone equally as handsome as Mr. Lacey?

She tipped his smiling image a saucy wink and grinned. Surely a man like him wouldn't mind treading the boards with a woman who'd once been an orange seller, step scrubber, glass collector, and since the age of fifteen . . . a whore.

She bit back a laugh. The man would no doubt run a mile from the likes of her. If not, she could be damn sure he'd toss her a coin to share a half hour of her time.

Laura lifted her shoulders. She could dream, couldn't she? Life could change in a single day. Wasn't that what Bette had told her ever since a brutal winter threw them together seven years ago, for the need of warmth and a shared corner under the shadow of Pulteney Bridge?

Sadness enveloped her. Yet, for all their efforts for a better life, a moral decision on Laura's part had left them once again struggling to keep a roof over their heads and food on the table. Their earnings had meant a comfortable life for a while—and now by doing the right thing, she'd caused hunger to knock inside their bellies once more. She tilted her chin. She refused to regret her decision to see a violent man imprisoned.

"Excuse me, young lady. May we get past? I assume you're not going in?"

She turned. The man stared her up and down, his face twisted into an expression of one surveying a dog turd. She scowled, but when his eyes met hers, she plastered on a wide smile.

"No, sir, I'm not." She glanced at the woman on his arm and her smile stretched to a grin. *Well, well, well.* "Hello, Ellen. Going up in the world, I see. Good luck to you. Never say that once you're a whore, there's not the possibility of becoming an upper-class whore, eh?"

"Why you—" The man lifted his hand as if to strike her.

Laura deftly caught his wrist in hers. "I don't think so, do you, sir?"

Their eyes locked as his arm tensed in her grasp. He pulled away and tossed her a violent glare. Satisfaction warmed her blood as Laura stepped back and gestured with a wave toward the door.

"You have a good evening, sir." She turned to her old friend. "And you, of course, Ellen. I'm mighty happy for your promotion."

Ellen lifted her nose in the air as though smelling for her next un-suspecting victim and flounced inside with her newest and maybe even exclusive client. Laura smiled through the glass doors until they disappeared up the grand carpeted staircase.

Exhaling a long breath, she hurried toward home as a strange fire simmered inside. Possibility was everywhere. Especially in a city like Bath. The theater. Upper-class gentlemen willing to spend money on a whore and a play. Her mind raced. She couldn't help thinking what was good enough for Ellen could be just as good for her. . . .

"Bugger." Laura sucked in a breath and put her cut finger into her mouth to stem the bleeding. "This knife's sharper than a pirate's sword. What did you sharpen it on, Bette? Your tongue?"

Silence.

Having expected an immediate retort, she spun around. "Bette?"

Fear ran up the back of Laura's neck as she rushed toward the bed where Bette lay, her thinning body as still as stone beneath the tangled sheets.

"No, no, no." The mumbled words tumbled from Laura's mouth

as she leaned over Bette and pressed the back of her hand to her friend's perspiring forehead. When she'd arrived home, Bette's skin wore the red flush of fever; now it shone a pale, pasty gray. "Bette? Bette, please. Don't do this to me."

Seconds passed like minutes before Bette emitted an explosive coughing fit that wracked her body and almost shook Laura off the side of the bed. Bette's spittle dashed Laura's cheeks and she hastily swiped at them, glancing at her fingers. She released her held breath when they came away clear rather than bloodied.

"Oh, love." She gathered Bette in her arms and smoothed her hand over her back in gentle circles. "Come on, now. It's all right. Everything's going to be all right."

Slowly, the coughing passed and Bette collapsed against the pillows. Her once-vibrant blue eyes were shadowed with deep charcoal smudges beneath, her once-ruby-painted lips so pale they were hardly visible. "You know as well as I do, nothing ain't right. I need to get out of this bloody bed and get some work."

Laura shook her head. "Don't talk daft. We'll manage. Things have a way of sorting themselves out. Isn't that what you're always telling me?"

"And look where that got me. God saw fit to strike me down with pneumonia. Bam, there you go, Bette Windsor, things have bleedin' well changed."

Laura tightened her jaw and pushed off the bed. "Stop with the sassing. This isn't like you. Don't let this damn pneumonia beat you." She fisted her hands on her hips. "We're going to get through this."

"Yeah? And how's that with me not working because no man wants to come within fifty feet of me, and you not working because you're too scared you'll find me dead when you come out of that back bedroom. We're going to die of starvation or living rough on the streets come November."

Laura glared. "I'm not leaving you. Not until I know you're better."

"And what happens if I don't get better?"

Her words were no different than what Laura had asked herself a million and one times over the last month. The signs were clear. Bette was fading fast, and if the number of men, women, and children who had been taken by bronchitis leading to pneumonia was anything to go by, it would kill her too. The lack of color in Bette's face over the last twenty-four hours sent a bolt of ice through Laura's blood, but she had to stay strong.

"We'll be all right. I just haven't figured out what to do yet. I don't want you listening to me grunting and gasping my way through the next bit of cash when you should be resting. Something'll come up. We're not in a situation where I have to go back to dropping my drawers in an alley either. At least not yet."

Bette's gaze hardened. "I ain't asking you to do that."

"I know you're not. You know what the streets are like as well as I do. I'll find another way."

The atmosphere in the dimly lit room pressed down on Laura's chest like a lead weight. Everything was going from bad to worse, and her friend dying would be the last straw after a year of endless struggle. It had been an age since she'd stood up in court and testified against one of her clients—thus sending their regulars scarpering like rats back to their damn upper-class drainpipes.

A ruckus drifted through the open window from the alley outside their door. Someone kicked over something metal, followed by a woman's shouting and the slap of a hand on flesh. A child cursed the sky blue and then nothing.

Laura smiled. "Life goes on, eh?"

Bette grinned. "It certainly—"

A cheery whistle and a knock at their door froze them. Laura stared at her friend. No one had knocked at their door wanting business for close on a week. She glanced at the carriage clock on the mantel. Certainly nobody past nine on a chilly October evening.

She slowly pushed to her feet. "Who—"

"Answer it." Bette lifted her chin and smoothed the bedclothes over her body. "Take him in your room. We need the money, darlin'. You'll have to leave me. Let's hope he's a quickie. Do what you have to and get him back out there. It's you I'm worried about, not me. You're wasting away. We need money. You need to eat."

Laura stood and stared through the living-room doorway to the bolted front door. The silhouette of a man's head and hat showed through the misted square of glass. "That's not a client."

Bang, bang. The caller hammered on the door.

Laura put her finger to her lips for Bette to button it and moved across the room. Snatching up the plank of wood she kept behind the dresser, she gripped it in both hands and crept toward the window.

"Open up, Laura, my girl. I know Bette's poorly and you need me." His voice drifted through the locked front door.

Laura cursed and squeezed her eyes shut. Malcolm Baxter was the last person she needed. A pimp to at least thirty other prostitutes who worked in and around the lower end of Bath. She and Bette hadn't needed him for the last five years and they wouldn't start now. She opened her eyes and faced Bette. Her friend shook her head.

Laura smiled. There was desperate and there was *desperate*. With a curt nod, she inhaled a long breath. "I don't need you any more today than I did yesterday. So get away from here and stay away. I know where you are if I change my mind."

"Everyone knows what you did, Laura. You ain't gonna get no more business when people know you shopped a client to the law."

"He deserved it. I've got no regrets. Now get out of here."

"You'll regret it when Bette dies because you can't get work to pay the doctor to come see her. You'll regret it when you have to move out of here and find yourself sleeping in a shop doorway."

His words slipped into Laura's blood. "Get lost."

"There's nowhere else in this city you can afford, Laura. You'll be homeless, mark my words." Malcolm laughed and slapped his hand to the door. "I'll come by again tomorrow."

His silhouette moved from the glass in the door and disappeared. She put down the wood and peered through the scrap of material at the window. Malcolm sauntered down the alley, tipping his hat to the beggars at his feet without tossing them a meager coin from his overflowing pockets.

She stepped away from the window and turned to Bette. "He's gone."

"Until tomorrow."

"Tomorrow is a new day."

"Yeah, and what will we do with it?"

The Theater Royal and Adam Lacey filtered through her mind. "I don't know yet, but giving in to Malcolm Baxter isn't the answer. I'll work something out." She moved to her friend's side and smoothed Bette's hair, damp with perspiration, from her face. "Let me warm up some broth and we'll worry about tomorrow when the sun comes up, all right?"

Bette's eyes drifted closed, her face pale with sickness and exhaustion. "He's right, you know."

Laura frowned. "Baxter?"

Bette nodded. "I wish we didn't need him, but I'm dying and it ain't making my passing easier knowing you'll be all alone with him sniffing around like a dog in heat." She opened her eyes.

Wisdom shone in her friend's gaze. Did Bette know? Did everyone know when their time was nigh? Had her father known? Her mother?

She shook her head, a single traitorous tear breaking over her lashes. "Don't say that."

"We have to think what to do. And think fast. My time's coming."

Ignoring the pain that slashed across her heart, Laura busied her shaking fingers by straightening the bedclothes, tucking them in warm and secure around Bette's thinning body. "Don't be daft. You're no more likely to give in to this than I am that bastard Malcolm Baxter."

Bette cupped a hand to Laura's jaw. "Look at you. You've got hair the color of polished bronze and eyes more violet than blue. If I had my way, you wouldn't be whoring at all. There never should've been a day you laid down with a man without his heart wanting to worship every inch of you. Find something else to do with yourself because I can't leave you until I know you're all right."

Taking her hand, Laura brought Bette's knuckles to her lips. "That's fine by me, because I don't want you to leave. Ever."

Bette's breath rasped as she huffed out a laugh. "I'll be leaving. Just not in peace until I know you're looked after."

Laura stared as tears fell from Bette's eyes and crawled like liquid silver down her cheeks. Seven years. They'd met on the street and never been apart since. In all that time, Laura had never seen Bette cry or falter. Her friend was dying.

Silently, she drew her legs onto the bed and gathered Bette in her arms. She laid her head beside Bette's on the pillow as they each lapsed into silent thoughts, fears, and plans. The minutes passed and eventually Bette's breathing slowed to the soft murmurs of slumber. Laura stared at the ceiling as twilight streaked through the window, casting the room in a soft semidarkness. Tomorrow she'd find work. New work. No more whoring. No more men.

Bette was right. Enough was enough.

Chapter 2

Adam Lacey moved in a ghost-like state toward his dressing room at the Theater Royal. His strained smile fixed in place and his heart beating fast, he continued forward, strangely numb to the shoulder slaps and handshakes he received from his fellow actors, the director, and the producer.

The corridor was rife with jovial laughter and chatter. The gas lanterns cast a golden hue, lighting the delighted faces and illuminating the company's satisfaction. Yet, he couldn't shake the feeling his performance could've been better. *Should've* been better.

He entered his dressing room, shut the door, and dropped back against it.

With the matinee over, only tonight's performance and one more week remained before the end of the show. The month-long run of performances had been better received than the company could have anticipated. The rave reviews in newspapers and favorable caricatures in shop windows all over town were testament to the play's success.

That was all well and good, but after the final performance, then what? He had no more work lined up. No producers waiting in the wings to grab him hungrily by the collar before anyone else thought to do so.

He pushed away from the door. His name was on the billboards outside the theater. His face graced the pamphlets. Yet, neither did anything toward alleviating the panic and fear his success could be ripped from him in a heartbeat.

Weeks of scraping around for new work, auditions, and rejection stretched in front of him, and fear clutched like a fist in his stomach. Where did he go next? How many people had told him the theater business was no better than a continual fistfight? Bare knuckles and blood were part of their world—success did not come to an actor taking handouts. Hard work and tenacity gave the only chance of longevity in the acting world.

He closed his eyes as self-hatred swept over him in a hot wave.

Were shortcuts not what he chased? Was that not the person he had become? Someone so impatient for elevation, he had made himself a rich widow's man-whore.

"What the hell am I doing?" Adam snapped his eyes open and snatched the powdered wig from his head. He slung it haphazardly upon the stand on his dressing table and dropped onto a blue velvet seat.

The steady thump of a headache snaked through his temples and he covered his face with his hands. Lady Harvard's money had paved the way for this job but, once again, guaranteed nothing. Taking her benefit had done little more than prove his lowly moral value. Was he not reinforcing everything his parents ever said about the theater business? That it was seedy and unsavory, and had very little to do with talent and hard work.

Raising his head, he looked to the hefty sheaf of papers stacked at the far corner of the table. Drawn together in a neat and tidy pile, and lovingly tied with string, they represented his dreams on parchment. His play. His manuscript. His soul's work. He ran his hand over the top sheet, before gripping the string until his knuckles showed white.

"One day you'll see the light of day, Lucinda. One day."

Frustration furled in his gut and desperation scratched at his sanity. Two years of putting pen to paper and he had created a heroine of such beauty and muster, tenacity and strength, she resided inside him like a living, breathing woman of flesh and consequence. Her story of struggle against adversity would bring him fortune one day. He was sure of it. He had to believe as much or he had nothing.

Standing abruptly, Adam yanked open the buttons on his waistcoat and strode to the wardrobe. Quickly removing his costume, he hung it neatly and turned away. He needed to get out for a while and take in some air. Early that morning, the scent of autumn hung heavy in the trees and the chill of a softly blowing breeze had whispered against his face. Now, as the clock on the fireplace mantel showed five, the bracing evening air would undoubtedly do much to clear his head.

Naked, he sat at the dressing table and seized some cold cream and a cloth. When he'd roughly scrubbed his face clean of makeup, he steadfastly avoided his reflection. There was no need to see himself laid bare. It was painfully clear what he'd find staring back at him.

A failure. A chameleon. An aspiring star who was little more than Lady Harvard's plaything.

Knock, knock.

Adam shot to his feet. Cupping his manhood, he rushed to the wardrobe.

"Who's there?" He grappled his legs into a pair of breeches.

"It is me, silly." The doorknob rattled. "Open up. I need to see you. I have missed you even though you have barely been a few feet away from me for the last two, excruciatingly long hours."

He closed his eyes against the fresh slash of pain that assaulted his temple. Lady Harvard. His investor. His believer. His lover.

"I am in the middle of dressing." He yanked a shirt from the wardrobe. "Why don't I meet you in the lobby for a glass of bubbly? I will not be long." He grimaced. The smile in his voice was strained and clearly forced.

The doorknob rattled again. "Open the door, Adam. Now."

Her chilly tone made him scowl. He was not in the mood for her histrionics, demands, or unique technique of ensuring she got her way. His penis shriveled as he stared at the door.

What was he doing? Why was he bowing and scraping to a woman who treated him as little more than a lapdog? He narrowed his eyes, wishing his glare would burn a hole through the door and straight into Lady Harvard's damn snooty nose.

Pride swelled behind his ribcage. There had to be another way. He worked hard. He had vision. He inhaled a long breath as his next step became clear. One way or another, he would manage without Lady Harvard's monetary support. It was time he moved on.

He strode forward and opened the door. She swept into the room before he had time to draw another breath.

"At last." Lady Annabel Harvard strode directly to his dressing table, her lavish sapphire blue skirts brushing the floor, her eyes flitting left and right. "I thought you might be hiding a woman in here."

He gripped the doorknob. "And if I was?"

She spun around, her livid green gaze shooting spears of rancor. "I beg your pardon?"

Adam shoved the door with his palm; it banged shut, and he came toward her. Determination burned inside. Anger and dented pride hummed through his veins, making him want to hold his head high and take back control. How had he succumbed to such a pathetic way of living for so long?

He halted inches away from her and satisfaction swept through him when she stepped back.

Her cheeks flushed pink and she swallowed. "Whatever is the matter with you?"

"I asked you a question. What of it if I chose to have a woman, a lover . . . a whore in my room?"

She huffed out a laugh. "Are you drunk?"

Adam smiled. "Drunk?"

"Yes, Adam, drunk." She moved past him, opening the space between them. She played her fingers over the thick braid of blond hair that lay over her breast. "I can see no other reason for you to be acting so beastly."

"As opposed to agreeing to your every whim, bringing you every drink or refreshment? As opposed to bringing your body to pleasure so you shout my name when the bedroom door is closed to the rest of society?"

For a long moment she said nothing, her mouth opening and closing in comedic rapidity. Then the inevitable tears glazed her eyes.

Adam sighed at the ceiling and turned before the onslaught of her dramatics filtered his conscience. His heart hammered with guilt that he would speak to a lady—even this *lady*—in any way other than respectfully. He closed his eyes. He had no other choice if he was to break the web she had wound around him with promises of escalation and fortune.

He was a fool. A fool who had been blinded by impatience.

She sniffed. "I assume you feel the play did not go well this afternoon."

He gripped the back of the chair at his dressing table. "It went well, so I'm told." He faced her. "That is not why I am being this way. I want out of this . . . arrangement, Annabel. I will find my own way. It was a mistake. My mistake. I should never have accepted your help this year past."

"Why on earth are you saying these things? I love helping you. . . . I love being with you. I do not support you out of the goodness of my heart. I believe in you."

"That may be, but from now on, I want to see my successes achieved by my own merits, rather than by what doors your money and name can open."

"But, Adam . . ." She rushed forward and clasped his hand to her breast. "How can this be wrong? You enjoy making love to me. You enjoy what I can give you. Do not walk away from it. I can make the world see your art for the brilliance it is. You know I can."

The soft cushion of her ample bosom heaved beneath his palm, but it did nothing to excite him. Realization dawned. The previous passions he had shared with her had been based on nothing but the potential of the promised success she claimed was at every corner.

He snatched his hand away. "I want you to go. Leave me." He softened his tone when a single tear left her eye. "Please."

"This is silly. You are feeling down and defeated merely because the play is coming to an end. We will find you more work. In the meantime, I will provide for you. There is no need—"

"There is every need." Irritation flared hot and fast in his abdomen, and he marched to the door. "There is every need because of the very word you have just spoken."

She frowned. "What word?"

"Provide, Annabel. I do not want you or anyone else *providing* for me." He yanked open the door. "Now go. Please."

She stood immobile. The tension weighed heavy on Adam's chest as he waited. Noise and laughter filtered into the room from the corridor. The clinks of glasses and the popping of corks offered little comfort or consolation to the fear that would not be silenced inside him.

"Fine." She snatched her purse from the chair beside her. "I will go. I will leave you to your melancholy. I will be waiting at the Rooms for supper and drinks after this evening's performance. We will talk this through and you will see sense."

"I will not be there."

She halted at the door. Her eyes darkened with anger and impatience. "Of course, you will. How can you not be? You are the show's star. People will expect you." She gripped his arm. "People of influence. Whatever has happened for you to risk throwing everything away, you must quash it and quash it now before you make the biggest mistake of your career."

He shook his head and pulled his arm from her grip. "Go, Annabel. Leave me be."

After another moment's hesitation, she left and Adam swung the door closed. He walked to his dressing table and looked into the mirror. Euphoria rushed through his blood and for the first time in weeks, he smiled.

Later that evening, adrenaline pumped through Adam's blood as he glanced toward the audience. The theater was packed to the rafters. The aisles, pit, and boxes overflowed with smartly dressed gentlemen and women mixing and blending with brightly dressed whores, ragged street thieves, and drunks. Some there to see the play; others to make a dime.

His smile faltered as his parents' disproval of his vocation seeped into his mind once more. Were the patrons there secretly wishing he would go wrong too? Prove himself a fraud who in reality couldn't act at all. . . .

He swallowed and widened his smile as the scene dictated.

Concentrate, you imbecile. Concentrate. You are a star. A star destined for London's West End. This is just the beginning. . . .

"You are my love, my savior, my all. Elisa, marry me." He dropped to one knee, grasping his costar's hand.

She clutched her hand to her ample bosom, her dark blue eyes shining with unprecedented joy. "Yes, of course, yes. A million and one yeses."

Adam leaped to his feet and clutched her into an embrace, his mouth covering hers.

The curtain fell for intermission.

He met Monica Danes's smile before she wrapped her arms around his waist, her cheek settling onto his chest. "You are Bath's jewel, Adam. You make this theater what it is."

He stole his arm around her shoulders and led her from the stage, exhaling a heavy breath. "I am not so sure about that. I have nothing else lined up once we wrap the show, and my money is dwindling badly."

She came to an abrupt halt and stared into his eyes. "Then you need to swallow your pride and rent something smaller than your current house. Show your parents you are not afraid of making sacrifices if it means you can continue to do what you love."

He clenched his jaw. "This has nothing to do with them."

Monica lifted her eyebrow. "Really? Then why do you talk about them all the time? My parents do not give me a second thought anymore and the action is reciprocated. Where is it written that children owe their parents anything? You need to do what is necessary before you end up with nothing."

He clenched his jaw. "I am doing my best."

"Good, because you're a talented actor. Moreover, you are the nicest, kindest man I have ever met. Someone, somewhere will snatch you up in a heartbeat. I promise." She pressed a hasty kiss to his cheek. "Now, I must rush before callback. The ladies' room beckons."

He stared after her as she disappeared down the steps and along the corridor. Five years younger, female and talented, Monica would not know what it was to be rejected and praying for work for a long time yet. Her words of flattery were more flannel than fact. Oh, he drew the women. The wealthy widows like Lady Harvard looking for company and money to spend, but he wasn't drawing the eye of a producer. From this day on, that would change.

Something was afoot. Something big enough that God had given him the push to rid himself of his benefactor and the grime that coated his conscience and good sense.

"We are back onstage in ten, everyone. Onstage in ten!"

The harassed call of the stage manager penetrated Adam's self-pity and he blinked, pulling back his shoulders. His ambition would forever override his fear. Onward and upward. Something would come along. If it did not, he was not averse to doing manual labor until something did. Theater was his life—and he would do anything to keep it so.

After a visit to the makeup chair and the bathroom, he was ready for the second curtain call. Inhaling a deep breath, he waited in the wings, his spine ramrod straight, his confidence renewed. He would not allow another moment of negativity to seep in him. He was on the precipice of something life changing. It simmered in his blood. Something would soon happen to turn that simmer into a burning flame.

The orchestra struck up with a bang and a crash, the curtain rose, and he ran onstage. The music filled his soul and the audience applause licked at his ego. People paid good money for an exemplary show, and there had not been a single afternoon or night he had not delivered just that. He addressed the audience and began his lines.

"If only hope rose at the same time each day as does the sun . . ." He stopped, further words catching in his throat.

She stood a little way from the front.

Her eyes alert and her smile lifting the corners of her mouth in such a way he could not be sure if she enjoyed or mocked him. Her soft study drilled through his chest and scratched at the place beneath.

My God. It is her. It is Lucinda.

Their gaze met and her smile slipped. Her eyes grew wide and she stumbled backward, apparently as dumbstruck as he.

"My Lord, is everything all right? You have paled awfully."

He snapped his head around. Monica dipped her head as she prompted him, the line improvised but clear in its message. Adam stared, his mind racing.

Talk, man. Talk. Act. For the love of God.

His heart pounded and his legs trembled. Somehow or other, he found his place and resumed his role. Everything inside wanted to look at the beautiful stranger again. To make sure she had not left. If she had, how would he find her in a city as big as Bath? Panic bled with excitement as he threw himself into this scene and the next, determined to finish the play as he always did. With his best.

The second half passed in a blur and he manically scanned the crowd as he took his final bow. She had gone. Nowhere to be seen. The curtain dropped. The assembled cast erupted into a furor of congratulations as Adam fought the urge to run into the audience to search for the girl who would play his Lucinda.

Come hell or high water, he would find the woman with the eyes as big as a doe's and hair the color of burnished bronze.

Chapter 3

Laura topped off her and Bette's glasses with a tot of ale from the bottle she'd picked up on the way home from the theater. It was probably an extravagance too far after the cost of the theater ticket, but life was taking a good turn and they deserved to celebrate. Exhilaration penetrated every inch of her body. What a place the Theater Royal had been! What a future it could hold for her. She took a slug from her glass before setting it down on the table. She could barely sit still for the excitement running through her veins.

"It's the answer, Bette." She grinned. "I know deep in my bones the Theater Royal holds the answer to our problems."

A rare light twinkled in Bette's eyes along with the flush of alcohol at her cheeks. "You look fit to burst. What in God's name happened while you were there? You see the queen or something?"

Adam Lacey's image rushed into Laura's mind, and she pushed it aside as she stood and twirled around, her arms wide. "I saw my future."

"On the stage? I'm not surprised. I see the way you gawp at that place every time we pass." Bette laughed. "You've got dreams bigger than the ocean, my girl."

Laura swallowed. Was she really that transparent? She waved her hand. "Don't talk daft. I'm talking about the laughter, the happiness, and the opportunities. Seeing Ellen a couple of days ago, dressed to the nines and preening like the cat that got the cream, was just the tip of it." She grinned. "God, there were whores everywhere. They were clasping the arms of gentlemen just as blatant as can be. Sitting

on their laps and sucking orange juice from their lips. Lord only
knows what their hands were doing." She winked.

"And that's what put such a smile on your face?"

Laura nodded. "Yes, because they weren't dressed in gaudy, flashy
cast-offs. They were dressed like ladies. Ladies with feathers in their
hats and jewels at their throats. Can you imagine? These men they're
escorting are paying for that. Paying to be seen with a well-dressed
whore. I knew it went on, but my God, to see it in reality was something else."

"It's still whoring, whichever way you look at it." Bette took a sip
of her drink. "Granted, I'd rather think of you rubbing shoulders with
gentry than with the likes of Malcolm Baxter, but still, didn't we
agree there are other ways of earning?"

Laura swiped her drink from the table and took another sip.
"Either way, I'm going back there tomorrow."

"To do what?"

"To find what the place has to offer *me*."

"You're thinking of finding one of those gentlemen for yourself,
ain't you?"

"Not necessarily." Laura glanced toward the window. How could
the idea to net the exclusive protection of a wealthy gentleman not
have passed through her mind before? Lord knows, whoring was the
only thing she knew for sure she was good at.

She faced Bette and shrugged. "I'm considering it, but that don't
mean I'll do it."

The minute she stepped into the theater, it was as though she'd
come home. Found where she was supposed to be. Never in her
twenty-two years of gracing God's earth had such a sense of belong-
ing swept her soul. The hustle and bustle of people around her, the
smell of rose water mixed with cigars, and the faint hint of alcohol
seeped into her pores and lit her ambition.

She drew in a breath. "I felt different when I was there."

"Different?" Bette frowned. "What sort of different?"

Laura smiled. Always her protector. "Like I belonged there. Like
I could spend every day and night inside those walls and never be
unhappy."

"I see." Bette shuffled back against the pillows, her gaze wary.

"I know something can happen for me if I can just find a way in."
She sighed. "All I'm saying is, if there's no other sort of jobs going
when I get there, I might need to find one of those wealthy gentlemen to pave the way for a while."

Bette's intelligent, rheumy eyes bored into hers and Laura steeled
herself, waiting for her friend's ever-growing cynicism. It was as
though, with every ailing breath Bette took, a little more of her
friend's positivity faded. She wouldn't let Bette convince her the
theater held little more than velvet curtains and costumes.

Bette slowly sipped her ale, her gaze steady above the mug's rim.
"I think you might be right."

Surprise jolted Laura and she stared. "You do?"

Bette emitted a croak of laughter and set her mug on the table
beside her. "I do. I think you'll find more than a gentleman there. I
think you'll find your life's destiny."

"What?" Laura snorted. "I'm not talking mystics and fancy
clothes. I'm talking good, hard work and paid in kind."

"Did you watch the show?"

Heat seared her cheeks. Damn it. The woman knew what Laura
thought before she did half the time. "Well, I saw some of it. How
could I not?"

"And what did you make of what you saw?"

She clasped her hands together, lest Bette see how they shook. "I
made nothing of it."

Bette lifted an eyebrow. "Nothing of the actors?"

"Nothing in particular."

"Nothing of the delectable Adam Lacey?" Bette winked.

Laura glared. "No."

The silence stretched out, but she refused to fill it. Bette might
know she'd stared at the actor's picture. So what? Hadn't a million
and one other women done the exact same thing?

She couldn't possibly guess how her feet had welded to the floor
like it was coated with melted wax when Adam Lacey met her eyes.
Bette couldn't know how when he looked at her, it was the first time
in forever Laura had stood before a man emotionally naked, vulnerable, and entirely his for the taking.

Bette cleared her throat. "Sing the song, Laura."

"What song?" She squeezed her eyes shut. *No, no, no.*

"Any song you heard there tonight."

She pulled back her shoulders. "Why would you want me to sing?"

"Because that's what you were born to do, my darling. You sing and move, dance and hum whenever you're not whoring, washing, wiping, or cleaning. You don't need to go to that theater for a gentleman, you need to go there and put yourself onstage. It's where you belong."

Bette grimaced and collapsed onto the bed, sucking in an audible breath.

Laura rushed to help her. "You're tired. Lie down and get some rest. We'll talk more in the morning."

"I'll rest when your voice is ringing in my ears and not before." Bette coughed, her breath crackling horribly beneath her ribs. "Sing me a ballad from the show. Send me to peaceful slumber with that sweet voice of yours in my head."

"Bette—"

"Please. Show me I know what I'm talking about."

Bette's eyes closed and her face fell into repose.

Tears smarted Laura's eyes and she swiped them away, her hand shaking. No tears, no fear. "Fine. There was a ballad."

A soft smile. "I know."

Laura inhaled a long breath and infused herself in the role so beautifully portrayed by the wonderful Monica Danes. She opened her mouth and the ballad's lyrics drifted like sweet oxygen from her lungs.

"You are the only one I see. The only one I long to hold. . . ."

As she closed her eyes, the orchestra resounded in her head. She smoothed her hands over her imagined gown of gold and scarlet velvet, and lifted her fingers to the pearls in her hair. Around and around she turned, her heart breaking for the coveted love of a man out of reach. A man encapsulated in the gorgeous form of Adam Lacey.

Opening her eyes, she stared in starry-eyed wonder around her. Gone were the bland walls and rickety furniture of her and Bette's abode. Instead, there he stood, high above her upon a stage festooned in exquisitely painted scenery lit by the golden hue of lanterns. Adam

Lacey's eyes met hers, and he stared as though she was the most beautiful woman in the whole of Bath and beyond. . . .

Heat suffused Laura's body and attraction pulled at her center. Oh, to have him hold her and speak those blessed lines!

She blinked and snapped her mouth closed.

Panic galloped through her blood. She and Bette needed food and money, not love and fantasy.

"Bette, this is madness."

Her friend's soft breathing floated over and Laura released her held breath. Bette slept.

The following night, Laura's nerves jangled as she shifted from one foot to the other outside the Theater Royal. The crowds waiting in line moved and chattered around her as they waited for the doors to open. The matinee performance was half the full ticket price, but it was still money she and Bette could ill afford to spend. Laura tightened her jaw. No, she wouldn't think that way. This was an investment.

If she wanted a job in the theater—or a gentleman of the theater— to keep Malcolm Baxter from their door, they had to put a bit of money out first. Clutching her purse, she breathed deeply in an effort to calm the nerves bouncing like a million rubber balls through her belly. She didn't know if she was more nervous about netting an unsuspecting gentleman or seeing Adam Lacey onstage again.

The look in his eyes from the night before had yet to leave her recollection for a minute. It was as though he knew her. As though he stared at a ghost. His eyes had grown wider and wider until his mouth dropped open and his body turned rigid. Why had he stared at her that way? There was as much chance of him knowing her as her knowing one of the royal princes.

A murmured cheer up ahead shook Laura from her thoughts and she stood on tiptoes to see what the commotion was about. The line was moving forward. The doors had opened.

She pressed her hand to her stomach and stepped forward. *No turning back now.*

Once inside, she resisted the urge to gape and gawk as she had before and forced nonchalance into her stance and demeanor. Pleased she'd chosen to wear her best frock from her wardrobe of relinquished cast-offs, she glanced about her. At least she seemed to be holding up to the standard.

She might not have the riches of the wealthy ladies with intricately beaded dresses and hats of the most beautiful design, but she didn't stand out as a street urchin amongst them either. Swallowing her nerves, she planted on a smile. She might be a whore, but tonight she sought more. Who knew what jobs the theater had to offer? There had to be something.

Clutching her ticket, she moved through the crowd into the theater proper and took a seat close to the exit. Her place by the aisle meant she could observe the comings and goings of the audience with minimal effort or the need for anyone to think her glances odd or suspect. She looked to the huge clock mounted on the wall above her. Another hour before the main feature was due to begin.

Plenty of time to survey the staff as they weaved among the theatergoers. Maybe she could catch the friendly eye of someone willing to help her secure a position. More and more people entered the auditorium, and even though several men and women appraised her through narrowed eyes, no one approached her. A relieved breath shuddered from between her lips.

At least she didn't look as though she was there scouting for business.

Worrying her bottom lip, she glanced around the theater once more. Something worthwhile had to happen that afternoon—no way in the world she could afford another ticket to return.

Maybe she should stretch her legs and have a wander. She had a good vantage of the people coming to and from the auditorium, but where was the staff? She glanced upward toward the boxes adjacent to the stage where waiters served glasses of champagne. She looked left and a woman offered some sort of confectionary to a richly dressed couple peering down their noses at her.

She could do that, couldn't she?

Laura Robinson could do anything she set her mind to. Standing, she left her ticket on the seat to reserve it and made her way down the aisle to meander across the walkway in front of the stage.

Smiling demurely, she fought her nerves as her confidence faltered.

Had her testimony against a client in court last year traveled along the grapevine and through the doors of the theater too? Did people know what she really was? She pulled back her shoulders. She was being paranoid. No one knew her here. She moved from the stage and strolled up the opposite aisle, her trained eye waiting for the slightest interest of a potential manager.

Her shoulder bumped something solid. She turned and came face-to-face with a young woman selling refreshments.

"Pardon me, miss." The woman tilted her basket. "Can I interest you in my wares? I've got oranges, nuts, sweets or chocolate . . ."

Laura stared. "My God, Tess?"

The girl's eyes widened. "Laura? Laura Robinson? You look fantastic."

Dropping her basket at her feet, Tess opened her arms and they embraced. Laura's heart swelled with fondness for Tess and the companionship they'd kept, along with Bette, years before. She swallowed. Times when their financial situation had been very nearly as bad as it was becoming now.

She pulled back and held Tess at arm's length. "How long have you worked here?"

The girl's pretty face lit up with pride, her dark eyes shining in the subdued light. "Close on a year."

"A year? And you're managing on the wages?"

"Of course." She glanced at Laura's dress, a hint of envy in her gaze. "I clearly don't earn the cash you do, but still . . ." She lifted her shoulders. "It means I'm out of . . . you know."

Laura knew exactly . . . and now it was her turn to stare in envy. "I see."

Tess's hands slipped from hers and she leaned down to retrieve her basket. "You don't seem to be doing too badly, though."

Laura's smile dissolved. "Bette's ill, Tess. Really ill."

Tess's face twisted in sympathy and she clutched Laura's arm. "She'll pull through, won't she? Bette's made of stronger stuff than any of us. Nothing will bring her down."

"With Bette ill and me not being as active as I used to, the money's drying up. I need to work and I came here hoping to get lucky. I need a job. A real job. I'd love to give up the whoring, but when I bumped into Ellen Jenkins outside the theater a couple of nights ago, I thought she might have the right idea."

Tess grimaced. "Hmm, I know what Ellen Jenkins thinks she is now and, believe me, escorting ain't no prettier than whoring. Not by a long shot. Those gentlemen aren't all they make themselves out to be." She scowled and glanced around. "Half the time they're a hell of a lot more demanding than the ones on the street . . . and stranger."

Caution rippled through Laura's blood. "What do you mean?"

"I mean a lot of them are married, with children, and have a taste for the vile. They've got demands that would make your stomach weak."

Laura frowned. "Ellen looked as though the money was dripping from her drawers."

"I wouldn't want no more part of that life if the money was dripping from my earlobes."

"I know, but—"

"Wouldn't you do anything not to have to do what you do ever again? To go home at night and know you've earned a crust by not laying with any man, boy, or grandfather?" Tess lifted her basket. "How would you feel about doing this?"

"Selling treats? I'd never make enough to see me and Bette right, would I? I'd have to sell night and day to pay the rent alone."

"I don't just do this, silly."

"No?"

Tess laughed. "Nooo, I take messages backstage. Set up meetings." She winked. "Gentlemen pay a lot to see the actresses alone. The women pay a lot more to see Adam Lacey."

Laura's heart skipped and she faced the stage. "Adam Lacey?"

Tess's breath whispered warm against her ear. "Do you blame them? Who wouldn't want a bit of alone time with Adam Lacey?"

Laura smiled as excitement whipped up a storm inside her. "Who wouldn't, indeed?"

Chapter 4

Protectiveness over paper. Who would have thought such a thing could exist?

Yet, the feeling hurtling through Adam's heart as he sat in one of the back rooms of the theater with his director could not be described as anything else. He tightened his jaw and studied the portraits of past stars gracing the walls. Undoubtedly, each one had come to Bath as young and as ambitious as he—and either gone on to tread the boards at London's West End or were now languishing on the slag heap. Acting was a two-way street, without junctions veering in alternative directions.

He was learning fast you either went up or down. There was no in between.

The scrunch and crumple of his manuscript pages in the director's hands veered his attention. For the last excruciatingly painful fifteen minutes, the man had scanned and tossed the sheets aside as though the words portrayed recipe instructions rather than the outpouring of Adam's soul.

"And you say you've no investment whatsoever?"

Adam met the cool study of his soon-to-be ex-director. A week to the finale of his current acting job and counting. The dire truth of his financial situation thumped him up the side of the head for the fortieth time that day.

He shook his head. "No, that is what I was hoping you can help me with."

Victor Talisman, currently Bath's most sought-after director, regarded him from beneath heavy lids. "The play's not bad, son, but it isn't brilliant either."

"I just need a bit of belief from someone. Someone willing to take an informed risk." Adam resisted the urge to clasp his hand to the back of Victor's absurdly thick neck and demand he see sense. Instead, he curled his fingers into a fist on the table between them. "If you could mention it to a few producers. Tell them I write. Tell them I have this play and, with the right amount of backing, you're confident the theater will run it for a couple of weeks to at least gauge the reaction."

Victor stood and ambled his stocky, five-foot-ten-inch frame across the room. He gazed out the window to the street below. "Do you know how many of these scripts get wafted under my nose every day?"

Adam stared at Victor's turned back. "I can imagine."

"I very much doubt that."

"Look, maybe I should not have commandeered you this way in between performances, but I've been trying to speak to you about this for weeks." Adam stood. "If you could just give me a chance. Or if *you* cannot, maybe speak to a few people at the Rooms tonight. If nothing else, suggest they read it."

Victor turned and ran his gaze over Adam from head to toe. He smiled and raised his eyebrows. "Well, your desperation doesn't help your case."

Soft light sparkled in Victor's eyes and Adam laughed, his shoulders relaxing somewhat as he glanced down at his clothes. "Maybe I should have approached you dressed in shirt and tails rather than my damn costume, but time is running out—"

"For whom?" Victor's smile dissolved. "Do you not realize you are on the precipice of your career? After your performance in this show, people will sit up and take notice of Adam Lacey. Mark my words."

Frustration raced through Adam, searing hot at his face. "So you say. Yet no one is knocking on my door. I need to work. I need to write."

He narrowed his eyes. "More than you need to act?"

"I . . ." Writing certainly mattered to him more and more over acting, but to admit to such could mean the end of further roles coming his way. He blew out a breath. "I cannot answer that."

Victor cleared his throat. "Seems to me, son, that's the bigger question, rather than whether or not you get your creation onto the stage." He wandered back to the table and picked up one of the many sheets he'd discarded.

Adam's stomach knotted with trepidation. He was desperate. He barely had eight weeks' rent left if he didn't find work soon. The familiar sense of failure engulfed him. He could not let Victor know of his situation. Confidence was key to a breakthrough in Adam's unerring quest for a backer. He shook his head.

"Acting will always be important to me, but I cannot deny how much I believe in this play and what it means to me."

Victor met his eyes. "Which is?"

"Everything. I have fought tooth and nail to avoid the regimental life my parents mapped out for me. I have come this far and I refuse to go back now. Roles are not guaranteed, but if I can make a success of my own creation, it will change everything."

Victor stared long and hard before he glanced back at the papers he held. "You've cast yourself in the leading role. What about everyone else? Forget the producers, Adam. There aren't many actors who will take a risk on a new play by a new writer. It could be months before you fill these roles. Not to mention stagehands, lighting, and scenery." He tossed the sheet aside again. "God's graces, man. You know the scale involved to put on a play as ambitious and complex as this."

"I appreciate that, but I also think the public is ready for a story such as this, don't you?"

Adam's heart beat hard as he detected indecision cranking and turning in the director's head as he considered.

Seconds ticked by and then Victor gave a curt nod. "I say forget the writing until you can afford to invest in it. Who knows? A year, two years from now, perhaps you can afford to run the show yourself. Nothing better than a man being in charge of his own work."

"Of course not, but——"

Victor raised his hand. "Come. Gather your manuscript together and put it away for another day. We have less than twenty minutes before you're due back onstage. I can't do anything to help you. I'm sorry."

Adam squeezed his eyes shut and fought to curb his temper. "Well, I would have always wondered if I had not asked. At least I gave you first refusal and the guilt you are out of pocket won't eat me up when my play is alive at the West End."

Victor grinned. "I like your positivity. Now, come, we must make haste."

"You go." Adam opened his eyes and forced a smile. "I'll be right behind you."

As soon as Victor disappeared into the corridor, Adam whirled around and pushed his hands into his hair. "Damn it to hell."

He marched across the room and whipped the disarranged sheets from the desk. He hurriedly gathered them back into a pile as best he could, already dreading the torture of putting them back in order for another long languish in obscurity. Roughly tying the string, he shoved the pile under his arm and strode from the room into the humdrum of the busy corridor.

The stage manager immediately clapped him on the shoulder. "There you are. Are you almost ready? Monica's scene starts in five. You're on next."

Adam waved in acknowledgment and continued along the corridor toward his dressing room. He marched inside and came to an abrupt halt.

God damn it. This is all I need.

The ladies had their backs to him, fiddling with a new flower arrangement on his dresser. His fragile temper could do without the provocation of another woman pushing her breasts in his face, clamoring for a damn autograph . . . or more.

Charm. He needed to maintain his charm, his public reputation at all times. He couldn't let anyone see the real him. That Adam Lacey would soon stick a pin through their fantasy of a rising star with the world at his feet.

He pulled on a wide smile. "Sorry, ladies, I have no time to visit—"

They turned in unison, but Adam focused on only one. "You."

The breath left his lungs and his smile faltered. Lucinda. Here. In his dressing room. Standing barely three feet in front of him.

"Mr. Lacey." Her cheeks darkened and she dipped a semicurtsy. The smooth skin at her neck moved as she swallowed. "It's an honor to meet you."

Adam found his feet and stepped closer. She was short—or at least compared to his five feet eleven inches. Petite. Perfect. Her eyes were huge and the color of lavender.

He laughed. "I cannot believe you are standing in my dressing room."

Her soft smile vanished and the color at her cheeks deepened as she turned to her companion. "I'm sorry. We brought you some flowers from a lady in the audience, sir. We didn't mean . . ."

Her companion looped her arm through that of the vision in front of him. "It's all right, Laura." She tugged *Laura* forward. "We apologize, Mr. Lacey. We'll be right out of your way."

They disappeared out the door, and Adam dumped his manuscript on the desk and hurried after them. Laura . . . Laura. His mind raced. She could not leave. He had to go after her. They had barely stepped into the corridor and he clasped Lucinda . . . Laura, at the elbow.

"Please. Would you join me for a drink after the show? Perhaps you'd like to accompany me to the get-together at the Rooms?"

Her eyes grew to the size of saucers. "Sir?"

He was scaring her. He was acting like an imbecile. A damn predator. He snatched his hand from her arm and raised them both in a gesture of apology. "I am sorry. I mean, would you . . ." He glanced from Laura to her companion. "Both of you, like to come with me? As my guests?"

Her friend squealed. "Yes, yes, we would. Oh, my. I can't believe—"

"No."

Adam looked to Laura. "No?"

She tilted her chin and brought herself up to her full height. Suddenly she seemed taller than she had in his dressing room. She shook her head. "No."

Her friend huffed out a laugh. "Laura, I don't think you understand what Mr. Lacey's asking—"

"Thank you, Tess, but I understand perfectly." Her gaze remained locked with his and Adam tried and failed to lessen the panic he knew would be evident in his eyes. She stepped back and did the damn curtsy thing again. "I thank you, Mr. Lacey, but I came here to work, not to take drinks at the Assembly Rooms. It was nice to meet you."

She spun around and marched away. Tess, her friend, glanced from Adam to Laura's retreating and perfect form and back again. "I'm sorry, Mr. Lacey. She's new. She doesn't understand—"

Adam grinned and shook his head. "It is fine. It is more than fine."

The girl smiled and moved to leave when Adam touched her arm. "Tess?"

"Yes?"

"If you can tell me where she lives, I would be forever indebted to you."

"I'll see what I can do." She tilted her chin, clearly mustering for as much pride as Laura had shown. "But I'm not making any promises."

Adam dipped his head. "I understand."

She took off along the corridor and Adam collapsed back against the wall behind him. His hand clutched the place his heart had been a few minutes before.

Laura.

Laura's legs shook as she hurried into one of the theater's many back rooms. She grabbed her basket. What had she been thinking, giggling and laughing along with Tess in Adam Lacey's dressing room? She swallowed as her hands trembled. She hadn't been thinking. She'd carried on like a naïve young girl in awe of a damn star. Well, it hadn't been stars in Adam Lacey's eyes—it had been lust. Pure and simple.

Disappointment lingered at the periphery of her heart and she pushed it firmly away. He was a man, wasn't he? What the hell else did she expect? Did she think he'd fall at her feet? Romance her? Laugh and ask her questions about her life? She was a whore. Men spotted whores as soon as they looked at one.

Tess hurtled through the door and Laura wiped away the tears that smarted her eyes.

"There you are." Tess pressed her hand to her heaving chest. "Why did you take off like that? The man's besotted."

Laura glared and hefted her basket onto her arm. "Besotted? The man is nothing more than a leech. A sexual deviant."

Tess's eyes widened and she laughed. "A sexual deviant? Mr. Lacey?"

"Yes."

"Don't be absurd. The man is a professional. He'd no more lust after the likes of us than he would piss in the street. The man keeps company with lords and ladies in most cases." She planted her hands on her hips, her eyes sparkling with excitement. "Which is why I won't believe for one minute you aren't the least bit curious why the sight of you set him to gushing the way he did."

Laura feigned interest in the contents of her basket. A spark of pride simmered deep in her belly. "Gushing? He wasn't gushing. He was toying with me . . . us." She met Tess's gaze. "Don't be fooled by him or any other man. You know what we are."

Tess's smile vanished. "Excuse me?"

The heat in her glare bore into Laura's conscience like a claw hammer. Just because she'd grown as jaded and cynical as a washed-up brothel madam, didn't mean Tess was. She slumped her shoulders and squeezed her eyes shut. "I'm sorry. Ignore me."

The silent seconds beat heavy in her ears. Her first day in a new life and she'd set upon the first person who greased the wheels of opportunity.

"Laura, look at me." Tess's voice was firm and clear.

Laura opened her eyes.

Tess tightened her jaw and crossed her arms. "First of all, I know exactly who I am. I'm a young woman making her way in the world. Always have been, always will be. Yes, I might've sold my body for a time to stay warm and fed, but right now those days feel a long way past. Now, you have to decide how you're going to start thinking about yourself."

"Tess, I'm sorry. I didn't mean—"

"I haven't finished. You need to start thinking about how to talk about yourself, because the way Adam Lacey just admired you had nothing . . . *nothing* to do with putting his cock inside you."

Laura flinched at the bluntness of Tess's words. "I never said he thought that."

"You didn't have to. It was written all over your face how little you thought of him. You didn't give him a chance to impress you."

The fight left her and Laura collapsed into a chair, heaving her laden basket onto her lap. "I didn't mean to run away like that. I didn't want to get angry or mean."

"Then why did you?" Tess grabbed a chair and dragged it along the floor. She sat in front of Laura. "Adam Lacey is the nicest bloke you'll meet, I swear to you. Considering his popularity around here, you'd think he'd be a right dandy, but he's not. He talks to everyone and anyone."

"So why get so excited about him talking to me? It was the ecstasy on your face that sent me flying out the door, not his. You can't blame me for thinking there was more to it, the way you stared at us as though your eyes might roll out of their sockets."

Tess grinned and wiggled her eyebrows. "I said, he *talks* to everyone. I didn't say he stares at everyone like he did you."

Laura frowned. "So I was right. He can see me for what I am."

"He didn't look at you for sex. You know that as well as I do. If the man had been scouting for sex, you would've put him in his place. The way he stared at you scared you as much as it shocked me. Admit it."

She was right, but there was no way Laura would admit that to Tess—or herself. "Why would he ask us to the party?"

Tess leaned back. "I've no idea."

Any residual notions of admiring Adam Lacey's acting skills or handsomeness disintegrated. "Then what's he playing at?"

"I don't know, but as sure as I'm sitting here, we're going to that party to find out." Tess pushed to her feet. "Come on. For now, we've got work to do."

Laura leaped up. "Tess, wait. I'm not going to any party. I've already told you how ill Bette is. I'm not leaving her to fend for herself while I go off to some theater carrying on."

"You can't not go." Tess's eyes grew wide. "What if he doesn't ask us again? It's not me he wants there, it's you, but I'll be damned if I'm going to miss out on a night of seeing all that finery. If you won't do this for you, will you at least do it for me?"

Snatching her basket back onto her arm, Laura tilted her chin. "I'm not going. You go. Enjoy yourself. Even tell me what happens. I'm not going." She inhaled a shaky breath. "Are you going to show me how to shift this lot or not?"

Their gazes locked.

Laura struggled to maintain a semblance of control as her heart raced and her hands shook. For all her words and fervor, the way Adam Lacey gawked at her remained painted in her mind as clear and vivid as a miniature portrait. He hadn't just admired her, he'd seen through her, to her very soul. It was as though he asked her a million questions. Where have you been? Who are you? What can you do for me?

The notion confused her. Shook her. Made half of her want to seek him out and the other half hide.

When no response came from Tess, Laura emitted a frustrated curse and swept from the room.

Actors speaking their lines and the accompanying clangs and hums of the orchestra drifted through the corridor as she stormed forward. The maze of doors and walkways threw her off balance. How did she get out of here? Back to the auditorium? Back to Bette?

She halted. Closed her eyes. No, she wouldn't run. When had she ever run from anything? So, she was shaken. Someone had managed to make herself stop. Make herself think. Make herself feel . . .

This was a new time. A new opportunity. This was for her and Bette. No more whoring. Wasn't that what Bette asked of her while she suffered and fought against the illness threatening to take her down?

Footfalls behind her made Laura turn.

Tess hurried along the corridor, her face etched with concern. She stopped and took her hand. "Where are you going? You're not leaving, are you?"

Laura released her held breath and forced a smile. "Of course not. It will take more than a man like Adam Lacey to make me run scared from a job."

Tess's shoulders dropped and a pretty smile lit her face and eyes. "I'm glad to hear it." She looped her arm through Laura's. "Let's go to work. These folks are ripe for the picking, I reckon."

Arm in arm, they entered the auditorium and the calls, laughter, and noise of the audience swept over Laura on a wave of possibility. The scent of tobacco mixed with the gas from the lanterns; orange peels mixed with the scent of chocolate from her basket. She stared resolutely forward. Adam's voice came from the stage to the left of her—masculine, clear, and entirely in control. She ignored the tightening in her stomach and the almost inhuman urge to look at him that pulled at every fiber.

She wouldn't give him the satisfaction.

"Laura?"

She started when Tess whispered urgently in her ear. "What?"

"Why are you staring ahead like you've seen some sort of ghost? We've got work to do." Tess frowned. "Are you all right?"

"I'm fine. How do we do this?"

"Well, there isn't much more to it than smiling and flirting with the gentlemen and acting envious of the women. The men want to feel as though you long to be with them. The women like you to want to be them."

Laura nodded. If she was good at nothing else, she was good at making people believe she was happy when inside she yearned to be a million miles away, doing something only other dreamers could possibly understand.

She drew in a long breath. At least this time she was dressed and no one was pawing at her cunny or kissing at her breast. For tonight, she was Laura Robinson making her way without any man's money or muscle.

Chapter 5

Adam meandered down the theater steps onto the street. Somehow, he had managed to get through the second half of the play without leaping from the stage and talking to Laura. He smiled. Despite the added energy to his performance, the agony of knowing she wandered amongst the audience and being unable to so much as look at her had been pitiful. Her presence, the anticipation of seeing her again, put a bounce in his step and set a strange fluidity through his limbs.

Intellectually, he was acting like a sap. Who had ever heard of someone seeing another person and sensing an excitement, a purpose, just by looking into their eyes? It was madness, but the wonder and surprise in her gaze was not a figment of his imagination. She had to have felt the connection too. It was their destiny to explore what it meant, surely?

He glanced left and right along the street before checking his pocket watch. By the time he had changed and was ready to leave, the theater had emptied of its patrons, along with Laura and Tess. Part of him knew Laura would be true to her word and not come to the Rooms, but he hoped Tess would at least deliver her address to him. Not that it mattered nearly as much now—he'd since discovered Laura worked at the theater. He would see her soon regardless.

His heart stuttered.

Which meant he would talk to her then if he could not tonight. Things had a way of turning out how they were supposed to. He would take the time to get his excitement under control and show her he was not a madman but a playwright. A playwright who, un-beknownst to her, had written a part for which she was perfect.

"Adam, you're waiting for me. You are surely the sweetest man in the whole of Bath."

He turned. Monica swept through the doors on Victor's arm. Adam smiled and offered her his arm too. Her fingers curled around his forearm, her pretty features alight with happiness. "Well, look at me, being escorted by two of Bath's finest gentlemen."

"And it is our pleasure. Isn't that right, Victor?"

"Absolutely." The director smiled. "Shall I send a message for my carriage or are we happy to walk?"

Monica tugged them closer. "Oh, I'm more than happy to walk and be seen considering my current situation."

Adam laughed. "You are an outrageous flirt, Miss Danes."

Her eyes widened. "Says he who is never without an adoring female answering to his every whim."

Adam pressed his free hand to his chest, feigning offense. "I am desperate for the attention of one woman and one woman only."

Monica's eyes sparkled. "Oh? And who would this honored woman be, might I ask?"

He winked. "That is for me to know and the rest of the world to . . ." Adam glanced over her shoulder and pulled his arm from Monica's hand as Laura came down the steps. He swallowed. "Laura."

She turned, her eyes widening for a brief moment before she pulled back her shoulders. "Mr. Lacey."

He blinked and collected himself. He extended his hand toward Monica and Victor. "Might I introduce Monica Danes and Victor Talisman."

Laura nodded and smiled. "It's an honor to meet you. The play is excellent."

"Thank you." Monica smiled. "You must be the last to leave. We finished well over an hour past."

Laura glanced toward the ground and back again. "I wasn't in the audience, Miss Danes. Tonight was my first night working here. I sell sweets and such."

"Ah, I see. That's why I haven't noticed such a pretty girl before." She tilted her head toward Adam. "As opposed to my fellow actor here, who has clearly noticed you to already know your name."

The lanterns cast Laura's face in an amber glow, so Adam couldn't be sure if she blushed as she dipped her head. "Well, it was lovely to meet you, but I must hurry home. Have a nice evening."

She moved to leave and Adam stepped forward. "Might I just have a very quick word with you?"

"I'm sorry. I really must——"

"I'll walk with you."

She stiffened and glanced toward Monica and Victor before facing him once more. "I thank you, Mr. Lacey, but really, I'm quite all right unaccompanied. Maybe we could talk when I'm next working?"

"Tonight will do just as well."

Her soft violet eyes turned to hard amethyst under the lamplight. Adam quickly faced Monica and Victor, and bit back the bubble of laughter in his throat at the sight of their identical expressions of interest and curiosity. He bowed slightly.

"I will catch up with you once I have seen Miss Robinson home."

"Of course."

"As you wish."

With a final frown at Adam and a hurried smile at Laura, Monica and Victor strolled away. Satisfied he was finally alone with her ran like hot, honeyed water through Adam's blood.

"Now then——"

"How dare you."

He blanched. Her face was set in stone, her eyes flashing a fury he had never encountered in a woman. "Sorry?"

"I said, how dare you." She poked a finger into his chest. "Let me tell you something, *Mr. King of the Theater* . . . I might have a life-long love of the stage, I might have totally and completely fallen in love with the costumes, the atmosphere, even the damn lighting, but no one—not even you—presumes to infringe on my time or company without my say-so. Understand?"

He stared at her lips and he wrapped his hand around the finger at his chest and held it there. "I am pleased to hear you are falling in love with the theater. In fact, I am more than pleased, I am ecstatic."

Her finger trembled in his grasp, but her gaze never wavered. "And why's that?"

"Because you belong on that stage. I knew it the moment I saw you."

She snatched her finger from his hand and huffed. "My God, you really are a piece of work. You must think I was born yesterday." She pulled her shawl tighter around her shoulders and stepped around him. "I'll bid you good night."

"Laura." His tone was firm. Probably firm enough to ignite that fiery temper of hers to explosion, but there was no way she was leaving. Not yet. He had to at least charm her into liking him more than hating him.

She spun around. "What's wrong with you? Why are you so intent on seeking my company? If there's something you want from me, why not be a man and just say it? You're toying with me like a cat after a mouse. I've seen more masculinity in a dog in heat."

He froze, stunned beyond laughter or offense. Her soft, dulcet tones had changed in her anger to that of an intelligent, knowing, and mature woman way beyond her youthful and beautiful looks. Yet, instead of lessening the fire burning inside him, her displeasure stoked it. Attraction licked at his insides and rode all the way to the center of his stupid chest.

He could not remember when last a female spoke to him in such a way. She was glorious. He laughed. "Well, I guess that told me."

"I'm serious, Mr. Lacey. For all your success and skill onstage, you know very little of how to treat a woman. I daresay the fancy, rich ladies who seek your company don't know any better or they'd run the other way."

The minx no longer scowled or spat feathers. Instead . . . she grinned. His breath caught. Her eyes sparkled and her gorgeous apple cheeks shone with a rich and rosy gleam.

He slowly approached her.

She tilted her chin, her smile still fully in place. "Are you daring to speak with me again?"

He considered every aspect of her face, especially her lips, before coming to a mesmerized stop at those deep violet eyes. "You are—"

The growl from deep within his throat was a new and fearful reaction. His mouth covered hers and he took without thinking. He swallowed her gasp and hitched her tight against him. His hands clasped a waist so tiny, so perfect, it fit in the splay of his hands.

He waited for her shove, her push—her slap, but it didn't come. Her rigid body turned pliant as the weight of her hands rested on his shoulders. She kissed him back. Matching his need with equal fervor. She moaned into his mouth with a passion that sped his heart. Her hot tongue touched his. The glide of her hands to his neck and hair sent tremors of desire thundering into his cock.

Abruptly, she pulled back. Satisfaction, desire and—dare he think it—need stormed in the depths of her eyes. Her lashes, as dark as night, sparkled with tears that shone like diamonds.

Adam shook his head. "Who are you?"

She grinned and swiped her fingers under her eyes. "More woman than you could ever handle, Mr. Lacey. Good night."

"Wait."

She brushed past him, her glorious behind swaying nonchalantly from side to side as she waved and disappeared into the darkness.

Laura pushed the key into the lock of her and Bette's house. The walk—or run—from the theater had done little to steady her nerves. What had she done? She'd kissed Adam Lacey. No, she hadn't kissed him. She'd *devoured* him. Yet, she couldn't fight the smile that tugged at her lips as she quietly slipped inside.

The breath-stealing emotions had brought tears to her eyes. Tears! Why had she reacted in such a way?

She bent over to untie her boots. *I know exactly why. The man kissed me like he wanted to possess me.* The tension between them had been like an exploding stream of fireworks.

Whoosh! Squeal! Bang!

She collapsed onto the bottom stair and covered her mouth with her hand to smother her laughter. Her heart raced, her cunny pulsed. It was a phenomenon. A miracle. She'd risen to his challenge and left him standing on the street alone. Now, though, she ached for more of him. God, she was terrified a man could evoke such need in her, such lack of control.

Her smile vanished as she glanced toward the living-room door. Attraction to Adam Lacey was the last thing she needed or expected.

In all her years as a whore, she'd turned numb whenever a cully touched, caressed, or sexed her. Her lack of sexual interest had been enough for Bette to infer on more than one occasion that Laura was meant to be with a woman. Except, of course, Laura always seemed to notice the man who ran the ironmongers down the street. . . .

She shook her head. *Noticed him* being the important thing. She'd more than noticed Adam Lacey.

The cracking and wheezing of Bette's coughing roused Laura from her muddled contemplation. She leaped to her feet and hurried into the living room that now also served as Bette's bedroom.

"Sorry I'm back so late." Laura sidled onto the bed and lifted a glass of water from the cabinet to her friend's lips. Bette's pallor was gray and sheened with sweat. "Here."

Bette shook her head and flicked her hand, gesturing for Laura to get rid of the glass.

Icy-cold dread seeped into Laura's stomach. Tiny blobs of blood crusted on Bette's mouth. She flitted her gaze to the covers to hide her panic. Smears of blood colored the edge of the sheets as though her friend had used them to swipe her mouth.

She looked up. Bette stared at her, tears glazing her eyes.

Laura swallowed. "When did it start?"

"It's nothing."

"It *is* something. It's something important." She clasped Bette's hand. "I need to get the doctor."

"What you need is to pray to God you don't get struck down, too, looking after me like this." Bette closed her eyes.

"I'm in and out of this house so much, there's little chance of me getting anything from you. Don't talk daft." Laura blinked against the hot sting of tears. "I just want to make a wish and have this go away."

"Isn't the doc coming tomorrow?"

"First thing."

"Good, then we'll worry what this blood means then and not before."

Laura bit back a sob. What would crying, screaming, or cursing do? Nothing. What would dancing and singing onstage or kissing a star do? Nothing. Heat burned like acid in her heart. She was selfish. Selfish and entirely unfocused on what was important. Bette.

Adam Lacey's dark brown eyes and heart-melting smile wouldn't fix her beloved friend. Money, safety, and security were what Bette needed. It was up to Laura to provide that until Bette was well again. Then everything would go back to normal. Back to the two of them against the whole damn world.

A tear dropped onto her clenched hands and Laura whirled away from the bed. "Are you hungry?"

"I'm bored and lonely. Tell me what happened tonight. Did you find a gentleman or, as I asked, land yourself onstage? Which one lucked out?"

"Neither." Laura squeezed one eye shut. "I kissed Adam Lacey instead."

"You kissed . . . Well, damn." Bette rasped out a laugh and Laura turned. She hadn't seen the wicked light that shone in Bette's eyes for such a long time. "When you said you were going to go after a gentleman's protection, I didn't think it would be the star of the stage."

Laura smiled. "This isn't good or funny. What was I thinking? More importantly, what was *he* thinking?"

"What are you talking about? Have you taken a look in the mirror lately? My God, Laura, you're prettier than any damn actress, princess, or lady. I give this Adam Lacey credit for seeing that from the moment he laid eyes on you."

"Or, rather, he could see I was a whore the moment he laid eyes on me."

"What?"

Laura's heart thudded with disappointment. "What if he knows what I am?"

"Then better to be protected by the likes of him than Baxter."

Laura's stomach twisted and she pressed her hand there. Of course he does. Was he laughing at her when he mentioned her and the stage in the same sentence? "You think that's it? You think he wants me for his exclusive pleasure?"

"Don't you?"

A slash of something she didn't want to contemplate struck her heart. "No, at least I hope not."

Bette raised an eyebrow. "So, what do you hope?"

Turning away from her friend's insipid gaze, Laura faced the window. "I don't know, but I'm not about to become Adam Lacey's whore, no matter what he might think. I've thought about what you said. I'm better than that. Hell, I'm getting too old for that." She faced Bette. "I did the rounds with Tess. I sold those wares, and laughed and joked with gentlemen and thieves alike. I was good at it. I sold the lot."

"All of it? Lord, I bet Tess was impressed."

"She was." Laura smiled and took some coins from her purse pocket. "Better still, I got enough from my cut to pay for the doctor tomorrow. I loved the atmosphere and listening to the play while I worked. It's perfect for me. I don't need to lay with a man anymore. Who knows where my hard work and charm can lead us, huh?"

Bette's smile was weak, but her eyes shone. "Who knows, indeed?"

Feeling better about the night and managing to ignore her dangerous liaison with Adam Lacey for the moment, Laura made for the door. "I'll go and boil some milk. It'll help us sleep better." She left the room and as the hem of her dress swished against the floorboards, she was reminded of the dress and cape Monica Danes wore when she stood beside Adam on the theater steps.

If Adam saw the dresses Laura wore and where she lived he wouldn't have the same glint in his eyes or passion in his kiss he'd had earlier.

Laura's hand shook as she filled a pan with milk and carried it to the stove. Since when had she cared what a dandy or toff thought of where or how she lived? Why had this man tilted her life off-kilter so potently and so suddenly?

Shaking her head, she hurried from the room and up the stairs to her bedroom. She got out of her clothes and into her nightdress, fighting thoughts of Adam Lacey, the theater, the music, and every other damn thing that hummed through her blood like a cruel and insistent reminder of the life she craved.

Ever since she was a young girl, abandoned by her mother and never knowing her father, she'd been drawn to the Theater Royal like a child to a toyshop window.

"You belong on that stage."

"You need to go there and put yourself onstage."

Adam's and Bette's words reverberated in her ears. The one thing life had taught her was that change happened in a heartbeat, without warning or preparation. Who was to say she wasn't supposed to be in the theater? Who was to say her life—her whoring—hadn't prepared her for such an event?

She took a long breath as she closed her bedroom door and descended the stairs. Wasn't her life a play of the highest drama? First living hand to mouth, she'd eked her way through. Last year brought the gentry into her life under the most unforeseeable circumstances and she'd dealt with it. Done what felt right.

Destiny rolled into a tight ball behind her ribs. Who was she to argue with her lifelong pull toward the theater? Tomorrow it was closed, but for better or worse, she'd go back the day after and embrace whatever it threw at her. Sooner or later, the true motivation of Adam Lacey's interest would be revealed. Moreover, she'd learn why God had steered her inside the Theater Royal a few days ago rather than years before.

Chapter 6

Laura stared anxiously at Bette as she slept. Her friend's labored breathing was steady but painful to hear as it eked to and from her tiring lungs. The doctor was due any moment. Laura returned to the window to look out for him. Last night, she'd stupidly thought Bette was taking a turn for the better with all her chatter and challenge about Laura working at the theater. This morning, her friend fared worse than ever.

When she pressed her hand to Bette's forehead, cheeks, and chest, her skin was hot enough to burn. Her pallor was pasty, and her lips dry and cracked. Refusing to eat and barely taking more than a sip of water at a time, Bette had little to no energy left to fight the bacteria inside her.

The sight of Dr. Penders coming toward the house sent Laura's heart flying into her throat and she blinked back tears. *Please, God, let him have come with a miracle.*

His sharp rap at the door snapped her gaze to Bette. She stirred but didn't wake. Loath to disturb her but knowing the doctor had a job to do, Laura stroked her hand over Bette's forehead.

"Bette? The doctor's here."

"Mmm?"

"The doctor. I'm just going to let him in. He'll want to talk to you."

Bette's eyes slowly opened and her gaze dazed. "Then let him in."

She squeezed Bette's hand, then made for the door and yanked it open.

"Dr. Penders, am I glad . . ." Laura's smile dissolved when she saw who stood behind the doctor, his snidey mouth stretched in a wide grin. "What are you doing here?"

Malcolm Baxter leaned around the doctor, his center-parted, oil-slicked hair making Laura grimace. He smiled, revealing the gap in his upper front teeth. "I saw the doc and thought I'd come and pay Bette a visit."

Not wanting to cause a ruckus in front of the doctor, Laura fought the urge to smack him in the face. "Well, wasn't that nice of you." She turned to the doctor. "Why don't you go on through? She's in the living room."

Dr. Penders removed his black top hat and cast a glance over his shoulder, his mouth twisted with distaste beneath tidy gray whiskers. "I told Mr. Baxter Bette wasn't up for visitors, but he doesn't seem to understand basic English."

Laura smiled. "Then I'll keep him here until he does."

The kindly doctor stepped inside.

As soon as she heard the doctor jovially greet Bette, Laura crossed her arms and fixed Malcolm with a glare. "Go away."

He raised his hands. "Is that any way to talk to a friend concerned for Bette?"

She gave an inelegant snort. "Friend? I don't think so. Get out of here before I'm forced to do something to wipe that smile off your face. You don't scare me, Malcolm. Now, go."

She moved to shut the door, but he stuck his foot in the way. His wolverine smile vanished and his eyes flashed cold with determination. "You need to listen to me before things get nasty."

Anger simmered hot and heavy in her belly. She fisted her hands on her hips and kicked his foot away. "I don't *need* to listen to anybody. Now, why don't you say what you came here to say and disappear? My best friend in the whole world is in there struggling for her next breath. I don't have time for your carrying on."

"I hear you've been sniffing around the theater for work."

Damn it. Who the hell had been talking to Malcolm about her? She tilted her chin. "And?"

"If you were looking for more up-market clientele, you should have told me first."

She scowled. "I don't have to tell you anything. I don't work for you and never will."

"Then maybe it's time you moved on. Here and abouts is my patch. Where *my* ladies work. I can't have you giving the impression it's one rule for you and not the rest. You're messing with my authority, and my patience has run out. You need to make a decision, or I can't be held responsible for what happens next."

"Are you threatening me?" Laura tightened her jaw. "You think I don't know it was you who got the other girls *messing with your authority* thrown out of their homes? Had their belongings stolen or tossed onto the street?"

"Well, if you know that, pretty Laura, why do you think the same hasn't happened to you and Bette so far?"

Her heart thundered as she glared at the dog turd standing in front of her. "You really think we'll eventually come around and give you a cut of whatever we earn?" She shook her head. "Over my dead body."

He laughed. "Don't you mean Bette's?"

Anger roared through her and she raised her hand to slap the damn know-it-all smirk from his ugly face. He caught her wrist in a vice-like grip and held it—hard. Her pulse beat under his palm.

"You listen to me." His eyes were cold with malice and his cheeks red. "I'm giving you one month to either get out of here or come work for me. One month and then Bette dying will be the least of your worries. In the meantime, I'll be watching you, and once I see you're off your high horse and spreading your legs again, I'll be back for a cut. If you don't pay me, you'll soon wish you were lying on a slab next to your precious friend."

He tossed her arm away and Laura stumbled backward against the doorframe. With a parting sneer, he straightened the cuffs on his jacket and stalked away like he was king of the world.

Shaking with rage and a hefty dose of fear, Laura crossed her arms and glared after him. She wouldn't give him the satisfaction of seeing her anxiety should he turn around. When he'd gone, she released her held breath and reentered the house. Shutting the door, she leaned against it and waited for the galloping in her heart to subside.

Tears gathered in her throat. What was she going to do with

Malcolm watching her every move? Would she be putting Tess at risk of Malcolm's attention if she continued working at the theater? She closed her eyes. She wouldn't put it past him to follow her there night after night. Damn him. Damn this life she and Bette were in, despite her efforts to release them from it.

The soft murmuring of Dr. Penders shook Laura from her contemplation and, forcing the frustration from her face, she hurried into the living room. The doctor had somehow managed to get Bette sitting up against the pillows and drinking tea. It was more than Laura had managed all day.

She moved to the bedside. "Doctor, you should've waited for me to make the tea."

He waved his hand. "The kettle was boiled. Don't worry yourself. You had more than enough to cope with getting rid of that Baxter character."

"Well, he's gone now. How's Bette faring, Doctor? Are there any signs of improvement?" She clasped Bette's free hand in hers.

His eyes softened and his brows drew together. "I'm afraid not. The pneumonia has spread to her lungs and taken up residence. I can give you a prescription for some decongestant. It might ease the discomfort."

Laura nodded. "I'll go into town as soon as you leave. I'll get whatever she needs."

"We don't have the money for no fancy medicine." Bette's words rasped against her throat.

She tightened her grip on Bette's hand. "We have the money for whatever you need to make you better."

Bette shook her head and closed her eyes. "Tell her, Doc. Tell her the truth."

Dread fell heavy into Laura's stomach. "What truth?"

Dr. Penders cleared his throat. "The truth that nothing is guaranteed. I hope and pray the drugs make a difference, but you, as well as Bette, need to know there is little I can do once the trouble settles in the lungs."

"I see." Laura straightened her spine. "That doesn't mean it's not worth a try, so don't worry, she'll be back to bossing me around in no time."

Bette shifted on the bed. "Laura——"

"Is there anything else I need to know?" Laura stared at the doctor, ignoring her friend. The notion of Bette giving up struck terror into her heart with overbearing ferocity. Bette never gave up on anything.

The doctor frowned. "Let Laura look after you. You need to fight this. Do you hear me?"

"I'm being realistic." Bette plucked at the covers across her lap. "We need to know so we can be prepared and make plans. That bastard, excuse my French, Malcolm Baxter will be back here tomorrow and the next day, until Laura succumbs to his demands. I'm as much use to her as a wet blanket. If I'm going to die, I don't want her wasting what little money we've got on nonsense."

Dr. Penders squeezed her hand. "Medicine is not nonsense and well you know it. Moreover, getting plenty of rest is paramount. As much sleep as possible with minimal disturbance or upset."

Bette lifted her hand from his and cursed.

With frustration set at a low hum in her blood, Laura cupped the doctor's elbow. "Let me see you out." She glanced at Bette. "Somebody has clearly got fever of the brain, too, if she thinks for one minute I won't be going to the pharmacy the minute you've gone."

Ignoring Bette's colorful protestation behind them, Laura led Dr. Penders to the door and opened it. "Thank you for coming by again. It means so much to me you're willing to come to this part of town to help us. There are many doctors who wouldn't."

He smiled. "Circumstances don't make the person. You and Bette are better people than most of the moneyed I know. You send a message for me if she worsens. I fear this has gotten a real hold on her." He drew in a long breath. "Be strong . . . but be prepared. You know where to find me."

Words stuck in her throat as he strolled down the alley, his aging frame stooped as though he carried the worries of the world upon his shoulders. Laura's view blurred. He'd told her in the kindest way possible there was every chance Bette would lose her battle.

Swallowing hard, Laura pulled back her shoulders.

She wouldn't let her best friend lay down and die. Not now. Not when they'd made the decision their whoring would end and a different future begin. She wouldn't take these new steps without Bette beside her. How would she gain pleasure from any new turn or opportunity without the person who never betrayed, lied, or disappointed her by her side? There was every chance she'd never again meet another person to love and trust like she did Bette.

She closed the door and snatched her coat from a hook in the hallway before walking into the living room.

Bette coughed. "Don't waste your money. Stay here with me and we'll have another cup of tea. I'll fight this thing. I promise."

"I know you will, but I'm going to the pharmacy all the same and you'll take whatever the doctor ordered."

The ensuing silence spoke volumes. Bette was scared. Really scared.

Shrugging into her coat, Laura fought her tears. "Shall I make you another cuppa before I go?"

Bette stared toward the window. "No."

"Fine. Then I'll leave you to rest."

"Just go."

Laura's head ached from the icy-cold tension emanating from the woman capable of making her laugh until she thought her sides would split clean open. She kissed Bette's perspiring temple. "I'll be back as soon as I can."

Bette grunted.

With her heart breaking, Laura left the house and hurried along the alleyway. If the worries of the world had stooped Dr. Penders's shoulders, she was bent double by the time she reached town.

Adam glanced up from his drawing-room desk to the wall clock above the mantel. It neared midday and he had barely filled a page and a half toward finishing his new play. Unheard of. The reason? Laura. He could not shake her from his mind or sensibility. Initially, she was a vision for his debut production, but now she was so much more. He wanted to get to know her personally. A passionate need burned in him through the night until he leaped from his bed and threw cold water over his face and neck in a bid to douse the fire.

He had never met such a woman in his life. He laughed aloud and stood. What eyes! What passion! What nerve!

The woman was built of a substance he could not name—but, by God, he liked it. Wanted it. Craved it.

With a woman like that beside him, it was possible he could touch the damn moon. What a formidable team they would be onstage. Her strength came through in her kiss and every touch. She no doubt possessed a rich story to have such a sense of self-worth.

He looked to the window. The sun shone bright in the sky, and birds flew and soared. No wonder his feet itched to do something. He would take a wander into town, stretch his legs through Parade Park, and maybe meander through the market. Nothing better than mixing with others to get the creative juices flowing. He had spent far too many hours cooped up inside writing or rehearsing his lines.

Before anything could change his mind, he marched into the hallway, donned his overcoat and hat, and stepped outside. The light seemed brighter than it had yesterday and the air clearer. Worry still lingered in the back of his mind because he had no further work lined up, but somehow the prospect did not feel as heavy a burden on this new day.

Things would come right for him, one way or another. He had severed his ties to Annabel and planned to pay back every penny she'd spent on him over the last twelve months. Two years had passed since his father cast him out of their family with a wad of cash and little else.

His father's words reverberated in his ears. "If you fail and come back, you will live by our rules, do as we say, and have no more theater."

Unable to stand his parents' resistance to his dreams, Adam rebelled and they had renounced him. He would never regret his decision. Even now, with his money dwindling to desperate levels. His pride and fear had led him to renting a house out of his means. His rationale had been that renting something more affordable might lower his chance of being taken seriously by a potential producer.

He marched along the street, his mind mulling over his decision to set out with the image he wanted to convey firmly established *prior to* auditioning. Rationalizing nice clothes and a good home would lead the theater's top people to take him seriously, he now realized he had been a fool. Never in his wildest imagination could he have anticipated the tens of people who would attend the auditions or that the competition would be so fierce.

His worst fears he would not be good enough were realized. Adam drew in a long breath as humiliation after humiliation haunted him once again. When his money ran out, Lady Annabel's continuous pursuit of him as her lover had been too hard to resist and he succumbed. Shame ached at his temples. The doors of opportunity had swung open freely on hinges greased with her money.

Was it any wonder he still doubted his ability? Who was to say the roles would not once again dry up without Annabel's assistance? Adam shook his head and pulled back his shoulders. No, he would not think that way. He had accepted long ago, the day either parent clapped him on the shoulder for a job well done was the day he married the "right woman" and bore them a grandchild. There was little chance of either happening this side of the millennium.

Marriage, family, and babies were as far down his list of priorities as taking tea with Annabel in the Pump Room. He had dreams, ambitions, and wishes—none of which involved a family. If a man had a family, he should be there for them. Have a continuous supply of money, a steady job so his beloved never feared for food being absent from the table or their child getting cold on a winter's night.

Acting would not provide as much, and yet he could not give up what he loved.

Shaking himself from his melancholy, Adam looked around as he entered the park. Bath was never quiet at any time of the day or night, but, on a day like this, it heaved with shoppers and people looking to enjoy the sunshine before autumn grew colder and stripped the trees, sending them scurrying for warmth and home comforts.

He tipped his hat to passersby who raised their eyebrows or whispered behind their hands as they recognized him. His ego inflated at the attention and diminished his fear of failure a little more.

Adam smiled when his gaze fell on some young boys tossing stones into the water or pushing wooden sailboats across the surface of the river that ran through the center of the park. He glanced at their mothers. Their backs were turned as they chattered in earnest conversation. No doubt gossiping about who was doing what with whom. What was it with women and their innate ability to zone out anything or anyone when a whiff of scandal was in the air?

A yell and ensuing splash behind him shot his heart into his throat and he spun around just as the women burst into hysterics.

One of the young boys who had been playing at the water's edge now struggled in vain against the weight of the current. His arms flailed and his open mouth took in the murky brown liquid time and again.

"Goddamn it." Adam yanked off his jacket and shoes.

He climbed onto the wall alongside the water and jumped. He sucked in a breath. The temperature was icy cold. Within two steps, its depth reached his torso. The boy sank beneath the murkiness once more. Gritting his teeth, Adam waded through the current and plunged his hands deep. He grabbed the boy's collar and hauled him into his arms.

Coughing and spluttering, the boy gripped Adam's biceps. The lad glanced over his shoulder and his coughing escalated to manic proportions rather than calming as it should've done. Adam looked ahead and grinned. A crowd had gathered at the water's edge. Clearly, the boy enjoyed an audience as much as Adam. He waded back to where he'd left his shoes and then stepped up onto the wall before releasing the boy into his mother's waiting arms.

"Oh, Laurence. Laurence, my baby." She gathered her son close, kissing his sodden hair over and over.

Adam smiled and shook the water from his hair. "He won't do that again in a hurry, ma'am."

She met his eyes over her son's head. "Thank you. Thank you so much."

"You are welcome." He winked at the boy. "Be safe, little man."

The boy nodded and turned his face into the crook of his mother's neck. Pretending not to hear his name whispered over and over as it filtered through the watching crowd, Adam sat upon the wall to pull on his shoes, his wet clothes dripping onto the concrete. Goose bumps erupted onto his cold skin, but the discomfort was worth it to know the boy was safe.

"That was quite the performance, Mr. Lacey."

Adam smiled and lifted his head. "Well, thank . . ."

Laura grinned at him and his heart stuttered. "Laura."

Her violet eyes flashed with amusement and her cheeks were flushed. "Is it really necessary to demand an audience's attention twenty-four hours a day?"

She held a basket over her arm, her smile wide. Adam stared, mesmerized as her glossy hair flew in tendrils from beneath her hat to lick at her cheeks. He blinked and shrugged into his jacket, his heart thumping uncomfortably. Was it fate that she kept coming unexpectedly into his path? Fate that the sight of her sent his thoughts shooting from his brain to his heart . . . to settle uncomfortably in his groin?

He stood. "I take attention wherever I can get it in most instances. Yet, leaping into icy-cold water on an October afternoon to save some rascal of a child from drowning is not my idea of fun."

She cast her appraisal languidly over his chest before meeting his eyes. "You do look a picture."

He laughed as he tried and failed to drag his gaze from hers. "I'm sure I do."

The tension escalated as the conversation lapsed.

Say something. Anything. Ask her to tea. Coffee. Dancing . . .

"Would you mind accompanying me back to my house so I can change?" He inwardly grimaced. *Good job, my friend. Why would she ever do such a thing?* "I mean—"

"All right, then."

He stared. "You would?"

Her eyes grew wide, as though the concurrence shocked her as much as him. She cleared her throat and her cheeks darkened further. "Yes."

Adam bit back a smile and straightened his jacket over his sodden shirt. The woman's pride was unparalleled. He offered her his arm. She looked from his arm to his eyes, her gaze lit with undeniable pleasure. She curled her hand around his forearm and stared ahead.

They strolled away from the people still carefully watching them. Adam could not dismiss the pride sweeping through him to have such a wondrous woman on his arm as he led her through the crowd toward the steps leading onto the street. Clasping her hand at his arm, he held her firmly, not wanting her to slip on the worn stones.

The heat of her study burned at his temple, but he stared resolutely forward. He didn't want her to sense his disbelief of what was happening. Nor for her to guess this was the first time he had taken a woman to his home so openly and freely. Cagey and territorial over his space, he rarely let anyone over the threshold for fear of having to share the life he kept private.

Yet now, he took Laura there. He waited for the trepidation, the regret, the abrupt change of heart. None came. Instead, excitement and pride thundered through him, making him want to run with her rather than walking at a pace nearly killing him with frustration. Closer and closer they came to his address and, with each step, his eagerness to be alone with her, to show her his work, grew inside him.

The pressure behind his ribcage was as welcome as it was painful. Was it madness to feel the prospect of a future he dreamed of could come to fruition because of the woman beside him? He had no idea why that should be so, but it was the truth.

What would make her go home with him unless instinctively, she, too, knew it was important she did so?

"What is it you have in mind to do when we get to your home, Mr. Lacey?"

Her voice and question chilled him. Her tone was almost amused, as though a silent joke at his expense hung in the air between them. Annoyance prickled the hairs at the back of his neck. Didn't she feel it? Didn't she know it was the natural order of things that they'd met at the theater?

"I have something I want to show you."

She guffawed. "I'm sure you do."

They neared the end of the street where he lived. He halted and looked directly into her phenomenal eyes. The skin at her neck moved as she swallowed, but she didn't turn or look away.

"I'm a playwright."

Her brow furrowed and the humor in her eyes vanished. "A playwright?"

"Yes."

Her hand slipped from his arm and she held her basket in front of her. "Why are you telling me this?"

He lifted an eyebrow. "Most likely for the same reason you so readily agreed to come home with me. I live just a little way along this street. Let us go inside and unravel the mysteries of our actions, shall we?"

Chapter 7

What was she doing inside Adam Lacey's house, sitting upright and rigid upon a settee she could never afford? Laura crossed and re-crossed her ankles as she glanced around his drawing room. His home was masculine, bare of trinket or flower, but compared to her and Bette's place, it screamed of achievement. He'd left her to go upstairs and change out of his wet clothes. She glanced at the wall clock. The ten minutes she'd been alone could've been an hour.

She needed to leave. Get out of there. Go back to where she belonged. Back to Bette.

Standing, she stepped toward the door just as it swung open and Adam entered. Her breath caught. The man was ridiculously handsome. His dark blond hair was darker than usual, after his unplanned swim, and his face scrubbed clean. Her gaze drifted, of its own accord, to the smattering of chest hair just visible at the vee of his open-necked shirt. The man was unfairly relaxed. Laura inhaled. Handsome—stupidly, stupidly handsome.

He halted, his smile dissolving. "You're leaving?"

He moved to touch her, seemed to think better of it, and dropped his hand to his side. Their eyes locked and silence descended. Her heart beat fast with the knowledge she would've given the world to stay there. Eye-to-eye, toe-to-toe with a man who fascinated and intrigued her.

She stepped back. It was too dangerous. The atmosphere between them too potent. Her attraction to him kicked and punched at her heart. It was strong enough to make her want to kiss him, touch him, and bring that dazzling smile to the surface over and over. For little more than another breath, she would risk everything to run her fingers over his biceps and up to the plane of his wide shoulders.

Laura blinked as her mouth drained dry. What had she been thinking by coming here? She hadn't been thinking. In that moment when he asked her to accompany him back to his home, nothing but desire had whipped through her. Nothing but interest had leaped in her veins and obliterated her common sense. The fervor and lust in his eyes bespoke of a man who clearly had an agenda entirely different from hers.

She looked past him to the door. "I have a friend. She's sick. She needs me and the medicine I bought before I came upon you at the park." She brushed past him, through the door and into the hallway. "I shouldn't have come here. I'm sorry."

"Laura, wait."

Ignoring him, she hurried toward the closed front door. She had to get out of there. If she looked at him again, she'd falter. Her rationale already hung on a hair's breadth. His footsteps sounded at lightning speed behind her and when she clasped the door handle, his hand closed over hers. She stared at their joined hands and her body heated.

"Laura. Please. I need to talk to you."

Swallowing hard, she forced herself to meet his gaze. His dark brown eyes shone with a pleading she hadn't expected. How was she supposed to refuse? He was the first man in forever to make her heart pick up speed and flourish her hope for something more. She slowly pulled her hand from beneath his and curled her fingers into a fist at her side.

"I don't understand this."

He frowned. "Understand what?"

She whirled away from him, clasping her basket to her chest like it would somehow protect her weakening heart. "Why I'm here. Why I can't stop looking at you." Heat pinched her cheeks as she faced him.

His features softened and his eyes brightened. "You can't stop looking at me?"

"As a star." Mortification he might think she saw him as anything more furled inside her stomach. Bette's disbelieving laughter rang in her head.

His gaze wandered over her face and lingered at her lips. "Come back into the drawing room with me. I want to show you something."

"No, I need to go. Whatever it is you need to show me, you can show me at the theater tomorrow."

"We won't have a moment to talk alone there. Please." He directed his hand toward the drawing room.

Indecision battled inside her. She should get home to Bette. She should put as much distance between herself and this man as humanly possible. The passion in his eyes and the excitement of his smile caused notions inside her she'd never experienced before. It was as though she'd known him forever; a kindred spirit, albeit one dressed in superior clothing and residing in a classier habitat.

She released her held breath. "What is it you want to show me?"

"My play."

"Your play?"

"Yes, I want you . . . I want you to be its star. With me."

Laura flinched as though he'd slapped her. She huffed out a laugh. "No, you don't. What is it you really want from me? I don't understand this. Any of it."

"I'm telling you the truth. Please, you have to believe me."

She stared. He seemed so sincere. Yet . . .

He gave a hesitant smile. "If I am not mistaken, you would love an opportunity like this, would you not?"

Her doubt faltered. What if he was serious? She frowned. "Are you playing with me, Mr. Lacey?"

His smile dissolved. "Of course not."

Laura shook her head. This was madness. She reached for the door, humiliation and anger burning at her cheeks. "I'm not a fool, sir. You're playing with me and it stops right here, right now."

"The minute I saw you staring up at the stage from the audience the other night, I knew."

She glared. "Knew what? That I would be the sort of woman to fall to your every whim? That you could easily cajole me into your home?"

He held out his hand, as if inviting her to take it. "Come with me. Please."

She looked from his face to his hand and back again. "You're wasting your time and mine. I have to leave."

He raised his finger. "Just wait here. One minute. That is all I ask."

She opened her mouth to protest, but he took off and disappeared into the drawing room. She glanced at the front door.

Open it. Go home to Bette and stay there. This is a ruse. He knows you're a whore. He knows, and it's just a matter of time before he tosses you some notes and asks you to service him.

With a shaky hand, she reached for the door just as Adam's heavy and hurried footsteps came into the hallway. Silently cursing, Laura turned. He held a bundle of papers about four inches thick. He met her eyes and grinned.

"Here. Here it is. My play." His eyes were wide with pride, his smile heartbreakingly boyish.

Her hand slipped from the door. "That's your play?"

"Yes."

Doubt and reservation mixed with interest and curiosity. Everything inside her told her to walk out the door. Yet, she moved toward him and as she did, he laid the stack of papers on a side table. He leaned his tall and muscular frame over the manuscript and lifted one sheet after another. His fingers worked feverishly, his handsome brow furrowed. Laura's stomach tightened at the sight of his concentration. His entire body hummed with a passion she'd never seen in anyone before. It was intoxicating. Infectious.

Her heart hammered as a yearning for more of this man pulled deep inside her. "Adam . . . Mr. Lacey—"

"There." He jabbed a finger on the top paper of the pile. "This would be your entrance scene. Read it. Read Lucinda's physical description. Read it and tell me what you think." He stood back, his palms raised in a manner of surrender. "After that, if you have no interest nor wish to read more, I'll let you go and not bother you again."

Cautiously, Laura approached him. When she was barely a foot away, she dragged her gaze from his and placed her basket at her feet. Straightening, she cleared her throat and lifted the paper.

Shame immediately burned hot at her face. She was a failure. An untrue person.

Anything could have been written there. How did she tell him she couldn't read when the man had penned over a hundred sheets full of words, descriptions, and directions? Odd words she knew and learned jumped from the page amongst others she didn't understand. The page blurred and heat burned from her toes to her scalp. Why had she thought she could be onstage when she couldn't read a single sentence in its entirety?

The seconds beat like minutes. The walls closed in on her and her breathing turned harried. She squeezed her eyes shut.

"Laura?" His breath whispered across the exposed nape of her neck and he stepped closer. "What is it?"

She shook her head. "I . . . I can't read this."

"What? Why? At least see what you think."

She squeezed her eyes tighter. "I can't read it."

"What do you . . . Oh."

Shame coursed through her body, but she forced her eyes open and faced him. "Maybe I'm not the woman for the job, after all."

His blank expression was inscrutable as to what he thought or felt. Dented pride was a horrible thing at the best of times, but when standing in front of a man so handsome, so interesting and charismatic to actually believe her worthy of so much more . . . it was unbearable.

"I'm sorry, Mr. Lacey. I really need to go."

He blinked and approached the door. "Of course. I'm sorry . . . sorry to have delayed you from your friend."

Pain struck her heart anew and tears burned. She picked up her basket and, with her head held high, strode silently from the house and onto the street. Adam Lacey's door closed behind her and Laura sucked in an anguished sob.

The following day, Adam sat in his dressing room pondering whether to seek Laura out before the show began or after. The revelation she was illiterate kept him awake for most of the previous night, despite the snifter of brandy—or three—he had consumed after she left his house.

Why had he not considered such a thing? Was he really so superior to not realize she might not have had the luxury of schooling as he had?

He stood and walked to his wardrobe, shrugging on a costume jacket. The show began in less than twenty minutes. Did he have time to talk to her? He stared blindly ahead as he buttoned the coat. No. He would wait. Bide his time.

Lord knows his lack of words when she confessed she could not read must have resulted in her never wanting to see his face again. Why in the world had he not said something? Anything?

"Fool. Damn stupid fool." He entered the bustling corridor.

There had to be ways to make her still consider the role of Lucinda, despite her lack of reading skill. She would not be the first actor to make a success from such circumstances. His shock and subsequent muteness had not been grounded in her lack of education, but in the fact such a thing had not occurred to him. When had he become so self-involved? He, better than anyone, knew success did not come on a plate.

He tightened his jaw. If Laura was willing to fight side by side with him, in a bid to make his play a success, who was he to say they would not break through barriers they both thought impossible?

He hurried toward Victor's room. It saddened him that someone who held herself with such self-respect, who possessed such a sharp lilt of the tongue and watched the world with knowing intelligence through her beautiful lavender eyes, had not received a formal education.

Upon reaching the director's room, Adam knocked.

"Come."

He pushed open the door and quietly closed it behind him.

Victor frowned over the papers in his hand a while longer before lifting his head. "Ah, Mr. Lacey. What can I do for you?"

Adam wandered farther into the room with his hands behind his back and his steps confident, as a cover to the deluge of nerves jumping in his body. "I am considering something and wanted to run it by you first."

Victor put down the papers he held. "Oh?"

Adam cleared his throat. "What's your experience with illiterate actors? Have you ever worked with any?"

The director frowned. "A few. Why?"

"I wonder of the work involved. How they go about learning their lines, and if it is ludicrously time consuming employing such a person."

"Why do you ask?" Victor narrowed his eyes. "Have you someone in mind?"

"Maybe."

"Is this about that play of yours?"

Adam circled the room. He was loathe to tell Victor too many details, considering he refused to back the project. People had a habit of talking about something with others even when they wanted no part of it. Only Adam would reveal the details of his production when the time was right.

"I am considering a character for something else I am writing and wondered of the plausibility. Despite my years in the theater, I have not worked with an actor who cannot read."

Victor studied him a moment longer before leaning back in his seat and lacing his fingers. "You'd need someone willing to sit with them and go over and over the lines until he or she has them memorized. Not only that, the person concerned would have to know every scene inside and out, including movements, props, entrances, and exits." He lifted his shoulders. "Everything's possible, but you must consider the hassle and commitment of giving this person a chance when someone who could read would save you a lot of money and time."

Adam frowned. "Why money?"

Victor laughed and pushed his bulk from his seat. He came toward Adam and slapped a hand on his shoulder. "Well, dear boy, I assume it won't be you who reads these lines over and over to this mystery person? Therefore, you'd have to pay someone to do so."

Adam swallowed. It would be him. Only him. Hours upon hours of making Laura believe in her possibility. His stomach twisted with excitement. He laughed. "Ah, I see. No, of course not. Anyway, the idea is for a character I am writing, not an actual person. That is excellent. Now I know exactly where I want to go with the scene."

Victor shook his head, his eyes shining with knowledge. "It's an actor, Adam. Don't think I don't recognize the excitement on your face." He blew out a heavy breath. "I'd like to congratulate you on finding this person, on finding the face you think perfect to portray your words, but I must warn you, without financial backing of a significant supporter, no one is going to give you the go-ahead to produce this play. You need to raise enough money to convince a possible investor you're willing to risk your hard-earned cash as well as theirs."

"And that's exactly what I intend to do."

Victor raised his eyebrows. "So you have further work lined up when the *Black Quay* draws to an end next week?"

Unwelcome heat pinched Adam's cheeks. "You let me worry about that."

Silent seconds beat out between them. "There's a small production planned in Bristol. I could put a word in for you. The role is somewhat smaller than you are used to nowadays, but money and exposure seem to be your priority, bearing in mind the aspirations you have."

"What is the role?"

"I'll make some inquiries." Victor strode to his desk and picked up several script pages. "In the meantime, you should concentrate on the here and now." He walked toward the door. "I'll see you out there."

Victor left the room and Adam stared after him. His resources were minimal. He certainly did not have money to throw into a project as big as he believed his play would be, but goddamn it, he would find a way. Laura's face drifted into his mind. Her eyes, her smile, her sass, and her humor. He had to work with her. Had to see her face and body move to his literary music.

He shifted as his penis twitched, despite his best efforts to convince himself his interest in her was entirely professional. He longed to smell the soft scent of lemon that lingered in her hair and stare into the violet dazzle of her eyes.

Straightening his shoulders, he left the room and moved along the corridor. Positivity and possibility bloomed behind his ribcage. Laura Robinson was the key to the play's success. He would convince her to trust him, then teach and encourage her until she embraced his play and her potential. Together, they could take Bath's breath away and leave them panting for more.

Chapter 8

Laura stared around the packed theater auditorium. All evening, she and Tess had flown about the place as if they had wings on their feet. The colder weather seemed to have increased people's appetites for treats and drinks, which was just fine by her. Her cut in the night's takings would hopefully cover the cost of Bette's medicine and leave enough left over to grab some supper on the way home.

Somehow she'd managed to work amongst the audience and still avoid looking at the stage and Adam Lacey's uppity face. She'd been taken in by his handsome looks and dazzling smile like a young, naïve girl, rather than an aging and knowing whore. When she'd told him she couldn't read, she should've slapped the shocked expression off his face.

Well, she didn't need an education to keep her and Bette fed and sheltered. She needed her wits and her belief something better would turn up. In the meantime, she'd handle Adam Lacey as best she could—with avoidance being at the top of her agenda. She sensed a dire and dangerous desperation in him. Her priority was Bette. Not Adam Lacey—and certainly not the stage.

Other opportunities would most certainly arise once Bette was fit and well again.

"Excuse me, miss?"

Laura plastered on a smile and approached the middle-aged gentleman hailing her from a seat farther along the aisle. "Yes, sir? What will it be? I have fresh oranges, the finest, most delectable chocolate . . ."

His eyes were wide with alcohol, his cheeks rosy red even in the semidarkness. "It's not your wares I want, my lovely."

Laura's smile wavered as her hackles rose. She wasn't in the mood for some leech after a piece of flesh. "No? Then why call me over?"

He whipped a sealed envelope from his inside pocket. "I wonder if you'd deliver this note to Miss Danes?"

A wave of relief that he didn't want a fumble rushed through Laura's blood. She grinned and took the envelope. "Of course, sir . . . for a price."

The man's smile widened and his color deepened. "That, my dear, goes without saying. Here."

He dropped some coins into her hand and she grasped them tightly. "Consider it done."

She moved to walk away when he gripped her arm. "Will you tell her I think she's the best actress in the entire world?"

Laura nodded. "Indeed, sir."

"And that I have money. *Lots* of money."

God, has the man no shame? "Of course."

"And you'll come straight back if she gives you a message?"

"Absolutely."

His hand slipped from her arm and he collapsed in his seat, satisfaction emanating from him as he slapped his hands together in a gesture of a job well done. "Lovely. Well, off you go then, my girl. The play will soon be coming to an end."

Duly dismissed, Laura turned. Arrogant sod. Did he really think the likes of Monica Danes would have even a passing glimpse for him? Stifling her laughter, she caught Tess's eye and held the envelope aloft, indicating she was disappearing backstage to deliver a message. Tess waved in acknowledgment, and Laura ducked through the corridor toward the actors' dressing rooms.

Music and chatter from the stage echoed through the halls. The current scene between Monica and her costar would last at least another fifteen minutes, so Laura stepped up her pace, safe in the knowledge she had enough time to leave the envelope on Miss Danes's dressing table and make a sharp exit.

She knocked softly on the dressing-room door in case Miss Danes's dresser or someone else was inside. When no one pulled the door open and everything remained ominously silent on the other side, Laura entered the room.

Her breath caught. Every girl's paradise was held within the four walls. Bottles of perfume and lotions and potions adorned every available surface. Vase after vase of beautiful fresh flowers dotted the space with bright pinks, reds, and purples.

Envy struck deeply as Laura wandered around the room, delighting in the scents and sights of a lady. She swallowed as longing rose up inside her for a life so very different than hers. A life where color and good times reigned rather than the browns, beiges, and grays of a lesser existence—a black and white sketch of struggle.

What she wouldn't give to be able to throw caution to the wind and pursue Mr. Lacey's suggestion of starring in his play. To sing and dance and deliver the lines of a playwright . . . Her smile dissolved. If Adam Lacey's reaction to her illiteracy was anything to go by, the dream would never become a reality. Well, he didn't know her, or know what she was capable of when she put her mind to it.

A rich sapphire blue dress hanging on the wardrobe door caught her eye. It was beautiful. Laura approached the wardrobe and ran trembling fingers over the sumptuous velvet bodice; the intricate beading and lace-edged neckline cut provocatively low. To wear such a dress would make even a whore feel like royalty. She shot a glance toward the open door and back to the dress. Lord, just to see what she would look like in such a frock . . .

She shook her head. What was she thinking?

Turning back to the dressing table, she focused on the task at hand. Taking the sealed envelope from inside her basket, she propped it up against some bottles in the center of the table. Humming a tune from one of the play's songs, she stepped toward the door but once more looked to the gorgeous dress Miss Danes wore for the ending scene.

"Darn it, if you only live once." She hurried toward the dress and pulled it down. Carrying it to the full-length mirror, she held it against her bosom and grinned. The color made her eyes huge, bright and wide, her hair, dark and rich. She closed her eyes and clasped the dress to her body as she sang around the room, improvising the actions she imagined the heroine executing.

Higher and higher she sang, louder and louder. The music in her head moved her feet, the words her heart. She was born to do this. The chance of passion and adventure filled her soul. The audience would clap and sing and cheer and wave as she acted night after night. With a final twirl, the song ended and she bent at the waist with a dramatic flourish. Bravo!

A slow clap snapped her upright. Heat burned her face.

Adam Lacey strolled through the door, his gaze burning with a fire that brushed over the surface of her skin in a heady wave. She swallowed and spun around to rehang the gown at the wardrobe.

"How long have you been standing there?" Her hands shook.

Silence.

She closed her eyes when the soft whisper of his breath warmed the nape of her neck. "Long enough to know somehow, some way, you and I are going to work this out. You are destined to be my heroine. You know it as well as I."

Her heart slammed against her ribcage and she drew in a long breath. What was it about this man that had her feeling so out of control whenever he came near? She controlled men, not the other way round. That's the way it had been since her mother first set her to work. This attraction was new and surpassed nerve-wracking. She wanted to run. Escape. Before she lost all sensibility and kissed him again.

She turned.

His chocolate brown eyes bored into hers. The seconds beat between them, heavy with tension.

"We can do this, Laura. We can make my play a reality. You are the one."

Words battled in her mind and lodged on her tongue. The soft whisper of his voice spoke of more intimate things than two actors performing. They suggested lovers having hot, unbridled sex. Her gaze fell to his lips. "I can't read."

"I will work with you. I will stay with you night and day until you know every word by heart."

Night and day. Darkness and candlelight, moonlight and roses. She firmly planted her hands on his chest and pushed. He didn't want to romance her; God only knew what he wanted.

"No." She marched to the opposite side of the room, opening the space between them so she could breathe again. "No."

He remained with his spine to her, seemingly frozen. His shoulders were stiff, the muscles in his back defined like cut stone beneath the soft silk of his shirt. She trembled with the inexplicable need to run her hands from his waist and up over his back. Desire pulled at her core and her nipples tightened. What was happening to her?

"Why not?" His voice was low and reverberated through the silence. He turned. "What are you so afraid of?"

You. She straightened to her full height. "I'm not afraid of anything. What you are asking of me, a complete stranger you know nothing about, makes no sense. I don't believe this pursuit of me has anything to do with your play."

He stepped closer and she shot out her hand.

"Stay there."

He halted. "It makes perfect sense that I want you."

She shook her head. "No."

"I saw you." His jaw tightened. "Goddamn it, I *heard* you. You can sing and you are beautiful. Please. Just try this with me." He glanced at her basket by Monica's dressing table. "Surely you would prefer to one day grace the stage than sell fruits and deliver messages? I can help you have the entire world at your feet."

Realization dawned and she fisted her hands on her hips. "You want me because you have no other options."

Two spots of color appeared high on his cheeks. "Of course, I have options. I am a star."

Satisfaction furled warm in her stomach. "You're a star right now, but maybe not forever. As you've rightly said, I love the theater. I know the theater. Stars come and go, Mr. Lacey. You have written a play and my guess is no one will take it on or act the roles you've spent so many hours creating. Am I right?"

He glared. "They will if they see you."

She huffed out a laugh. "You've lost your mind."

"If you stood before a director and sang like you did a moment ago, you would be onstage before you could draw your next breath."

Why is he saying these things? How can anyone be so cruel?

She shook her head. "Do you think just because I'm new here you can attempt to charm and pursue me until I end up in your bed?" She glared as a bolt of humiliating pain quivered through her chest. "You have absolutely no idea who you're dealing with, so I suggest you go and find another plaything."

Her wavering strength returned and Laura marched forward to snatch up her basket. When she straightened, his hands firmly clasped her waist. "When I look at you, the last thing I see is a plaything." His eyes were so dark, they shone almost black. "I look at you and I see my success. I will not lie to you. Everything you say is true. I have no investor. I have no one who wants my play to become a real thing. Alive and dominant onstage." He inched closer. "But I believe in it with my entire heart and soul. I also believe you are the key to it coming to fruition. Stop hiding. Tell me why you will not take this risk."

Laura's breath hitched as her legs trembled. Why couldn't she take her eyes from his? Why did she want to inhale him like oxygen? "Mr. Lacey—"

He gently shook her. "Tell me."

Tears smarted her eyes. "I can't leave Bette. I'll never leave Bette."

His gaze immediately softened and his grasp loosened. "Bette?"

"My friend. My ailing friend." She slid from his hands and moved to the door.

"Laura?"

Squeezing her eyes shut, she turned. "What?"

"I am coming home with you when I have finished tonight."

Panic hurtled through her blood. "Don't be ridiculous."

"I am coming home with you and we are going to talk about this. I assume this Bette is at your house?"

She swallowed. "Yes, but—"

"Then I will see you after the show."

He swept past her and into the corridor. Laura stared after him. Now what was she to do?

She couldn't believe this was happening. Laura glanced at Adam from beneath her lowered lashes as, arm in arm, they left the glitz of the Bath Theater Royal, toward the lowlier part of the city.

True to his word, he'd apprehended her as she'd come out of the theater. Purposely taking her time after the performance drew to a close, she'd offered to cover Tess's part in cleaning up under the guise of thanking her for getting her the job. As Tess was hankering after sharing a drink with a good-looking stagehand, she'd leaped on Laura's offer.

Stalling and taking on double work had given Laura the time to come to terms with what would happen if Adam Lacey kept to his ludicrous suggestion. Even if his intention to come to her home was strong, it was unlikely he'd wait around on a cold, wet night like tonight.

Just another thing about the man she'd been completely wrong in assuming. He'd been waiting for her on the theater steps.

She shivered and he clasped her hand tighter where it lay on his forearm. "Is it very much farther?"

The lanterns were fewer as they neared her home, and she hazarded a guess he grew more and more regretful of his decision to accompany her. Pride rose. She and Bette might have little money, but they remained their own women who paid their rent and bought their food. No one, not even the complex Adam Lacey, would make her ashamed of what was entirely theirs.

She glanced at him. "We're almost there."

He stared into her eyes and smiled, his teeth showing white in the semidarkness. "Good."

She cleared her throat. "It's nothing as grand as your house, but it's all ours."

"Then you should be rightly proud of that." He sighed. "It's that sense of independence I hanker for desperately."

"What do you mean?"

"My parents have never believed in my acting. My money is at an all-time low and my options even more so. At first my parents thought my acting was something I had to get out of my system before I found myself a nice wife and settled down."

"And now?"

"And now, and for a long while, they have realized I won't surrender to their wishes."

"You've no money?"

He stared ahead, his jaw set. "No."

Laura didn't know whether to laugh or cry. For all his pompous attitude, it appeared the man had relied on his parents for a long while and now found himself broke. She slipped her hand from his arm as regret he wasn't as perfectly strong and capable as she'd imagined lodged like a rock in her throat.

"I have disappointed you."

She lifted her shoulders as they neared the alley where she and Bette lived. "Maybe. A little. But it's none of my business how you choose to lead your life. Independence was something forced on me. I didn't have the luxury of choice."

He laughed. "As was my dependence."

The carefree tone of his laughter would've been taken as nonchalance by someone not used to the wiles and wills of a lonely man. Lonely men were the backbone of her life, and to hear heartache in Adam's voice disturbed her. She halted at the entrance to the alley and faced him.

"Our circumstances are entirely different."

He shifted from one foot to the other. "My father is a very successful man. Retail. He owns several shops both in Bath and Bristol. I have been educated and cared for, but my parents have never *seen* me. They do not *know* me and never will. I think any man or woman who bears a child and does not truly see them should never have been given the blessing of parenthood in the first place."

The conviction in his words penetrated through her skin and bones to her rapidly beating heart. Her mother never saw her either. She only saw the profit to be made in her fifteen-year-old daughter's body. She saw nothing past the money Laura could make. Never in her life had she considered her mother's neglect in the way Adam spoke of now. The beatings, yes. The hunger, yes. The humiliation . . . but never the blindness.

"I . . ." She nodded and tilted her chin to look deep into his eyes. "I agree."

For a long moment, they stood toe-to-toe, eye-to-eye, neither moving nor—on Laura's part—breathing. Slowly, he leaned forward and kissed her. His lips were velvety soft, gentle, and loving. Her stomach knotted and she gripped his biceps.

She'd think afterward. She'd worry later. Right now, the silent connection was too intense, too important to ignore. He saw her. She saw him.

They parted, and he brushed a lock of hair from her cheek. "Show me where you live, lovely Laura."

She smiled and inert shyness flooded her to see such appreciative study in his intelligent brown eyes. "Right this way."

He stepped back and nerves bounded inside. She forced one foot in front of the other. Bette would, no doubt, be sleeping, and when she awoke to the sight of Adam Lacey in their living room, a heart attack would most likely take her beloved friend rather than the pneumonia she fought.

They reached the front door and Laura took her key from her drawstring bag. With a final glance at Adam, she pushed the key into the lock and entered her home. She listened to his footsteps behind her. The door clicked closed and he exhaled into the darkness.

She wouldn't consider what such a heavy breath meant. Instead, she pulled back her shoulders and waved toward the kitchen. "Why don't you go through. I'll just look in on Bette and then put the kettle on."

"Laura?"

"Yes?"

Determination whirled in his eyes. "I want to meet your friend. I need to speak with her."

Laura opened her mouth to refuse, to tell him to leave Bette alone, but no words formed. She slumped in defeat and led him toward the open living-room door.

Chapter 9

Adam entered Laura's living room and blinked to adjust his eyes to the darkness. The sliver of moonlight that darted across the rug at his feet and the flickering flame of a candle by the side of a bed in the far corner provided the only illumination. The air was thick with the sour stench of illness and the room cold. He glanced toward the fire grate. The embers were low and only a meager amount of kindling was stacked in a wooden box on the hearth; there were no thick logs like those that adorned his fireplace uptown.

Self-realization twisted in his gut. Was he any wealthier than Laura to afford the luxury of heat? Most likely not—he lived under a veneer of pretense while Laura eked out a living as best she could. She stood for hours serving and smiling at the wealthy men and women who came to the theater—more often to socialize, flirt, and turn tricks than enjoy the production—and for what? Little money and even less appreciation.

He had no right to call himself a man. Things had to change. *He* had to change. Tightening his jaw, Adam approached the bed, aware Laura watched him from the doorway. She had to think him more capable than he currently believed himself. With her beside him, God only knew what the future could hold for them both.

The woman lying beneath the covers moved and her thin arm reached for the candleholder beside her. "Laura?"

"I'm here, Bette." Laura spoke from behind him.

Adam cleared his throat and purposely stepped into the light when the woman lifted the candle. "Hello, Bette. I'm Adam Lacey, I walked—"

Her sharp intake of breath sliced through the room. "Adam Lacey?" A second or two passed before her raspy exhalation followed. "Am I dead?"

He glanced at Laura and she merely lifted an amused eyebrow in response.

Bette coughed. "If you're standing in our living room, dressed as you are and looking fifty times more handsome than Laura told me, I've either died or I'm dreaming."

Relief rushed from his lungs and Adam laughed as he stepped closer. "You're not dead. I'm glad to hear Laura described me as handsome."

A shuffle of skirts behind him and Laura brushed past, none too gently nudging him out of the way to get to her friend. "I never said you were handsome. Not once. Bette, Mr. Lacey——"

He cleared his throat. "Adam."

Laura shot him a glare over her shoulder. "*Adam* insisted on walking me home, but now he's leaving."

"No, I'm not."

Bette grinned before a coughing fit engulfed her.

His smile vanished. The hacking sounded so raw and painful, it made him want to clutch his chest. The woman could not have weighed more than seven or eight stone. The efforts racked her entire body. Leaping forward, he cupped Laura's elbow and moved her to the side.

He gripped Bette's skinny frame and gently maneuvered her until she sat upright against the pillows. He smoothed his hand in firm circles over her upper back until the coughing eased enough he could reach for the glass of water at her bedside.

"Okay, Bette, enough of that. Come on now, drink this."

He tipped the glass to her lips and she managed several sips before she collapsed against the pillows, her shoulders rising and falling from her exertion. Frowning, Adam pressed the back of his hand to her forehead. "Do you have any more candles? I can hardly see a thing in here."

Bette managed a half smile. "What do you want to see? Surely not my ugly mug?"

Adam smiled. "It is in your best interest we increase the light in here."

"Why's that?"

"Darkness can make a man think it is time for bed." He winked. "You surely do not want to risk me climbing in beside you?"

Bette chuckled hoarsely.

Adam turned to Laura. "Do you have more candles?"

Her eyes were shaded in the semidarkness, but he could have sworn a tear glowed bright in the corner of her eye. He reached for her hand, but she stepped back, the glow of the candle beside her now lit her suspicious gaze as it locked on his. He frowned. "Are you all right?"

She laughed, glanced toward Bette and back again. "Of course. Candles. You need candles. Just . . . just wait there. I'll be right back."

Adam raised his eyebrows at her retreating back as though the devil chased her. Shaking his head, he faced Bette. Her smile was wider than the Avon Gorge.

"What?"

"Lord, if you haven't put the wind up her."

"Laura? I think not. I do not see how anyone, man or woman, could put the wind up a woman like that." He tugged a chair closer to the bed and sat. "I have never met anyone more in control of what she will or will not do."

"Hmm . . . well, for a start, we keep the candles in that bureau over there. God only knows where she thinks she's going. You've put her in all sorts of a fuss." A glare and set jaw replaced Bette's smile as she narrowed her eyes. "What are you doing here, fancy Adam Lacey? Moreover, what is it you want with my Laura?"

Adam stared. If such a notion were possible, Bette's eyes were even more steely and determined than Laura's. He leaned his elbows on the bed, the musty smell of dank sheets and sweat lingered. He had to make this woman see what he could do for her and Laura.

"I want her to star in a play I have written. I want her to see how beautiful and talented she is. She is a born actress, whether she realizes it or not."

She raised an eyebrow. "You think she don't know that?"

Adam straightened. "She has acted before?"

Bette's eyes gleamed. "Yep."

"Why did she not say so? Why would she be working selling oranges?" He frowned. "You are toying with me. Forgive me, but why would a working actress live here? In these conditions?"

Bette grinned and let out another croaky burst of laughter. "She's an actress from her toes to her scalp."

The inkling he was entirely missing something pummeled into his brain just as Laura appeared in the doorway. "What are you two talking about?"

He stood and opened his mouth to speak, but Bette got there first. "I was just telling Mr. Lacey what a good actress you are, and we don't need the likes of him telling us what we already know."

Laura's entire body turned rigid and she scowled before brushing past him toward the bed. "Not funny, Bette."

She laughed. "'Course it is."

An incessant banging at the front door froze Laura to the spot. Everything stilled. The volume of the ticking clock on the mantel increased. He looked from Laura's wide-eyed stare to Bette. The woman's gaze was locked on Laura, her eyes reflecting a mix of question and challenge. What was he missing?

He nodded toward the hallway. "Aren't you going to answer that?"

Bang. Bang.

Still no one moved. Adam stepped to leave the room. "Fine. I'll answer it."

"No."

"No."

Laura and Bette's voices joined.

He planted his hands on his hips. "What is going on? I came here in good faith and now I feel as though you two are about to pull out some scheme to have me strung up by my trousers."

"Shhh." Laura flapped her hand back and forth. "Just simmer down. Wait."

Another knock at the door was followed by clanging metal resounding in the hallway. The caller had evidently lifted the letterbox in the front door. "Only me, Laura. Open up."

Adam raised his eyebrow. "Who's that?"

"No one." Laura's whisper was urgent. "Quiet."

Irritation swam in his veins as Adam looked from one woman to the other. The man's voice at the door held an underlying threat, an intent to do Laura harm. If she or Bette thought he would stand there rather than get rid of an unwelcome visitor, they had better think again.

"I hear you're working at the theater now, Laura." The man growled. "Now, what did I tell you about that, eh? You think you can get away from working for me that easily? I'll find out the gentleman who's keeping you, and then we'll negotiate. I'm sure if I tell him for a bit extra charge you'll give him a service he'll never forget . . ."

The remainder of the man's tirade faded into the background of Adam's consciousness as he stared at Laura. She stood stock-still, her eyes locked on his. Indecision battled in his heart, and confusion blurred his concentration. Disbelief overrode everything. *Laura's a whore? That is what Bette was inferring when she said she was an actress?*

The letterbox clattered closed and he blinked out of his stupor as words and questions bounced and leaped in his head. What was he to say to her? Did her life before she met him even matter?

Bang. Bang.

Metal clanged once again.

"You're a whore, Laura." The visitor laughed. "*My* whore now Bette ain't strong enough to keep you protected. You think you can go it alone when she's dead?" He laughed again. "Now you'll really get a taste of being alone in the big, bad city."

Irritation gave way to rage, and Adam emitted a low growl before charging forward.

"Adam. No, don't." Laura grasped his arm as he strode past her.

Without thinking, he cupped her face in his hands and looked deep into her eyes, his body trembling with suppressed anger. "It doesn't matter. I do not care. It damn well doesn't matter."

He snatched his hands from her face and marched to the front door. He yanked it back on its hinges. The man stumbled backward and down the steps, tumbling onto his ass in the dirt. Light from the lanterns at Laura's door shone on the scumbag.

Adam glared. "Get up."

The man scowled. "Piss off. This ain't the business of no punter. Whether or not he's dressed like a dandy."

Adam clenched his jaw. "Get up before I drag you up."

The light around them grew stronger as doorways opened and more and more people stepped out of their homes. Adam leaped onto the moron and wrenched him upright by his lapels. He reeked of cheap cologne and hair cream. His whiskers were sleek and shiny like a cat's; his cold eyes were green and calculating.

Adam glowered. "What do you want with Laura?"

The man coughed and spluttered as though Adam was already choking him. "Get off me, you toff."

Adam's body tensed as pain thumped at his temple. "Answer me. What do you want with her?"

A slow grin curved the bastard's lips. "You soft on her, mister? Is she spreading those fabulous legs of hers for free?"

Adam shook with rage as he stared into the scum's face.

"Hit him."

"Slap him."

"Kick him in the cock."

Shouts of women and children filled the alleyway. Did they know this man or were they just braying for blood? Anyone's blood. Poverty bred contempt; anger and frustration led to decisions that could not be altered or changed. He blinked and fought to focus above the fury roaring in his ears.

Tightening his grip on the man's jacket, Adam shook him. "Who are you?"

He grinned. "I'm the main man around here. That's all you need to know."

"The hell it is." Adam tightened his jaw. "Tell me your name."

"You shouldn't go wasting your time on the likes of Laura Robinson and her friend, Bette." He sneered. "For all her stupid aspirations, Laura ain't nothing but a dirty whore—"

A curtain of red colored Adam's vision as he wrenched his arm back and slammed his fist into the cretin's face. Bones cracked and blood flew. He threw another punch into his gut and the son of a bitch doubled over before falling to the ground. Adam pulled back his leg, preparing to land him a hard kick in the ribs.

"Adam! Adam, stop."

He snapped his head around. Laura rushed down the steps of her house. She stood in between him and the scum at their feet, her hands splayed on Adam's chest and her eyes pleading with him. "Stop. You have to stop. Think of the play. Your career. Don't do this. You have no idea what he's capable——"

"That's right, pretty whore. You tell your fancy man what I'm capable of."

Adam pulled her to the side, his heart beating like a drum. The man had clambered to his feet and now faced them, his chin tilted in defiance. Adam smiled and took a step closer. His smile stretched to a grin when the bastard inched back.

"I asked you a question." Adam pushed his finger into the man's chest. "Who are you?"

"I'm her goddamn keeper, that's who." He laughed and looked over Adam's shoulder toward Laura. "Tell him, sweet cheeks. Tell him you'll soon be working for me."

Adam lashed out and gripped the bastard's neck. Cartilage moved and creaked beneath his fingertips, but still he squeezed harder. "Who. Are. You?"

As the scum's face turned dark red and his eyes bulged, something inside Adam told him to loosen his grip before he throttled the bastard, but he couldn't. He wanted to choke him. How dare he speak to Laura like that?

"His name is Malcolm Baxter." Laura grasped Adam's forearm and he slightly loosened his grip.

"Why is he here?" He kept his eyes locked on Baxter.

Her gaze bore into Adam's temple. "Because he preys on whores with promises of protection and housing, only to have them living eight or nine to a three-bedroom house and taking all their money, leaving them pittance for food and heat."

Her hand slipped from his arm and she circled behind Baxter, her eyes ablaze with anger. She stopped at his side and pushed her face close to his. "Then he takes a free lay and beats them when he realizes their dress is torn or threadbare, as though it's the woman's fault rather than his."

She turned from Baxter, and Adam stared into her violet eyes, his heart beating fast to see such pain and rage reflected back at him. "I'm a whore, Adam. A whore from the age of fifteen right up until a couple of months ago. Go home. Go home and leave me alone."

His breathing turned harried as she strode back to the house. Anger ebbed and flowed in his blood. She had no idea who he was. No idea how he had done little more than whore himself for the last twelve months—albeit with a wealthy widow. He understood her pain, her frustration, and how little it took to make a person feel worthless.

Her door slammed and he whipped around to Baxter.

He grabbed Baxter's lapel and slammed his fist into Baxter's gut once more. The air rushed from his lungs before he erupted into a barrage of coughing and spluttering. Adam gripped his hair and yanked him upright.

"You listen to me." He spoke slowly and carefully, despite the cat-calls and shouts coming from the growing crowd of spectators. "I am going to get Laura and Bette out of here. They will not be back. If you happen to pass either of them on the street and so much as look at them, I will hunt you down and kill you." He yanked on Baxter's hair again. "Do I make myself clear?"

"You really think Laura will leave with you?" Baxter smiled, blood framing his front teeth. "That girl is a sentimental fool. She'll not leave her friend, neighbor, or the damn kid who sits at the end of the alley trying to catch a coin or two from a passing gentleman. She's her own worst enemy. She ain't got no one but Bette looking out for her. You'll have your fill and then toss her aside just like her mama did."

"The hell I will. That woman is phenomenal." Adam trembled with rage. "Maybe up until now no one has taken the time to show her that. Maybe no one has bothered to see her for who she really is." He tapped Baxter none too gently on the cheek. "That is fine. I am here now and I am telling you, Laura Robinson's life is going to change forever."

Adam landed Baxter a final punch in the stomach and he went down like a lead weight. With his shoulders straight, Adam climbed the steps to Laura's door, raised his battered hand, and knocked.

Chapter 10

The knock on the door jangled Laura's stretched nerves tighter. She snapped her gaze to Bette's. "What if that's Baxter rather than Adam?"

Bette glanced toward the window. "If I know Baxter, he would've been carrying a damn knife." She grimaced. "Chances are that won't be Lacey on the other side of the door."

Laura closed her eyes as nausea rose on a vile wave in her stomach. "Don't say that."

The letterbox clanged open. "Laura? You have to let me in. Please, listen to me."

She opened her eyes and Bette blurred in Laura's vision. Adam. He was all right. She rushed from the living room into the hallway and pulled open the door. He stood there, his hair disheveled and his gaze desperate. Why was she so stupidly happy to see him? So moved by his actions to defend her? Why did she want to kiss him until she couldn't breathe?

"Laura, please. I am serious. It does not matter to me what you might or might not have done——"

She grabbed his jacket and pulled him inside. With her eyes locked on his, she slammed the door shut. Her heart beat fast and her body quivered with raw desire and an overwhelming relief he was unharmed. Without further thought or sensibility, she pushed him against the wall and stood on her toes. "You're alive."

He laughed. "Well, of course, I——"

She pressed her lips roughly to his, consuming and branding. The same powerful sense that a happy future was possible when they'd kissed before overtook her heart again. Her body shook for him.

Wanted him. She held on to his arms and kissed him harder, deeper. Their tongues tangled and their hands discovered. As his fingers traveled over her back and hips, Laura mirrored his exploration. He was hard, strong, and muscular. Her mind soared to imagine the feel of his smooth, bare skin beneath her palms.

He gripped her waist and steered backward until her bottom touched a table against the wall. He gently cupped her jaw as he continued to kiss her, his lips firm and possessive.

They parted and their breathing filled the small space. She kept her eyes firmly closed, not wanting to see him. Not wanting to linger on the reality that even though he defended her honor, he could never be hers. So why did that only make him more attractive?

His lips gently kissed her neck. A soft, silent question. She tilted her head to the side, allowing him access and confirming her permission. The tentative nip of teeth and caress of tongue lingered lower to her collarbone. She released her held breath and moisture coated her most intimate place—a new and exciting response to a man after experiencing such dry and unfeeling sex for more years than she wanted to remember.

Bette.

Laura snapped her eyes wide open and pushed her hand to his chest.

He stepped back. His eyes were hooded with desire, his chest rising and falling. "Laura—"

She touched her fingertips to her tender lips and shook her head. "I don't know what I'm doing." She stepped away from the table. "We can't do this."

She hurried into the living room and climbed onto the bed beside Bette. She gathered her friend—her strength—into her arms and pressed a kiss to Bette's hair. With her arms wrapped around the familiarity she'd come to rely on, Laura released her held breath and met Adam's stare as he stood in the doorway.

She swallowed. "He's all right. Adam's all right."

Bette patted her leg. "But you're not. You deserve this, you know."

"Deserve what?" Laura frowned, her heart racing. What was Bette saying? Did she suspect what Laura already knew? She was falling head over sense in lust with a star of the stage.

Adam's face was in shadow and his shoulders high. A stance of determination. Her stomach twisted with trepidation when he entered the room. With his face lit by candlelight, he glanced from her to Bette and back again. He opened his mouth and then clamped it shut. Laura tensed, thankful for Bette's silence, although it must have been nearly killing the woman to be keeping her thoughts to herself.

He circled the room. Once. Twice. He came to a standstill and faced them.

Laura sucked in a breath. "You should go."

"I will once you are ready to come with me."

She blanched. "Come with you? What on earth are you suggesting?"

Bette struggled away from Laura's embrace and hitched higher against the pillow. She coughed. "You want Laura to go with you?"

"Of course he doesn't." She squeezed Bette's hand but couldn't drag her gaze from Adam's. "You need to leave. Knowing Baxter, he'll be back here at first light. No doubt with some of his paid cronies to see if you're still here. If they find you, you'll be lucky to walk away with your kneecaps intact." She slid her arms from Bette and left the bed, forcing false conviction into her voice. "Go. Please."

He crossed his arms, his jaw tight. "Pack a bag for you and Bette. You are coming with me."

Her heart pounded. "Have you lost your mind? I'm not going anywhere."

"I am not leaving you here. It is not safe. I want you both to come live with me."

Bette's crack of laughter encapsulated Laura's state of disbelief perfectly. She shook her head. "You really are living in a world of your own."

He glared. "Why stay in a place without heat and light when I have plenty of both. Why stay where Baxter can come and harangue you anytime he sees fit?"

Unease whispered a warning over the hairs at the nape of her neck. She fisted her hands on her hips. What did he want from her? Was he insane? Dangerous? Yet the thought of accepting his ludicrous proposal inched into her consideration. It was as though the soft touch of his lips and the gentle tone of his words battered through her defenses and blinded her beyond all reason.

She dug her nails into her palms, struggling to retain a semblance of rationale amid the sexual chaos battling around inside her. "You're saying you want two whores to pack up and come live with you? Just like that."

He looked from her to Bette. "Yes, I know the journey across town will be hard for Bette to endure, but I can arrange for a carriage. Please, just say yes."

She gave a wry smile, ignoring the twist of trepidation in her stomach. "And what of your career? Your reputation? Don't you think inviting us into your home will raise a few eyebrows amongst your society? Or does that not matter to you?"

"I will deal with that."

She huffed out a laugh. "I get the impression nothing matters to you past your career. What is it you really have in mind for us, Mr. Lacey? Because, right now, I'm not buying this offer comes from the goodness of your heart."

God knows, I wish it was. . . .

The ensuing silence spoke volumes and Laura narrowed her eyes against her disappointment. She opened her mouth to tell him to leave again when Bette's huffing and puffing stole her attention. She turned. Bette was in the midst of untangling the bedclothes from her legs and moving from the bed.

Laura rushed forward. "What do you think you're doing?"

Bette halted, her face red with exertion, and exhaustion showing in the dark shadows under her eyes. "The man's asking us to go live in his house. I'm getting out of this damn bed before he changes his mind."

"Are you insane? You carry on like this you'll make yourself more poorly than ever."

Bette glared. "We're going. I want out of this damn alley and away from Baxter. For both of us."

"But—"

"No buts. I've made up my mind." She gripped the bedpost. "Let's do this. Right now. I want you safe and happy. There's more chance of that happening at Mr. Lacey's home than here."

"You're ill. Have you forgotten that?"

"How could I with you reminding me every damn minute? I won't lie in this bed when we have the chance to get out of this godforsaken place. Don't even think about trying to stop me."

Laura stared. Words failed her. Never in a month of Sundays would she have thought Bette would agree to such an outrageous suggestion—further proof of just how ill she truly was. Laura started when Adam touched her elbow.

"Laura, look at me."

She turned but didn't really see him. "This is madness." She shook her head. "Less than a week ago, I left this house to go to the market. That was it. Go to the market and come home again with food for my dearest friend. I went to bed and prayed to God, asking Him to do something, anything to make Bette well again. Now tonight, you're suggesting it's perfectly sane for us to pack up and move in with you."

"Maybe your prayers have been answered in a way you cannot see or accept."

She glared. "Don't mock me."

"I'm not. I am *begging* you. If you do this, it will mean I can work with you night and day on the play while Bette rests in warmth and comfort."

"Work with me? But—"

He grasped her hands. "I want you in my play."

Irritation soared into her blood and hurt into her heart. None of this was about her or Bette. It was all about his stupid damn play. "Go. I want you to leave. It's nearing midnight. Just leave and I'll see you tomorrow at the theater."

She turned her back to him and faced Bette. "Get back into that bed. We're not going anywhere. I've lived my life my way for a long time. I don't need this from another man who thinks of nothing more than what use I can be to him." She whirled around. "If you think for one second you can waltz into our life and turn it upside down, you are sorely mistaken."

Bette tugged on her arm and Laura turned. "What?"

Bette pinned her with a glare. "And what about me?"

Aware of Adam watching them, Laura silently pleaded with her friend not to fight her on this. "I'm doing this for you. Can't you see he wants something from us?"

"How much longer do you think I'm going to last?"

Laura's stomach knotted with fear to see such coldness in Bette's eyes. They had barely shared a cross word in all the years they'd known, worked, and lived with each other. "What do you mean?"

"I'm sick and I'm dying." Bette's voice cracked and her eyes turned glassy with unshed tears. "The blood is still coming up when I cough. My chest hurts and my lungs are clogged. So if Mr. Lacey wants you, damn well let him have you. For me. Let me die in a home instead of a damn hovel."

Bette put her bare feet on the floor. Laura said nothing when Adam came from behind her and clasped Bette's elbows, helping her stand. The lack of control tasted bitter. There was no other option than to grant Bette anything she asked. Deep in her heart, she couldn't deny Bette grew frailer every day. Odd bouts of attitude showed her determination to fight, but the lapses when she didn't move or talk lasted longer and longer.

Blinking against the cruel sting of tears, Laura touched Adam's back and he straightened. She stared into his handsome face. "Leave us to get ready. Get a carriage, a horse, whatever you think it is that will get us from here across town. We'll be ready as soon as we can."

He smiled and blew out a breath. "You won't regret this. It will be a lot of work, but we're going to make it happen."

"If by *it* you mean your play, I think you've lost all grasp on reality. I'm agreeing to come home with you for one reason and one reason only. Bette. My friend. The only person I've been able to rely on my entire life." Tears clogged her throat. "I don't trust you. I don't believe in fairy tales or heroes on horseback. This is the real world. Sooner or later, you'll show who you are and rest assured, I'll see you clearly the very first time that happens."

He stared, his gaze intense with determination. "I've already shown you who I am. More times than I've ever shown anyone." He turned to Bette. "I'll see you soon."

She gave a curt nod. "That you will."

Laura stared at a spot on the wall as he swept past her. Once the front door opened and slammed shut behind him, she faced Bette. "I can't believe we're doing this."

Bette grasped her hand tightly. "This is the right thing to do.

Come hell or high water, I swear to God that man is going to change your life."

Laura sniffed. "I agree. The question is, am I going to end up worse off than I would have if I hadn't walked into that theater? Maybe there was good reason why I never dared stepped inside there before."

Bette's hand slipped from hers and she hobbled away, holding on to the furniture as she lurched to the door. "I see good things in your future, missy. All the good you've done is going to come back and sweep you right off your feet."

Bette left the room and Laura looked toward the window and the pitch-black night beyond. "Maybe he already has."

Adam stood at his dining room table and fiddled with the Michaelmas daisies he'd put in a vase and placed in the center. Why wouldn't that damn bloom stand straight? His hands shook and he swiped his arm over his perspiring forehead. Since when did he fuss over flowers or get nervous in his own home? What in God's name had he done?

The dining-room door swung open and he snatched his hand from the vase, plastering on a wide smile.

"Ladies, good morning." He gestured to the table. "Are you hungry?"

Laura led Bette carefully by the arm into the room. Her friend's inner strength and fortitude were still as strong as they had been when they'd left their house the evening before. Arguing with Bette's determination to come downstairs had been equally as futile as Laura's protestations about them coming to Adam's home, so she'd given up.

She nodded toward the table. "Did you do all this?"

He glanced toward what he considered a minimal breakfast, but judging by the expression on Laura's face, it was far too much. "Do you not like toast and eggs? I can find some meats? Or cheese?"

Her smile was tentative, but when she met his gaze, a quiet joy shone in her eyes. His heart twisted. God, she was beautiful.

She laughed. "You are full of surprises, Adam Lacey."

He released his held breath and grinned. "Long may it last. I have to do something to keep you on your toes, as you do me. Come. Sit down and make yourselves comfortable."

Laura glanced at Bette, a tinge of red darkening her cheeks. "Bette insisted on getting out of bed, but I wonder if she could take a tray on her lap at the settee? She's as stubborn as a mule . . ." She narrowed her eyes. "And mules should not be seated at a breakfast table."

Bette huffed. "But they should at a settee?" She shook her head and winked at Adam. "The girl needs her head looked at if she thinks I'm going to sit in that bedroom rather than breakfast with you down here. I'll leave it for you to decide where I sit, Mr. Lacey."

Adam stepped forward and took Bette's arm. "It's Adam from now on, and I think a tray at the settee is perfect. Especially for what I have planned after we've eaten."

Steadfastly avoiding their study, Adam led Bette to the settee. Once she was seated, he hurried from the room and into the kitchen. After grabbing a tray from the dresser closet, he rushed back into the dining room, part of him fearing they'd be gone when he returned.

He exhaled. "Here we go. Now, then, tea or coffee?" He glanced at Laura. Her expression had changed. She now looked at him as though he were an interloper rather than the host. No doubt the two women had exchanged words in his absence. "Won't you sit?"

She raised her eyebrows. "Don't you want me to serve Bette?"

Adam frowned, his smile faltering. "Why would I want that?"

Her blush was the prettiest thing on her yet. It was the softest pink, as opposed to the angry red he'd caused time and again. Or even the scarlet flush of desire after they kissed . . . the pink revealed her embarrassment, her insecurity. Adam's heart lurched. "Laura?"

She shook her head and waved a hand. "I'm being silly. I just didn't expect someone like you to serve, that's all."

Amused, he turned to the table and picked up a fork, spearing some bacon. "Someone like me?"

A beat of silence passed before she cleared her throat. "Someone famous. After all, you and Monica Danes are well-known around here. Or are you going to be so modest as to not admit that?"

He placed some scrambled eggs and toast next to the bacon and turned. "The day I can't serve myself or my guests, and instead rely on someone else to do it for me, is the day I give up acting and start scrubbing pots and pans to bring my feet firmly back to the ground."

He set the plate on the tray and poured some tea into a cup. "My parents are the snobs in the Lacey family, not me. I've seen enough of that superior nonsense to last a lifetime."

Her ensuing silence left Adam wondering what his words meant to her. He approached Bette, where she'd gotten comfortable on the settee, and placed the tray on her knees.

"There you go. That should put some color back into those gorgeous cheeks of yours."

Bette laughed, the rasp hoarse against her weak chest. "Lord, now I see why you've got Laura all of a dither. You surely are the most cocksure charmer to ever grace God's earth."

Laughing, Adam turned. He'd gotten Laura all of a dither. Thank God, because that put it mildly for what she was doing to him.

She'd taken a seat at the table. The bronze tendrils brushing her cheeks had fallen forward, obscuring her face. Adam smiled. Judging by the way her shoulders were hunched barely an inch beneath her earlobes, she'd only too clearly heard what Bette had said.

Was it egotistical to appreciate the knot of satisfaction that curled in his stomach?

He approached the table, purposely sitting beside her rather than opposite her. Not only did he want to be as close to her as possible, they had a better view of Bette should she need anything, tire, or take a turn for the worse. Guilt he might have compounded her illness rather than helped it during the chilly journey across town lingered in his conscience.

"Adam?" Laura's voice broke through his reverie and she touched his hand lying on the table. "Thank you."

Her violet eyes were wide with happiness. The sight of her in his home, sitting at his table, took his breath away. All he could think was how right it felt to have her there, to see her looking at him that way, a smile at her mouth and her body at ease.

He smiled and stared at those damn clever lips of hers. "You're welcome."

Breakfast passed in amicable conversation. Adam laughed as he hadn't in months over Bette's stories and Laura's protestations. They were a comedic double act one minute and sisters-in-arms the next. The love, respect, and care they held for each other came from them in waves. He'd never seen such commitment for one another from two people in his entire life.

He'd never wanted it or sought it before, but now that he'd witnessed the beauty in Laura's relationship with Bette, it made him yearn for the same level of intimacy with someone.

He struggled to drag his gaze from Laura's profile. What would happen to her if Bette died? What would happen to this woman who emanated such goodness, such determination and tenacity? Would she wither inside and lose the integral piece of her that made her shine from the inside out? Would her spirit be crushed, never to return?

A sudden clatter of cutlery broke into his thoughts and he blinked. Bette was struggling to put her tray on the table in front of her. He and Laura simultaneously leaped to their feet and left the table.

"Whoa there, Bette. I've got it." Adam reached her first and just managed to take the tray before it tumbled from her hands.

A raw and violent coughing ensued. Whilst Bette struggled to catch her breath, he and Laura did their best to comfort her. When Bette had calmed, Laura grabbed cushions from the surrounding armchairs and plumped them behind her dear friend.

"Right, lean back." Laura's voice cracked. "Adam knows we're grateful for him opening his home to us, but enough trying to act as though you're fit and well. You're not." She swiped her trembling hand over her face. "Once you've got your breath back, I'm helping you upstairs to bed and you'll stay there."

Adam stood back. Laura shook from head to toe, her fear for Bette clear in her shaky gestures and quivering voice. Did she already know what Adam had only guessed? He swallowed the fear that Bette had only days to live and clapped his hands.

"Right, well, seeing as Bette is under orders, I'm going to take advantage of having her commandeered to the settee."

Laura faced him and her pretty brow creased. "What do you mean?"

He forced a smile to his lips and enthusiasm into his voice. "I want to prove to you that you are capable of being an actress. A great actress."

She looked from him to Bette. "What's he talking about?"

Bette smiled and collapsed against the cushions. "How should I know? The man has two whores living in his house as though it's the natural order of things. He's a mystery to himself, I shouldn't wonder."

Grinning, Adam moved to the center of the room and held out his arms. "This, Laura Robinson, is your stage. Today is your first acting lesson."

"What on earth—"

He dropped to one knee. "Oh, Mrs. Johnson. Please, please believe I did not mean to kill your cat."

She laughed. "What are you—"

"He was in my path. I accidentally trod on his tail. The bugger shot across the pavement and under the wheels of a passing carriage before I could think to stop him."

She continued to smile and then comprehension lit behind her gaze. She narrowed her eyes, her smile turning to a scowl as she fisted her hands on her hips. She stamped her foot. "That, my boy, isn't good enough. My cat, my dear baby Robert, was everything to me." Slowly coming toward him, she bent over him. "I will see you strung up by the neck. You see if I don't."

Time stood still. They stared into each other's eyes. Boy to Mrs. Johnson. Not Adam to Laura. Two actors portraying two characters. The atmosphere was electric. Adam's heart beat hard and his excitement grew.

Laura blinked and emitted a delighted burst of laughter. A sound that told him she had tasted the sweet flavor of the stage and wanted it with a passion. Told him she held the fever for what could and would be hers.

Chapter 11

As Laura stepped from the gig outside the Theater Royal and slid her palm against Adam's, the stares of the people milling around brought sharp heat to her cheeks. The fantastical bubble she'd lived in for the previous twelve hours popped. What happened between her and Adam behind closed doors was one thing, but in view of his adoring public, quite another. What would he do now that people could see them? Would he reject her? Ridicule her?

He tucked her arm into his elbow and pleasure knotted her stomach as he led her up the steps as though they were a courting couple. She inhaled a long breath. So far, so good. Although she had no idea how she was supposed to react to the curious stares of the people meandering around the foyer.

She risked a glance at his profile. She'd never met a man like him. Not only had he taken her and Bette into his home, he'd generously paid for a woman to nurse Bette and keep her company whilst Laura and Adam went to work. What kind of man did such a thing on top of everything else he'd already provided?

Laura released her held breath. A man like Adam Lacey, that's who. Could she really believe his intentions were about both their futures rather than just his?

He steered her through a door that led backstage. As they started along the corridor, she concentrated on keeping her head aloft without revealing the turmoil of disbelief hurtling around her abdomen. Surreptitious glances were directed their way from cast and crew as her fondness and respect for Adam escalated. Both sentiments were inappropriate and futile. She was old and experienced enough to know his true motivations would become clear sooner or later. She must keep strong and not get distracted. His actions could only be for his benefit. Not hers or Bette's.

"I'd better go and find Tess." She eased her hand from his arm.

He halted and looked deep into her eyes. "Of course."

She dragged her gaze from his and studied her hands. "Adam, I know you think I can act in your play, but—"

"Not think, *know.*" He touched his finger to her chin and lifted her head. "Trust me. This will happen because I will make it so."

She closed her eyes. She couldn't think straight when he looked at her. "I'm grateful you've risked scandal and whispering by inviting Bette and me into your home, but as soon as she's well, we'll find somewhere else to live. I don't want to bring you trouble."

"You won't."

She opened her eyes, willing him to listen. "When Malcolm Baxter discovers we've gone, he'll come after me, you, or us both. I won't risk your safety that way. Bette and I will find somewhere else or, if not, we'll go back to the alley and deal with whatever Baxter throws at us. We've faced worse adversities, believe me."

"Such as?" Anger shone in the dark brown depths of his eyes, and Laura resisted the urge to shiver.

"It doesn't matter. Anyway, this isn't just about Baxter, it's about Bette and me too. We like being independent. Being on our own is the only way we've ever known and what I hold dear. We've needed our total independence to survive. It's others' interference that ruins things."

His cheeks darkened. "Letting you stay in my home is not about charity or even an act of heroism. I believe we were meant to meet, and I believe you are meant to be Lucinda."

Disappointment scratched painfully across her heart that he should mention Lucinda once again. She was stupid to think he looked at her as anything more than an actor in his play. She pulled back her shoulders and inhaled a long breath. "I can't read and I'm a whore. You're kind to let us stay. Kind to feed us and make us laugh, but I'm scared this fixation I'm Lucinda is little more than a pipe dream. What if I disappoint you? I've no idea if I can do this."

"Then all we need to do is prove you can. We can sit and act together until you know and love my play as I do. Then you will believe."

He pressed a brief kiss to her cheek and took off, marching along the corridor, leaving her confusion and doubt flailing for anchor. His hospitality and acting as her savior from Malcolm meant so much to her. Tears smarted her eyes. Yet, she still couldn't allow herself to believe he saw her as anything more than a whore.

"Laura?"

She started and stood ramrod straight, plastering on a smile. "Morning, Tess. How are you?"

Tess frowned and looked along the corridor toward where Adam had disappeared. "How am I, she says." She turned back and glared, grasping Laura firmly by the arm. "My office. Immediately."

Laura laughed as Tess propelled her along. "You have an office now? My, my."

Tess stared resolutely ahead and Laura grimaced as anxiety knotted inside her stomach. Was she about to lose the only job she'd ever had outside of whoring?

"Tess, slow down." Laura tugged her arm back. "You're nearly breaking my arm."

They reached the room where their baskets and evening supplies were piled on wooden tables. Tess released her and jabbed her pointed finger toward a vacant chair. "Sit."

Laura considered arguing but, judging by the scowl on Tess's face, a fistfight might well ensue if she did. She sat and crossed her arms. "What?"

"What's going on between you and Adam Lacey?"

What should she say? Did Adam want anyone to know he'd homed two whores?

Tess squeezed her eyes shut. "Laura . . ."

Warning and impatience were dominant in her tone. Laura unfolded her arms and stood. "Nothing."

"You were seen getting out of a gig as bold as brass with him. My God, girl, you were seen coming into the theater on his bloody arm." Tess stared at her in disbelief. "And you say *nothing* is going on?"

Intuition told Laura to keep the developing relationship—if what they shared could be considered a relationship—between her and

Adam a secret. At worst, its revelation could ruin his career; at best, it could be so short-lived, it would be nothing more than a pleasant memory come nightfall. She brushed past a goggle-eyed Tess toward the table.

"I was walking along Milsom Street on the way here and he pulled up alongside me and asked if I'd like to share his gig. It's pouring. The man was being polite." She turned and winked. "And since when does a girl refuse the opportunity to be seen with a man like Adam Lacey."

Praying Tess fell for her display of sassiness, Laura grabbed some oranges and filled her basket. The silence was suffocating.

"He offered you a ride . . ." Tess sniffed. "Fine. If you want to keep things to yourself, that's up to you; but you should be warned, if I saw you, others did too."

Foreboding seeped icy cold into her blood and she turned. "What's that supposed to mean?"

A gleam lit Tess's eyes. "Everyone's talking about the fact Mr. Lacey has stopped keeping company with certain upper-class ladies of the house. If people see him with you, they'll put two and two together and come up with six."

"Meaning?"

"Meaning, folks will be asking what you're doing that those fancy ladies won't."

The suggestion was clear and whether rightly so or not, indignation seared Laura's cheeks. "I'm not his whore."

Tess raised her hands. "Never said you were. I'm just giving you a bit of friendly advice. It's one thing to keep occasional company with people above our station. It's another to spend time with them publicly. Adam Lacey is a cut above, Laura. A man who, up until a couple of weeks ago, was undoubtedly servicing none other than Lady Harvard." She inhaled a breath through clenched teeth. "You don't want to be getting on the wrong side of her in a hurry."

Laura turned to her basket, feigning disinterest. "I've no idea who Lady Harvard is, but she's got nothing to worry about on that score. Adam Lacey is a kind man who offered to get me here and out of the rain. Nothing more."

"So there's no truth to the rumors bouncing around here since the day you started?"

Laura whirled around. "What rumors?"

She shrugged. "People talk. They've seen the way he looks at you and the way you look at him. Are you really expecting me to believe nothing else came of the night he asked you to accompany him to the Rooms?"

Memories of their kiss heated her body, but Laura tried to keep her gaze steady. "What do you want me to say, Tess? I'm not his whore, and he's in no way paying or keeping me, do you hear?"

Time halted and Laura cursed her constant need to defend herself at the slightest provocation. Would where she'd come from and what she'd done to earn a crust ever fade? She wanted a good life as much as the next person, but every time she took a step forward, she battled the suspicion she deserved to stay in the desolation and filth she was born into.

Her mother's words echoed in her head. *Once a whore, always a whore.*

"Hey." Tess stepped toward her and held Laura's upper arms. Her gaze softened. "I didn't mean anything more than concern by questioning you. Adam Lacey is nothing to be sniffed at. If he likes you, enjoy it while it lasts. I'm just warning you there are people—people with connections and money—who might mess with whatever is going on between you two, all right?"

Laura glared. "There's nothing going on between Adam Lacey and me."

Tess stared at her a moment longer before she gave a curt nod and released her. "Good. Then there's nothing else to say."

She turned away just as a young stagehand appeared in the doorway. He smiled. "Laura?"

"Yes?"

"Monica Danes has asked if you'd come to her dressing room."

She froze. "Monica Danes?"

"Uh-huh. As soon as you can, she said." The boy tipped her a wink and disappeared.

Laura stared at the empty doorway. What did Monica Danes want with her? She faced Tess, and her friend quirked her eyebrow. "Nothing going on, huh?"

Scowling, Laura snatched her full basket from the table and marched toward the door. There was only one way to fight indecision and that was to choose a path and follow it.

Her current path brought her to a stop outside Miss Danes's dressing room.

Laura took a breath. Her life changed beyond recognition whenever she was at the theater, but every time she looked into Bette's eyes, her friend's suffering brought back to reality. While there was still a breath in Bette's body, Laura would do what she could to make her better.

Maybe right now, this meant keeping her friend warm in Adam's spare bed. She raised her hand and knocked on the door. In all likelihood, Ms. Danes wanted her to fetch and carry something or maybe pass on a message to a gentleman who would later grace the audience.

"Come in."

Swallowing hard, Laura opened the door and entered. Miss Danes sat at her dressing table, her personal dresser at her feet, adjusting the actress's shoes. Miss Danes met Laura's gaze and her face immediately lit with the same welcoming smile she'd given Laura at the theater steps a few nights before.

"Laura, you came. Thank you."

She executed a semicurtsy. "Of course, Ms. Danes. I got a message you wanted to see me?"

She waved toward a chair. "Yes, yes, I did. Please, have a seat." Miss Danes turned to her dresser. "I think they're fine now, Stephanie. Thank you."

The young woman, a similar age to her mistress, smiled and moved to the wardrobe where more than one flamboyant, jewel-colored dress hung.

Laura stared at them as the yearning to wear such a frock rose once again.

"Laura?"

She blinked and grimaced as a way of apology. "Sorry, Ms. Danes. Those dresses are just so beautiful, I stare every time I see one."

She laughed. "And I am lucky to be the one who gets to wear them. . . ." She rose from her seat and approached a side table. Lifting a ceramic pitcher, she poured a glass of water. "Although, if Adam has his way, I understand you might be wearing one not too long from now."

He told her about me acting in his play? She swallowed, struggling to keep her face impassive. "Adam, miss?"

Miss Danes lifted the glass to her lips, watching Laura over the rim. She took a delicate sip and laughed. "There is no need to act innocent with me. I am Adam's friend. Always will be. If he thinks you can act, then you can. If he wants you in his play, I will do anything to help make that happen."

Laura fought the urge to flee the room. "Why would you do such a thing? I've told him the idea is ridiculous. He really shouldn't—"

"Why?"

Laura stared. "Pardon me?"

Miss Danes strolled toward her. "Why is it ridiculous? You are a beautiful woman. You're also strong and full of tenacity, according to Adam. Plus, you have a clear love of the theater and everything it entails."

Pride burned behind her ribcage and Laura tightened her jaw. "Has he told you I can't read?"

"Is that the only reason you are dismissing his wishes out of hand?"

She held Monica Danes's questioning stare. "Wouldn't it be reason enough for anyone?"

"If you want the stage badly enough, *nothing* will stand in your way. The question is, how badly do you want it?"

Laura glanced toward the dresses hanging at the wardrobe as regret wound tight in her stomach. "I have a friend who needs my mind on her right now, not some fantasy." She stood. "Did you want me for anything else?"

"Adam has told me about your friend. He has also told me about Malcolm Baxter."

Embarrassment burned Laura's cheeks. "That's my personal business. He had no right—"

"He had every right." Monica sat at her dresser and eyed Laura through the mirror's reflection. "He also told me what you did for a living before you came here."

Anger and humiliation rose hot and fast. Laura narrowed her eyes. "I have no shame in making my way any way I see fit. If there's nothing else, I really should be getting back to doing what I'm paid to do."

She turned and marched to the door. Just as she reached it, Miss Danes's voice stopped her. "I wasn't always an actress, you know."

The insinuation hung heavy in the air and Laura slowly faced her.

Miss Danes stood and took Stephanie's hand. The two women stood side by side. "Neither was Stephanie always a dresser. Stephanie is my best friend and was once my lady's maid before we left my parents' home so I could pursue my stage career. We'd do anything for each other, as I gather you would for your friend."

Laura looked from their joined hands to Monica's face. "What does any of this have to do with my friendship with Bette?"

"Adam can make you a star, Laura. You have to believe this is possible. Can you honestly tell me your friend would rather you continue to sell from your basket than take an opportunity such as this?"

"Of course not. But she is so unwell." Tears burned Laura's eyes. "I have to do what is guaranteed. Selling these wares is a guaranteed income. An income I don't have to lay with any man for."

"I understand that, but Adam has asked me to help teach you your lines in his absence. If for any reason he is called away or finds work, he would like me to step in and help. Between the three of us—"

"Between the three of us?" Laura slipped her hand from the door handle and strode back into the room. "Why do I feel as though I'm being duped? That this is some sort of ruse?"

"Because you do not trust Adam or me. Why should you?" She looked at Stephanie. "Show her."

Stephanie put her hands on the tiny buttons at the back of Miss Danes's dress and one by one popped them open. She turned her back to Laura.

"I knew Malcolm Baxter once upon a time too."

The scars that marred the actress's otherwise creamy-white skin were old, but deep. The bumpy lacerations shone pink under the muted light of the room, raised and angry at the edges. They could've been made by a knife, a belt buckle . . .

"I don't know what to say." Laura's heart beat fast.

Miss Danes turned, her blue eyes ablaze with determination. "This is what Malcolm did to me as his sweetheart. God only knows how he treats the women who make him rich. I hate him, Laura. He duped me into believing him a gentleman, as he did my parents. Now I'm free of both him and a mother and father who refused to hear a bad word about it."

Laura lifted a hand to her throat. "Your parents believed Malcolm over you? Didn't you show them what he did?"

Miss Danes gave a wry smile. "Oh, he did this after I left him, not before."

"I'm so sorry."

"No, never say sorry. You say you'll do anything to show the likes of that man and anyone else who has said you're worthless, you are worth far, far more than they could ever imagine. That's why I want to help you and why you should want to help yourself."

Stephanie silently buttoned Monica's dress as Laura's heart beat out of control. "Does Adam know? About Malcolm?"

The delicate skin at Miss Danes's neck shifted as she swallowed. "No, and he never will. Our inability to trust is understandable, and you are a savvy girl to question me, Adam, and anyone else who offers a hand of kindness. But . . ." Her eyes softened. "Sometimes a person comes along and they're real. They're real and you must take what they offer." She smiled. "Will you take what Adam and I are offering? Please?"

Chapter 12

Laura paced from one end of Adam's drawing room to the next. He'd disappeared upstairs to do goodness knows what, leaving her alone to wait for Monica to arrive. Having taken a leap of faith and agreeing to play Lucinda the moment Monica stripped herself bare, emotionally as well as physically, Laura was determined to try her hardest to make Adam's belief in her worthwhile.

She refused to be added to the number of women who'd been battered and bruised . . . even murdered, without any opportunity of escape. Adam had given Laura a chance out of the life she'd always known and today, the three of them would begin their first reading together. She glanced across at Bette, where she lay on the settee, covered with a blanket. Her friend's eyes were narrowed as she watched her.

Laura frowned. "Why are you looking at me like that?"

"You're wearing a hole in the rug." Bette nodded toward the seat beside her. "Come and sit. You've got nothing to worry about. You'll show Adam and this Monica woman what you're made of. Make no mistake about it."

Laura perched on the edge of the armchair. "I hope so."

"So you say Monica Danes had a proper relationship with Baxter? That they were lovers?"

Laura nodded. "She comes from a middle-class family. The type I imagine Baxter likes to think he belongs with."

"Did she know what he really was while they were courting? That he's nothing but a damn pimp working his whores to the bone?"

Laura shook her head. "Not at first. She was in love with him. He promised her the world. God only knows how the piece of scum blindsided her parents, but he clearly did. He promised her she could act and pursue her dreams and he wouldn't stop her. What she didn't know was how he earned his money."

Bette inhaled a long breath. "I suppose when she found out, he wouldn't let her go without a fight."

"Exactly." Admiration for Monica shot adrenaline into Laura's blood. "But she fought back and eventually got free. She's made her success regardless. I admire her for that. I think she could be a good person to know and befriend."

"Then what is it that has you pacing the room like a caged tiger?"

"Nerves, I suppose." Laura sighed. "I just worry I'll let Adam down after everything he's risking."

"The man isn't risking anything. He wants you because you fit what he had in mind for his play. I'm a good judge of character, and that man ain't got no ulterior motive. He's one of the good ones."

"What if I'm nothing like he imagines me to be?" Laura glanced toward the drawing-room door. "What if I mess up every line? Or worse, don't remember a single word?"

"You're taking the first step. That's all that matters. For all we know, this could be the start of the rest of your life. If you haven't learned anything over these past weeks I've been ill, you should've learned how quickly our time can come to be with Him upstairs. He doesn't always give us a warning."

Laura clasped Bette's bony hand. "I've also learned how to be strong. Like you. I'm doing this for us both. Don't think I'm giving up on a better life when you're fighting this pneumonia with everything you've got."

Bette gave a wry smile. "That I am, but I wish God would give me a break every now and then. There's only so much a woman can take."

Laura gently squeezed her fingers. "You're looking better today than you have for the past two weeks. Adam was right. Being here, in a warm house, and getting some proper food has worked wonders." She drew a long breath. "Which is why I'm going to do my damnedest to be everything he wants me to be in this play. It's the best way I can thank him for having us here."

"And what about what's going on inside that heart of yours?"

Laura opened her mouth to deny any growing care toward Adam, then slumped her shoulders. If she did, Bette would see straight through her. She swallowed. "I like him. More than I should."

Bette smiled. "Who says how much you should like him? The man is as handsome as they come and generous to a fault, and if what I hear is true, he sets the Bath stage alight. What's not to love?"

Laura stared. "Who said anything about love?"

Bette grinned. "You're smitten. I see it every time you look at the fellow. Don't run and hide from it. Embrace it. When have you ever taken such a shine to a man before, eh?"

Despite her lingering fear of the unknown, the excitement shining in Bette's eyes swelled Laura's heart. She laughed. "I haven't."

"Well, then. Just take each day as it comes."

Laura dropped Bette's hand and stood. "You and I both know there can be no future with him. We're from entirely different places. It's attraction, and there's a good chance that man wants me in his bed . . ." She smiled sheepishly. "And God only knows I'm starting to want to be in there with him."

They both burst into laughter just as the knocker on the front door sounded. Their laughter halted and Laura's heart leaped into her throat. "Oh, God. That must be Miss Danes."

"Then help me sit up. I don't want some grand actress seeing me slumped on the settee like I'm ready for the knacker's yard."

Laura plumped the cushions and pushed them securely behind Bette's back. She'd just straightened the blanket across her knees when the drawing-room door opened and Monica entered with Adam following close behind. She smiled widely as she glided into the room. "There she is. The star of the show."

Returning her smile, Laura walked into Monica's outstretched arms and they hugged. When Laura pulled back, the genuine fondness in the actress's eyes settled Laura's nerves—a little. Was this something she'd have to get used to from now on? People wanting to help her rather than take from her?

Monica looked to the settee and eased her hand from Laura's to approach Bette. "And you must be our audience for the day. Bette, isn't it? Adam has told me how poorly you've been."

Laura stood stunned in silence as Monica sat in the armchair opposite Bette and took her hand.

"Isn't she wonderful?" The warm whisper of Adam's breath across Laura's ear sent a tremor through her.

She turned. His face was inches from hers. The subtle scent of man hovered beneath her nostrils and she swallowed the urge to kiss him. She forced a smile. "Monica's more than wonderful. She's genuine. Something I'm learning may actually exist outside of Bette and me."

"More than that, she's willing to do whatever it takes to help my play come to fruition."

Laura looked deeply into his eyes. "As am I. I'm finally starting to believe this is possible. That I can turn my back on my old life and start anew."

"Good." His gaze wandered over her face. "Because you and Bette are more than welcome to stay here as long as you want. I want to keep you safe and happy. Help Bette get well again."

Her body heated under his heavy-lidded stare. God, how she longed to kiss him. The desire darkening his eyes to the color of melted chocolate couldn't be mistaken. "Laura——"

"When you two have quite finished staring into each other's eyes, shall we get started?" Monica's laughter drifted across the room.

Laura immediately stepped back.

Adam grinned and faced Monica. "Lord, you certainly know how to spoil a moment. How do you know we hadn't already started and I wasn't attempting to seduce Lucinda with the utmost charm and cunning?"

Monica raised her eyebrows. "Because that was Laura standing there giving you as good back. Lucinda would've been blushing like a damsel."

Forcing a laugh, Laura released her held breath and went to stand beside Monica. Bette watched Monica with a look of uncertainty and it brought Laura back down to earth with a bump. She couldn't get carried away. Her and Bette's lives had been a long trek of disappointment and lessons learned. Rushing headlong into an affair with Adam or believing Monica's motives were solely founded in her hatred of Malcolm would be hasty and foolish.

If she lost her head—or heart—too soon, she and Bette would be right back where they started. With no money, home, or person to rely on other than each other. She pulled back her shoulders. Over her dead body would she and Bette go backward.

Adam clapped his hands. "Right. Shall we get started?" He moved across the room to his writing desk and picked up two thin piles of paper. He handed one to Monica. "I've copied out the first scene for you. I thought it best we learn everything in chronological order, regardless of whether or not you're in the scene, Laura." He faced her. "That way, you'll know exactly what is happening and why, throughout the entire play."

She nodded through the barrage of nerves bouncing around inside her.

"I will spend every minute with you over the next three days. We will go over and over your lines until I have to leave for this blasted audition in Bristol. While I am away"—Adam cast a brief smile at Monica—"Monica has agreed to sit with you as much as possible, at the theater and here, in between you and her working. Does that sound like a suitable plan?"

Laura fought the urge to flee the room. The entire notion of what she was taking on was overwhelming. She nodded. She could do this. "Of course."

"Good. Then let's get started." He snapped the papers in his hand. "Act one, scene one. The hero, me, is walking along the Thames. It is nearing two in the morning and he is waiting for an accomplice who will help him break into a tavern that is locked up for the night. The surprise is that his accomplice is a woman." He grinned at Laura. "You. Or rather, Lucinda."

Laura frowned as she considered this. "But didn't Monica say Lucinda is the type to blush? I hardly think a woman like that would be willing to help a man break into—"

Monica raised her hand, cutting off Laura's words. "She blushes when she is in the hero's arms. When he is looking to ravish her. In every other aspect of her life, she is entirely in control. Do you see?"

Laura cursed the way her stomach knotted. She glanced in turn at each person in the room. Did she see? Monica had just described Laura. She forced a smile. "I see perfectly."

Adam grinned. "Fabulous. I will start and Monica will speak your lines. Then we will try a scene together once you have memorized a few words at a time."

Monica moved to stand opposite Adam and they began. Laura risked a glance at Bette. The knowing way Bette wiggled her eyebrows and smirked set Laura's cheeks to burning as if her friend held a flame to them. Clearly, Bette found it amusing Adam had written a play about the woman now falling in love with him.

Laura poked her tongue at Bette and returned her concentration to Adam and Monica. Bette sniggered quietly and Laura scowled. Sometimes Bette could be a royal pain in the ass.

Two hours later, Adam could barely contain his excitement as he followed Monica from the drawing room and closed the door. They walked to the front door. Laura was reacting to the task of learning her lines and direction with more aplomb than he could have imagined. The woman was phenomenal. Whatever challenge was set before her, she conquered. His heart pounded and his attraction soared. She was a new and exciting inspiration.

He stepped ahead of Monica to open the door. The bright October sunshine flooded the hallway, echoing his mood. "So, what do you think?"

Monica smiled and cupped his jaw in her hand. "I think you were one hundred percent right. She's perfect."

He grinned. "I have never been so sure about anything in my life. You know I could not do this without you?"

"Of course you could, but I am more than happy to help. This play deserves to be seen by thousands, and if I can have a small part in making that happen, all the better."

"Thank you." He pressed a brief kiss to her cheek.

She glanced toward the drawing room. "So, you really intend on letting Laura and Bette live here?"

His smile slipped. "For now, yes."

She frowned. "For now?"

"My money's running out at a rate of a hundred knots." He blew out a breath as frustration wound into a tight ball behind his ribcage. "The lack of funds does not concern me as much as ensuring Laura does not feel tied to one thing or person. The minute she thinks I want her here for anything other than the play, she will be gone."

"Why would you think that?"

Adam sighed. "There is a distance in her. She is keeping me at arm's length, and now that I know what she did before she worked at the Royal, I understand it. The last thing I want to do is frighten her away."

Monica smiled. "So I assume what she fears is true? You want her for more than the play?"

Adam's groin tightened with desire and he smiled. "I have never met anyone like her."

"And if it was anyone else, I would be happy for you, but it is one thing to work with a woman like Laura, quite another to fall in love with her." She squeezed his hand. "She is different than you, Adam. She has undoubtedly seen things you could not possibly imagine. You must not crowd her."

Irritation skittered along the surface of his skin and he pulled his arm from her grasp. "I will not."

"Good. Because it is important she stays here with you. For as long as possible."

The tension in her grip and the urgency in her voice alerted Adam to Monica's rare distress. He frowned. "What is it? What makes you say that?"

Her cheeks flushed and she glanced along the hallway once more. "I am just saying Laura deserves this opportunity. She is a nice girl. This could be the same chance for her that I had." She met his eyes. "You supported me and requested nothing but my hard work, in return." Her eyes darkened. "As opposed to the way Annabel Harvard supported you, in exchange for you being at her beck and call. You have made a break from her and, Lord knows, I do not want you to go back." She shook her head, her shoulders slumping. "Laura deserves this escape too. So does Bette. Between us, we need to find a way to ensure that happens."

Guilt scratched like a hundred knife tips in Adam's throat. He was going to Bristol for an audition, but what would Monica say if she knew he had also arranged to see Annabel again? Heat seared his cheeks and he opened his mouth to confess he planned to meet Annabel, but Monica moved toward the door.

She stepped outside and turned. "Laura is lovely, but bide your time. What will be, will be."

His stomach tightened with trepidation. He could not have agreed more, but there were so many graver things at stake than his feelings. He took Monica's hand, willing her to understand without actually having to confess the truth. "I am going to do everything I can to keep Laura here, but if you know something about her I do not, you should tell me now. I feel your concern is founded in fear rather than Laura's chastity."

She sighed. "It is not about Laura. Not directly."

"Then what?"

She glanced over his shoulder into the house. "It is Malcolm Baxter."

Adam glared. "Baxter?"

She nodded. "If he finds out Laura is living with you instead of surrendering to his demands, he will hurt her. Then he will hurt you. If she means as much to you as I think she does, keep her safe."

What is she saying? Did Monica . . . "You know him, don't you? You know Baxter."

Monica's eyes glazed with unshed tears. "Just keep her safe."

"What did he do—"

"Bye, Adam."

She hurried down the steps and Adam slumped against the door frame, letting her go. What good would it do to harangue her for information about a man she would rather forget? He clenched his jaw. So Baxter had not only threatened Laura, he had also hurt Monica. The man was living on borrowed time. One way or another, Adam would catch up with him. Whether that be the next day, week, or year.

A scuffling behind him pulled him upright and he turned. Laura was helping Bette upstairs. He quickly shut the door. "Here, let me."

Laura smiled as they continued to the upper floor together. "Bette's finally agreed to go to bed and rest. We can continue rehearsing as soon as I have her settled." She met his eyes. "I think I've remembered quite a few lines already if you want to go through them?"

He smiled. "I would love to."

They got Bette comfortable atop the bed and covered her with a blanket. She shooed them out the door and Adam took Laura's elbow as they descended the stairs and went into the drawing room. He released her as he closed the door.

She wandered across the room and picked up her copy of the script. Her beautiful brow drew into a frown as her gaze darted over the words she so clearly yearned to read. She was a wonder. A beauty. A woman he could no longer deny he fantasized taking to bed and making her his. God, to see her looking at him with desire rather than contained circumspection felt as desirous as his need to have her star in his play.

Inhaling a shaky breath, he approached her and drew the papers from her hands.

Surprise glowed in the violet depths of her eyes.

He ran his hands up and down the smooth silk that covered her upper arms. "When I leave for Bristol in a few days, promise me you will stay here."

She laughed. "If all goes as I hope for you, you'll leave the director flabbergasted at the audition, land the role, and be happy in the knowledge you have work for another couple of months. We couldn't possibly stay here without you. It's too much."

"You can."

Her smile faltered. "Adam, this is serious. It makes sense Bette and I move out of here whilst you are gone."

She moved to the settee and sat, turning her face to the window as though she dare not look at him.

He sat beside her. "I want you here. Where I know you will be safe."

She faced him and tears sparkled in her eyes. "Thank you, but I haven't been a burden to anyone for a very long time. I haven't allowed myself to be dependent on anyone for this very reason."

"What reason?"

Color darkened her cheeks. "I haven't felt this cared for before, and it would be foolish for me to grow used to it. Part of me knew before we even came here it was madness to do so. You know that."

Adam smiled. "Do you have any idea how beautiful you look with the sun coming through the window like it is right now?"

She smiled. "You're changing the subject."

"What if I am?"

Laura gave him a teasing glare. "Flattery will not always get you want you want, Mr. Lacey."

His smile faltered as shame furled inside him. Wasn't it flattery that made Annabel agree to see him in Bristol? He dropped Laura's hand and pushed to his feet. He approached the window. "There is something else I need to tell you."

He turned.

She lifted an eyebrow in expectation and pulled up straight, her back stiff, as though ready for a blow.

Adam hesitated. He suspected if he had the guts to admit to his weakness of contacting Annabel, Laura would tell him he had made his bed and now he must lie in it.

Nerves jumped in his stomach and he strode toward her. Taking her hand, he urged her to her feet and pressed his lips to her knuckles before looking into her eyes. "There is a possibility I have an investor for my play."

"You do?" She squeezed her fingers around his hand, her beautiful smile lighting her eyes. "That's wonderful news. Is it Victor? You wore him down and now he's stopped being such a stubborn oaf and acknowledged your talent?"

The smile at his lips trembled, but no joy filled him as it so clearly did her.

She frowned. "Adam?"

"No, it is not Victor. It's someone else." He swallowed against the dryness in his throat. "It is nobody you know. They would like to meet with me when I go to Bristol."

"Well, that's wonderful news. Why aren't you happy?"

He forced a smile. "I am."

Concern darkened her eyes. "Please don't worry about Bette and I having to leave. I wasn't expecting this to last forever—"

"No, you must stay." He gripped her waist without thinking. "You leaving is the last thing I want."

Her gaze wandered over his face before she straightened in his grasp and determination clouded her eyes. "Tell me why you aren't leaping around this room like a man possessed? You've worked so hard trying to make people listen to you about your writing. You're willing to spend hours teaching me lines. Why would you look the way you do when you have a potential investor?"

He closed his eyes. The woman's astuteness was more disarming than any weapon. "I'm worried."

"Nerves are expected when you are—"

He took her hand and pressed a kiss to her palm. "I am worried when I get back you will be gone. Do not leave me, Laura. Say you will be here when I get back."

Chapter 13

As happy as his words made her, Laura's ever-present rationale took over. "Adam, you have a lot at stake by having us stay here. What if you get the part? How long is the play in Bristol to run? One month? Two?"

He lifted his shoulders. "Eight weeks, I think. It doesn't matter."

Laura shook her head. "I won't let you risk ruining your reputation. The public loves you. Women adore you and want to be with you. Do you really want to be associated with two women society will forever view as whores?"

"What if Baxter comes after you? How can I go to Bristol without knowing you and Bette are safe or even where you are living?"

The anxiety in his eyes clawed at her heart. "I didn't come here expecting you to change your plans."

He tightened his grip on her waist. "Why don't you turn this around in your mind and conscience, and view my supposed generosity as me investing in my career? I want this to work. I want you in my play. I do not care what people think or say. I know you want this as badly as I. Let's just take one day at a time. If things are not meant to be, God knows we will find out soon enough."

Laura's mind whirled. Since when had she shied away from a challenge or the derision of others? Weren't her feelings for Adam, rather than the sharp tongues of gossips, what truly made her want to put distance between them? While she'd endured numerous counts of humiliation, his rejection of her would be far worse. He already meant so much more to her weakening heart than any bastard gent out for a quick thrill. The notion of a middle-class actor and a whore without means ever being a real couple was laughable, and she needed to accept that if she was to keep her heart intact.

She swallowed. "Adam, I'm not a grand lady or a friend. I'm not even a relative. I'm a whore who works at the theater selling wares. It's one thing for me to be here and risk scandal with you to bear it as well, but if people discover you have entrusted me in your home whilst you are out of town, they will assume—"

"That we are lovers? That I have marriage intentions toward you? Let them. Let them think what they want. I am going to Bristol and will hopefully come back with an investor and a few months' work to fund my play without help from anyone else." He shook his head. "I am on the brink of achieving what I have always dreamed of. A life of my own making. If you leave, you will not come back. I know it. Worse, I may never find you again. I want to go to Bristol secure in the knowledge you will be here when I return."

Laura looked into his eyes. The fear that his passion and desperation were borne from his infatuation of her being Lucinda rippled through her once again. Could she accept this might always be the case? Unfairness struck a cruel slash across her heart, yet his obliviousness to her feelings for him was undoubtedly a good and safer route to follow.

That she'd forever regret not taking this opportunity to change hers and Bette's life forever continued to beat at her conscience. "What will we say to people?"

He shook his head. "Nothing. Everything. I do not care. I learned long ago the only way to move forward is to care less and less what people think. Surely you understand that more than anyone?"

Heat struck her face at his insinuation. She glared. "Because I'm a whore, I suppose."

He closed his eyes. "I did not mean that."

"Yes, you did." Humiliation twisted a knot in her stomach. "That's exactly what you meant."

He opened his eyes. "I meant you have known poverty, known the streets, known what it is to eke out a living. This is a chance to do something more. Laura, I am begging you, please, take it."

Anger and self-worth mixed with fear and longing as her heart beat faster. He had so much more to lose than she did. Whether they succeeded or failed in this fantastical endeavor, wouldn't she and Bette have somewhere decent to live for a while? Wouldn't it provide the perfect habitat for Bette to recover?

She met his eyes. They pleaded with her. "If I stay, you cannot hold me responsible for any irreparable damage to your career. I've warned you—"

"I do not care."

Her hands trembled as flutters of excitement churned in her belly. She had to do this. Had to stand up and grasp this chance. She drew in a long breath. "Fine. Then we will stay."

His brow smoothed and he grinned. "You will?"

She forced a smile. "How can I not?" *Despite the risk to my stupid heart.* "If my being in your play is important enough you'll risk your parents' wrath and society's disgust, who am I to argue?"

He laughed. "I will look after you and Bette, come what may. I promise."

Without a word or warning, he pulled her tight to his body and, after a moment's hesitation, he kissed her. She foolishly allowed the moment to continue. The scent of musk and man drifted mercilessly, the strong confidence of his hands gripping her, owning her, was more sensual an experience than she could remember wanting.

She'd seen love in the eyes of others, knew it existed. Now there was every possibility she was falling into the same trap she only had once before. Yet, it wasn't hearts and flowers as she'd always dreamed; it was terrifying and left her completely out of control of her sanity and actions.

His tongue teased and tormented the edge of her lip. Her nipples tightened as she fought every primal instinct in her body. Resistance was futile. It was beyond the realms of her imagination Adam would ever care for her the same way she did him. He was in love with a character. Not her. For now, though, she was powerless not to take this moment. To keep the soft caress of his lips as a memory for the rest of her life.

The passion pulsed between them and Laura slid her hands over the muscled planes of his shoulders. They were rock hard beneath the thin silk of his shirt. Any second now he would stop the madness, step back, and realize what he was doing.

He pulled her closer and kissed her deeper. Laura exhaled a soft moan. The anticipated pleasure of basking in this simple yet erotic need from him, of what she'd imagined it would be like to be desired by him, was too much to resist. She hungrily slipped her tongue into his mouth and gripped her fingers in his hair. He pulled back to feast on her neck.

"I want to make love to you, Laura. I have to."

The soft brush of his breath and the urgency of his tongue ripped through her common sense, obliterating it and leaving it shattered and useless at her feet. She'd take, for her. She wanted this on a physical level . . . nothing more. She could do this and not suffer because of it. Hadn't she experienced more heartache through her struggles to be fed and warm than she ever had at the hands of a man? She knew how to rise above such futile emotions and accept the physical was more often than not a means to an end.

You fool. You damn fool. Stop this. Stop it now!

She stepped back. "You don't want me. You want Lucinda."

"I want *you,* Laura. You excite something so deep in me I feel I might die from it. That moment I saw you in the theater . . ." He shook his head, his gaze caressing her face, hair, and lips. "I knew. I knew you were there entirely for me. For us."

She wet her lips and fought for the words to deny the exact same bolt of lightning hadn't hit her where she stood. "It's lust, Adam. Nothing more."

His face flushed. "I have no idea what this is, but it is so much more than lust. Let me show you what you mean to me, what you do to me. Please."

The ardent intensity of his eyes and the tightened line of his jaw hitched her nerves and inflamed her desire. He was so masculine. So damn sure of everything he did and said. Her heart hammered and her center pulled with unsated desire. "I'm not yours."

"I know that."

"This is my decision. I'll make love with you, Adam . . . but to do so is my decision."

He nodded, his gaze dropping to her mouth. "Yes."

Her stomach twisted with a yearning so deep, her breath turned harried. "Then let's go to bed."

He lifted her into his arms. With her legs slung over one arm and his other secured around her back as though she weighed little more than a feather, he carried her from the drawing room and upstairs. Laura's heart raced and her body came alive with arousal like she'd never known. She wanted to feel his skin under her fingers, his mouth on every part of her.

She closed her eyes and mind to the doubts that threatened and kissed his jaw as he carried her into a room and gently lowered her to her feet. She opened her eyes and his lips found hers as his hands worked on the buttons at the front of her dress and hers at his shirt. It would take forever for him to undress her and impatience made her step back. She trembled. "Let me."

As fast as she could, without completely abandoning all decorum, she shed her dress and crinoline before bending to untie and remove her boots. At last, she tossed them aside and looked up. Adam pulled open his shirt and yanked it from his trousers. He took off his boots and dropped his trousers and underwear. Her study dropped to his groin. Her breath hitched. God, he was beautiful. Her cunny twitched as she lifted her chemise over her head and stood naked before him.

His gaze moved to her breasts, to her revealed bush, and his eyes darkened with desire. "Look at you."

Laura smiled as she stepped into his arms. He cupped her breast in his hand, his thumb roaming over her nipple until it hardened. She quivered like an inexperienced woman, confused yet desperate for a lover's touch. Her heart swelled with the desire to know this man. No matter how many times she told herself this was physical, that she was in control, the welcome relief that her years of whoring and her mother's derogatory words hadn't hardened her heart was overwhelming. She was falling desperately in love.

Slowly, Adam steered her backward. She surrendered her intuitive need for control and let him lead her. The tip of his cock touched her belly and his moisture wet her skin. She relished the tingling of warmth readying her core. They reached his huge bed, its surround elegantly worked in golden brass.

She hesitated. She had never bedded with a man in such romantic grandeur. "Adam, I don't think—"

"I want you in my bed. I want you where no other woman has lain with me. I want you to understand this is not about the play." He ran his gaze over every inch of her face. "This is not about the theater, or Lucinda, or what happens tomorrow. This is about you and me. Now."

Her heart melted as sanity fled and she nodded. Was he saying her affection was reciprocated? Joy and yearning filled her with a rush of heat and she kissed him.

He eased her back onto the bed. It was as soft as duck down beneath her. She sank into the coverlet as he lay down beside her. His hands roamed from the curve of her breast, over her ribs, to her waist and hip. Their kiss deepened. She clawed her hands up his biceps and onto his incredible shoulders once more.

Without warning, he plunged two fingers deep inside her most intimate place and Laura stared into his eyes, her mouth agape and her arousal soaring. The intense mix of tenderness in his eyes and roughness of his touch was more than she could stand. Her impatience heightened and she reached between them to grip his hardened cock. He was big and wide in her palm and she massaged him, running her fingers over his balls and across his thighs. Satisfaction furled in her stomach when his breathing turned harried.

He rubbed her expertly. Faster and harder. Their breaths became one until she wanted to scream aloud from the agonizing torment. She wanted him inside her, deep and unyielding, yet she wouldn't confess her yearning aloud. He had to want her and take her as he dreamed and wanted. She was surrendering everything to him and he was taking a huge risk having a whore in his bed——no matter how much he wanted her to believe otherwise.

"I have to have you." His breath whispered hot against her breast before he sucked her nipple into his mouth.

"Then have me, Adam. Please."

He lifted his head and looked into her eyes. "Do you want me as I want you? Truly?"

She nodded. The threat of his rejection vanished. Sincerity and vulnerability shone in his eyes and she understood, in that moment, he wanted her as equally as she wanted him. Who was she to say this wasn't just as terrifying for him? She wouldn't be a person so jaded by mankind to paint another's feelings in ignorance. He smiled and kept his gaze on hers as he slid between her open thighs.

With the tender persuasion of a true gentleman, he teased his cock against her most sensitive spot before sliding lower and entering her. Relief pushed a rush of air from her lungs, which he captured in a kiss.

Together, they moved. Thrust for thrust, she held him as he took her deeper and deeper. Their need increased in intensity, as did their sexing until nothing could have stopped her from going over the edge for the second time in her life.

"Oh, God, Adam . . ."

The words whispered from her lips as she came. A second passed before he thrust hard to the hilt and, sucking his breath between his teeth, he emptied his seed inside her. He collapsed with his head at her breast, his fingers trembling as he gripped her thigh.

"Laura."

She closed her eyes and held him to her, hoping he couldn't hear her heart breaking. The last and only time a man had truly made love to her, the act had planted the seed of a baby. Her baby. Her precious baby that never lived . . .

Adam woke to gray morning light coloring the room. He turned his head to the side, hoping she would still be there but knowing Laura would have fled his bedroom as soon as possible. He rolled over to put his face to where she had lain. The pillow was cold and he squeezed his eyes shut. She must have left hours ago. Scared of discovery . . . or scared of him? What would happen now? Would everything change between them? He had promised Monica he would not pressure Laura with his intensity and now he had made love to her.

He rolled over onto his back and strained his ears to any noise from within the house. Any noise that would tell him Laura still remained and had not fled more than the bedroom.

Nothing.

He groaned. "What in God's name have I done?"

He scrambled from the bed and wrapped himself in his robe. He strode across the room, opened the door, and stepped onto the landing. Laura's and Bette's bedroom doors were open. His heart pounded as he hurried first into Laura's room. Her bed was neatly made, everything in its place.

"No, you promised. You promised you would stay." He moved to the dresser and yanked open a drawer.

Laughter bubbled in his throat as relief rushed through him. Her cotton underwear lay neatly folded inside. He left the room and once he reached the stairs, the muted sound of female chatter filtered from the kitchen. He rushed downstairs and followed Laura's and Bette's voices.

He stood at the kitchen door. "Good morning, ladies."

Bette sat at the table while Laura fried eggs at the stove. She turned and their eyes locked for a moment before she snatched her attention back to her task. "Good morning."

His stomach rolled with uncertainty and Adam forced his wavering smile to stay in place as he faced Bette. She studied him with wizened intensity. "Good morning, Mr. Lacey. Did you sleep well? You certainly woke in a hurry." She lifted an eyebrow and ran a glance down the length of him.

He tightened the belt of his robe. The teasing tone of her voice left no doubt she knew of Laura spending time in his bed. He swallowed and pulled out the chair beside hers. "I did. And how did you sleep?"

Her eyes glinted. "Not too badly . . . considering some strange knocking on my wall during the night."

He glanced at Laura. Her shoulders were up around her ears. "Is that so?"

Bette reached for her tea. "Yep, went on for a mighty long time before everything fell silent. Whoever made the noise had some tenacity, that's for sure."

Laura slammed a plate of toast and eggs on the table in front of Bette. "Eat."

Bette winked at him and Adam bit back a laugh. When he looked up, Laura glared at him with enough venom to down a horse. He cleared his throat. "Why don't you sit and have your breakfast? I can make mine."

She smiled sweetly. "No, you sit there. I'll see to you."

Bette sniggered.

Adam glanced at her bowed head. The woman was ill, yet her humor and torment were rife. It was no wonder Laura cherished the ground she walked on. With all the hardships they had undoubtedly had to endure, Bette's wickedness would have gone a long way in keeping the desperation at bay.

Laura put two laden plates on the table and slid into the chair opposite him.

Adam picked up his knife and fork, and cut into his egg. He brought it to his mouth and chewed, his gaze on her flushed face. "This is delicious, thank you."

Finally, she met his eyes. Even with Bette's teasing, happiness brightened her eyes. "You're welcome."

He smiled and the next few minutes passed in silence as they ate.

"Nurse and I are going to take Bette for a stroll in the park this morning." Laura reached for her teacup. "What are your plans today?"

"I am meeting Victor for a spot of lunch later to discuss the audition in Bristol. I need this part just to keep me in finances, and any direction he can give will help me secure it." He paused. "Would you consider joining us?"

She halted with her fork halfway to her mouth. "Pardon?"

"I would like Victor to meet you." His mind drifted to the dreaded meeting with Annabel and he drew in a shaky breath. "I would like to make a last-ditch attempt to get him to invest in the play. I am convinced if he meets you, he will succumb."

Her eyes gave nothing away. There was no judging what she thought about his leaving for Bristol now they had made love. He wanted to talk to her. He could not leave without ensuring she knew how important the previous night was to him.

Upon her continuing silence, Adam cut into some toast. "I am meeting Victor at the Pump Room at midday. Do you think you will be back from the park by then?" He looked up.

She stared, her violet eyes wide with uncertainty. "I'm not sure it's a good idea—"

Bette coughed, the sound raw once again. The day before it had seemed marginally better and Adam frowned. "Are you not feeling any better than yesterday?"

She pressed her hand to her mouth and waved dismissively with the other. "Don't you go fretting about me. I'll be right as rain soon enough."

"I could get the doctor to come and see you. That cough—"

"Will see itself right." She inhaled a raspy breath and reached for her knife. She pointed it at Laura. "You go with Adam and meet with this fancy director. After everything the man is doing for us, the least you can do is suck up to some rich toff who has the money to make his play happen. I'll go with Nurse to the park and you go with Adam. I'm sure the two of you have plenty to discuss before you see this director."

Laura shook her head. "I'm coming with *you*. Adam is perfectly capable—"

Bette pinned her with a glare. "I said, go."

Two spots of rose darkened Laura's cheeks, and when she looked at him, he raised an eyebrow. What had gotten into Bette?

Laura shook her head and raised her hand in surrender. "Fine. I know when I'm not needed. I'll join you for lunch, Adam. Only, Lord knows what you think I can say or do to change Mr. Talisman's mind."

Bette grunted her approval and bit into a slice of toast.

Adam smiled. "That is settled, then. I will leave you ladies to it and get duly washed and dressed."

Neither Bette nor Laura offered a response. Adam glanced from one woman to the other—sometimes it was best to steer clear of women poised for a fight.

Chapter 14

Adam stole another glance at Laura and pride yanked at his chest. Her shoulders were pulled back and her demeanor spoke of a lady used to taking lunch in the Pump Room. The faint blush at her cheeks was the only indication this was not the norm. He smiled. No matter how uncomfortable or unusual this situation was for her, she dealt with it as she did everything else—with carefully poised determination.

He touched her hand lying on the dining-room tabletop. "Are you all right?"

She smiled, her beautiful eyes soft with amusement. "Yes, at the moment. If you ask me the same question when Mr. Talisman arrives, it's likely you'll get an entirely different answer. For now, though, I'm fine."

"Well, you look as though you belong here, so enjoy it."

She glanced left and right, and he followed her gaze. The uppity and curious stares of different women and the blatantly lustful glances from several gentlemen came at Laura from every direction. Adam narrowed his eyes. She deserved to be admired and looked at with respect. The only possible reason they had to study in such a way could be the less expensive cut of her dress, or maybe the inferior quality of her hat and shoes. He would have liked to deliver them each a slap.

He faced her. "When we finish lunch, I am taking you shopping."

"You will do no such thing." She stared down one particularly haughty woman sitting at the table alongside them. "I know exactly what you're thinking. There isn't a woman or man who could intimidate me in a place like this, believe me."

Adam looked around. "I do not doubt that. You are fifty times the lady of half the women in here. You deserve the clothes to prove it."

She dragged her glare from the woman who now looked engrossed in her menu. "Thank you for the offer, but the next dress or hat, shoes, or parasol I own will be bought with *my* money, not yours."

He smiled. "Ah, that insufferable independence of yours rears its head once again."

"Indeed, it does."

Approaching footsteps turned their heads and Adam was not surprised when Laura's hand whipped from beneath his. Victor Talisman's gaze shot from the table to Adam as he drew to a stop beside them. "Well, good afternoon. I hope I am not past our scheduled meeting time?"

Adam pushed to his feet and clasped Victor's hand. "Not at all." He gestured to Laura. "May I introduce Miss Laura Robinson. She—"

"Works at the theater." Victor dipped his head, his forehead creasing with a frown. "As an orange seller, I believe."

Laura smiled. "Yes, sir. I do. It's nice to meet you."

Although tempted to jump to Laura's defense, Adam swallowed back his words. She bore Victor's disparagement with confidence, and Adam suspected any intervention on his part would earn him a swift kick to his manhood.

Victor took a seat, shook out his napkin, and draped it across his lap, his eyes still on Laura. "Well, you'll have to excuse me if I say how unorthodox this is to see you here together. I'm most definitely intrigued."

Adam sat and raised his hand to the waiter. "All will shortly come clear, Victor."

The next few minutes passed with the ordering of drinks and a light lunch of soup to start, followed by a salmon tart for Laura and Somerset ham for the gents. Once the waiter left, Adam placed his elbows on the table and laced his fingers.

Victor raised his eyebrows expectantly. "Well? Are you going to shed light on why you asked me here?"

Adam cleared his throat. He needed to proceed with honesty. The wily older man was respected in the theater industry for his fairness. He would listen to Adam, if nothing else came of the meeting. He met the director's eyes. "I guess you have already surmised why I brought Miss Robinson along today?"

Victor glanced at Laura, his expression nonchalant. "I have an idea, but as you're my friend and one of the finest actors in Bath, I'd like to think you'd do your utmost not to jeopardize your advancement. I hope this meeting has something to do with this play of yours as opposed to the gossip surrounding the time you and Miss Robinson have been spending together."

Adam looked at Laura. Her face had reddened, but she carefully continued to study Victor. Her self-containment was all the permission Adam needed to further press the director for support. He lifted his chin. "Miss Robinson is my Lucinda, Victor."

Neither surprise nor disbelief altered Victor's expression as he appraised her face and hair and lingered a while longer on her lips. "I see that."

Possibility twisted inside Adam's gut. "I'm glad. She is perfect."

"How do you feel about Adam plucking you from obscurity and presenting you with an opportunity of a lifetime, Miss Robinson?"

She coolly met his gaze. "I feel grateful and duty bound to do my best for him. Admittedly, I'm still shocked he would choose me from the many other actresses who'd want this chance—"

"Other *actresses,* Miss Robinson? Aren't you an orange seller and not an actress?"

Adam shifted in his seat. "Miss Robinson—"

"I've wanted to be onstage my entire life, sir." Laura smiled. "If Mr. Lacey thinks I can do this, then I'll do my utmost to prove him right. The one thing I am not is a person who gives up. I want a better life and will work as hard as I can to get it."

"I see." He turned his attention to Adam. "I'm assuming Miss Robinson is the actress of your imagination whom you said couldn't read?"

Adam dragged his gaze from Laura's profile, his heart picking up speed. He did not want her subjected to Victor's negativity. This was not why he brought her there. He wanted the man to see what was possible. How Laura could light the stage like a sunbeam on a dank, dismal day. He tightened his jaw and pummeled his rising irritation into submission.

"She is, but I am confident she will prove an impeccable student. She has already committed lines to memory from two scenes and we have rehearsed less than a single day."

The waiter reappeared. Silence bore down as he served their soup and filled their glasses with water. Once he'd left the table, Victor picked up a spoon and stirred his soup. "Why don't you just ask me the question that brought me here, Adam?"

Adam picked up his spoon. "I need your investment. I know you've already refused me, but I want you to come to my house and see Laura work. I swear, if you do that, you'll understand how she can make this play remarkable."

Victor lifted his head and stared into Adam's eyes. "I already see the potential of what you're proposing."

Laura's sharp intake of breath sounded across the table. "Really?"

Victor smiled. "Yes, if nothing else, the determination in your stature is halfway to making Lucinda come alive, my dear." He turned to Adam. "That doesn't mean I'm willing to part with my money. Not this time."

Adam frowned as frustration simmered like fire in his chest. "Not this time? If I don't get this play to the stage, there will not be a next time. If I do not have the money to support this venture, how can you expect me to write another play? I have approached everyone I know. I would not have come to you a second time unless I had to."

"I'm sorry. The risk is too great. I don't have the money to support a play that may never get a single showing. I recommend you go to Bristol and see a few people there. I'm willing to put my name as a reference for any interested investors you might find, but I don't have the cash to help you. I'm sorry."

Adam looked to Laura and sympathy shone in her violet eyes. Her sympathy was the last thing he wanted. He wanted her to see him as her provider, her hero. To trust he would make this happen for him—and her.

"I have already written to as many people in Bristol as I possibly can and nobody is willing to back me." He concentrated on Victor. Looking at Laura was just too hard. "For the love of God, do not make me beg. You must have less faith in me than you have led me to believe over the years."

The older man tore off some bread and shrugged. "I have faith, just not the money. There is nothing else for it but to work your behind off until you have the money to do this yourself." He smiled at Laura. "I'm sorry, my dear, but it seems your visions of grandeur are to be extremely short-lived."

Her eyes widened and Adam inwardly grimaced.

He knew that look. "Laura—"

She pinned Victor with a glare that would've scared children from the workhouse. "My visions of grandeur, sir?"

Victor laughed. "I merely mean to state—"

"My ideas of grandeur stretch far and wide, but let me tell you this, Mr. Lacey will find a way of getting his play to the bright lights of London, let alone Bath or Bristol. I'll see to it myself, if necessary."

Victor swallowed his bread and smiled. "I see. Well, I wouldn't even hazard a guess as to how you would make that happen, but I admire your gumption."

Adam's fragile threads of temper snapped. "Do not talk to her that way. Laura is one of the most hard-working, honest, and determined women I have ever had the pleasure of meeting. She does not deserve your derision or lack of respect."

The director turned, his blue eyes darkening. "Then you have no need for my money, or me, do you? The pair of you clearly have the resources and integrity to make this happen of your own will."

Anger pulsed in Adam's blood and he rose, his appetite gone. "Indeed, we do. Come, Laura."

She dropped her napkin on the table and pushed to her feet. When she looped her hand through the crook of his elbow, Adam straightened his spine as his confidence grew. Together, they would make the play come to fruition. "You will regret not backing me in this, Victor."

The director glanced at their joined arms and shook his head.

"You're a superior actor, Adam. A damn fine writer even, but first and foremost, I've been in this business a mighty long time and I fear you'll not get what you want here in Bath or anywhere else, for that matter. Writing is an art form. There are men and women who do nothing else but perfect that craft day and night. You cannot expect your first effort to be snapped up and produced."

Adam glared. "I would accept that if I had not seen your reaction to it when you first read it. I know you think the play has potential. You just do not have the courage to take that leap."

Laura tugged on his arm. "Adam, let's go."

Victor smiled. "Take the girl's advice. I'll see you soon."

Frustration hummed through Adam, making him tremble. "It is a sad day when a man of your vision becomes so jaded he no longer provides a new writer a chance. I wish you luck, because without risk, nothing is possible."

The director's smile vanished. "Theater needs money. The cold, hard cash of the Royal Family and all the aristocracy. I want everything for you and more, but sacrifices have to be made and egos damaged for anyone to progress. Do not make the mistake of upsetting people along the way."

Adam gripped Laura's hand on his forearm. "Fine. Then I will find my investor in Bristol and take pleasure in proving your theories wrong upon my return."

Victor waved his hand. "You do that, my boy." His disparagement drifted over Laura from head to toe. "Because you've most definitely found a diamond in the rough. She's exquisite. I wish you well."

Laura snatched her hand from Adam's and put her palms on the table. She leaned forward until her face was inches from Victor's. "I'm more than exquisite, Mr. Talisman. I'm strong and I've lived a life that's made me want to finally take the world by the neck and squeeze something more out of it. This will happen for Mr. Lacey, and it will happen for me. I wish you good day."

She whirled away from the table and brushed past Adam toward the exit. Ignoring the stares and whispers of the ladies surrounding them, Adam faced Victor. "Whatever lies in Bristol holds the key. I hope you don't live to regret this."

Victor glared. "I could say the exact same thing to you. Tread carefully, my friend. Very carefully."

Ignoring the shiver of trepidation that skittered up his spine, Adam gave a dismissive snort and headed for the door after Laura.

The following evening, Laura smiled as she collapsed on Adam's drawing-room settee, exhausted from their previous hours of re-hearsal, her mind full of lines and choreography. "I swear I'm too tired to even stand upright at the theater tonight." She laughed.

Adam dropped down beside her and took her hand in his. "I am hoping it will not be for much longer you will have to work the stalls. Before we know it, you will be onstage where you belong."

She stared at their joined hands clasped on his lap, as a further surge of love warmed her heart. "I'm going to miss you when you go tomorrow."

"You just keep practicing those lines. I will be back before you know it."

She nodded, not daring to look up and risk him seeing pathetic love shining in her eyes. Since their single night of lovemaking, he had neither attempted to bed nor kiss her. The absence of intimacy spoke volumes and, try as she might, Laura couldn't fight the humili-ation she'd surrendered to him too easily and desperately.

"Laura?"

"Mmm?"

"You are learning your lines quicker than I ever dared imagine. You told Victor just how you feel yesterday. Things will work out. I promise. I am willing to do whatever it takes."

"I know that."

He touched his finger to her face and lifted her chin. Laura closed her eyes.

"Then why won't you look at me?"

She opened her eyes. His gaze shone with tenderness in the lamp-light, concern in their dark depths, and his brow furrowed. "What is it?"

Insecurity and an unwelcome stupidity rose like a rock in her throat. "Why did you bed me, Adam?"

He stiffened. "What?"

She stared at him directly in the eyes. "I want to know. I'm not saying I was an innocent party to what happened. I wanted it too. I just wonder what your reasons were so I'm clear." *Liar. You want him to say it meant something. That he's as equally out of control as you.*

For a long moment, he said nothing, and Laura's heart kicked painfully with each beat.

His jaw tightened and a barrage of emotions swept through his eyes. Each more bewildering than the one before.

Nausea rose bitter in her throat.

"I see." Laura pushed to her feet as traitorous tears burned behind her eyes. "Thank you. Your silence has made things perfectly clear. I just needed to know." She moved toward the door.

"Laura, wait."

She turned.

His mouth opened and closed, but no words came forth.

Laura huffed out a laugh as pride swelled hard and fast, turning her breaths harried. "I just didn't want you to leave for Bristol without speaking of it, that's all. For the last few days since we slept together, the topic has been like a huge boulder wavering between us. I just needed it to be pushed in one direction or the other before it fell and someone got hurt."

He strolled toward her and her heart beat faster.

"Now we know where we stand. No one gets crushed."

He came ever closer.

She forced herself to stay in the same spot. *Say something, you cad. Say you used me.*

His gaze wandered languidly over her face and he took yet another step closer until a whisper of breath couldn't have passed between them.

"I took you to my bed because I wanted you." His breath danced across her lashes. "I took you to my bed because the sight, scent, and sound of you drive me insane with need." He dropped his mouth to her jaw, nipped and kissed his way to her neck. "Yet I dare not do so again for fear I will lose the best thing that has happened to me in a long time. I want you to believe our lovemaking is about you and me entirely, not the play. I saw the hesitation and fear in your eyes before our passion took over. I want you to come to me of your own free will next time."

Tenderness seeped into her heart and desire poured into her core. He cared for her. Moreover, he respected her. She tilted her head back and smoothed her hands over his arms as he continued to feast on her neck. "We're adults, Adam," she whispered. "We can do what we like as long as we both know where we stand."

He eased back and looked deep into her eyes. "You want me again?"

Yearning ran like hot liquid through her blood, causing her breasts to rise and fall. She swallowed. "Yes."

He clamped his mouth to hers and his hand kneaded roughly at her breast. The strength of his lust sent her arousal out of control and she thrust her tongue into his mouth, tugging impatiently at his shirt. How could she not want him? He believed in her. Escalated her potential. Made her feel like a woman every time he looked at her.

She clawed at his shirt and he moved her backward until the hard wall met her spine. Time stood still as he opened the buttons at her throat and pulled her dress wide open; she yanked and tugged at his shirt. Her mind emptied of everything but Adam and the animalistic need to have him before he left for Bristol.

"Laura. My sweet, fiery Laura." He gathered her skirts and maneuvered his fingers beneath their voluminous curtain.

Her heart pounded and her excitement grew. His hand smoothed up her thigh, higher and higher; then he plunged two rigid fingers deep inside her. She dropped her mouth open, her head falling back against the wall. "Adam."

He leaned lower and kissed the revealed skin at her chest and collarbone, all the while massaging her into a frenzy. The delicious sensations of her building release gathered strength and rolled through her over and over on a trembling wave. She reached for the front of his trousers.

Adam growled against her breast. "No, you. Just you. I will not take you again until I come back from Bristol." He met her eyes, his face contorted with desire and flushed with a passion that bordered on frightening. "When I come back, I will be yours to own. Just not yet."

She attempted to protest, to question, to ask what he meant, but his ardent strokes were impossibly good and she clung to him as sexual satisfaction ripped through her very core, soaring through her blood and into her heart. She shuddered and gasped, thankful his mouth swallowed her groans lest she waken Bette from her slumber upstairs.

How had this passion grown so quickly? Had she lost her mind? She panted with need and confusion as the sweet ripples of her orgasm slowly ebbed and flowed through her. When they'd passed, Adam smiled and brushed the fallen hair from her eyes.

"We are in this together. I promise."

Hope edged at the periphery of her heart and she nodded. "I trust you."

Please, God, don't let me be wrong to trust him. . . .

Chapter 15

Later that night, Laura clasped a note in her hand and headed toward the door that led to the backstage corridor of the Theater Royal. Her body still hummed from Adam's earlier seductive and expert attention. Her heart, on the other hand, was a mess of insecurity. Adam's strange insistence they wouldn't make love until he returned from Bristol lingered in her mind. What had he been thinking when he said that? Why did Bristol hang between them as a barrier to the physical . . . or was it the emotional?

She shook her head and pulled an invisible—if flimsy—protection around her heart and focused on the job at hand. The gentleman who'd given her the note for Monica had been good-looking, obviously moneyed, judging by the amount of champagne he'd requested for him and his friend, but more importantly, had eyes that spoke of kindness.

Laura smiled. She hoped he turned out to be a gentleman in his attentions toward Monica and not the devil in disguise. After spending time with her, Laura really wanted to see her new friend happy and smiling with a man who cared for her. She turned the corner toward the stars' dressing rooms.

The sight of Malcolm Baxter drawing Monica's dressing-room door closed with meticulous care caused Laura's heart to stop as she froze to the spot.

Dressed in smart trousers and a jacket with his hair neatly combed, Malcolm could easily have been mistaken for a gentleman rather than a pimp. What was he doing here?

For a long moment, he loitered there, his gloved hand clasping the door handle and his head bowed.

Time stood still as he straightened and turned. His eyes met Laura's and his face showed a fleeting moment of surprise before a wide grin split his expression. She silently counted to five as he strolled toward her. Trying and failing to will her feet to move, she longed to brush past him as though his presence didn't bother her one bit. Her feet remained stuck to the floorboards.

She pulled back her shoulders and waited.

"Laura." Baxter stopped in front of her, his cold blue eyes appraising every inch of her face, lower to her revealed cleavage. "You are looking quite spectacular."

"Thank you." Her voice was clear and smooth, despite the suppressed hatred causing her legs to tremble.

"Your new career suits you." He glanced back toward Monica's dressing room. "I have just been speaking to Miss Danes. We're acquainted . . . from the past." He raised his eyebrows. "It was actually you we were discussing."

She narrowed her eyes. "Why?"

"Because you matter to me, why else?"

"What do you want? You know I work here. You could've come and found me without bothering Miss Danes."

His smile stretched. "Oh, I didn't bother her."

Laura glared, anger burning like fire in her chest. "I doubt that."

Still smiling, his eyes shone with malice. "It seems you've had quite an effect on her. She even asked me to leave you be." He laughed. "For some reason, she thinks I might have cause to hunt you down. Can you think what might have given her that idea?"

Their eyes locked and revulsion twisted a knot in her stomach. "I'll ask you again, what do you want?"

"I see your landlord has leased your home to another whore."

Laura tilted her chin, battling the fear that she and Bette had made a huge mistake by giving up their place, their independence, in favor of Adam's generosity. "And what of it?"

"You're a fool if you think a star of the stage can give you more than I can. You're a whore. A whore without a home. Once Lacey has tired of you, then what?"

"If that happens, it will my problem to deal with, not yours. Go away, Malcolm."

She moved to walk past him and he shot his hand into the air. She froze. His eyes lit with glee, his smile wolverine. "The whore in your sad excuse for a home knows which side her bread is buttered. She knows her place. Doesn't try to mix with people above her station. You might as well kiss these actors' asses"—he leaned closer, his whiskey breath making her want to gag—"or suck their cocks for all the attention they're going to give the likes of you."

She fisted the note for Monica tighter in her hand. "Go to hell."

"And how's Bette? Is she dead yet?"

Her anger soared, and before she could stop herself, Laura jabbed a finger in his chest. "Don't you even speak her name, you—"

He gripped her hand in the ironclad vice of his, spun her around, and yanked her arm up behind her back. She sucked in a breath as fear shot like a boulder into her throat. Panic rushed through her when he shoved her forward, ramming her cheekbone against the corridor wall. Tears of humiliation burned like needles at her eyes when people hurried past without stopping to intervene.

"Once a whore, always a whore. Look how the people walk by knowing you deserve to be shown a bit of roughness to keep you in your place." Malcolm licked a trail of warm saliva along her ear. "I want you to come and find me at the end of the show. I want your earnings from tonight and every night. After that, I'll be back once a week to collect whatever I feel appropriate. You avoid me, cause me trouble, or go to the law, I'll come back and take my frustration out on your new friend Monica Danes. She hasn't your gall, Laura. She's a lady and doesn't fight like a cat. She does as she's told."

He sucked maliciously on the skin at the side of her neck, branding her, before shoving the side of her head so her cheek banged against the wall a second time. He chuckled before releasing her.

His footsteps slowly faded as she stayed there, her heart racing and her body shaking. When she closed her eyes, a tear slid down her cheek.

Stand up. Stand up now.

Summoning every inch of her self-preservation, she pushed away from the wall and swiped at her face. With her hands trembling, she tilted her chin and strode toward Monica's dressing room and knocked on the door. What if he'd left Monica beaten and bloody behind the door?

"Come in."

Relief at the sound of Monica's call pushed air from Laura's lungs as she entered. Monica stood in front of a full-length mirror and her smile was instantaneous when their eyes locked, despite the painfully obvious shakiness of Monica's gestures. "Laura. What a surprise. How are you?"

She tightened her jaw. "I just saw Malcolm. In the corridor."

Monica stared for a moment before she nodded and took a seat at her dressing table. "I see."

Unsure whether to approach her and offer comfort or keep her distance, Laura hesitantly stepped forward. "Are you all right?"

"I'm fine. Judging by the mark on your face, Malcolm took more of his anger out on you than me. Why don't you sit down? There is no need to hide anything from me as far as he is concerned. The man is an animal."

Laura gratefully sat on a chair beside her friend. "He wants my money."

Monica nodded. "I know. The question is, what are you going to do about it?"

She stared. Anger, frustration, and, more than anything, determination shone in Monica's arresting blue eyes.

Laura frowned. "What did he say to you?"

"Nothing of any importance."

She reached for Monica's hand. "If he threatened to hurt you after everything you've done to help me. . . ."

Monica glared. "He hasn't hurt me. That man will never hurt me again."

The tension around them pressed down on Laura's chest and she released Monica's hand. "I won't pay him what he wants. Not now. Not ever." She swallowed the bitterness that dried her mouth. "I owe him nothing. I've never worked for the man. He's after me now because Bette's dying. He thinks I won't survive without her, so I'm easy pickings."

"And will you? If she dies?"

Pain stabbed deep in Laura's heart and she looked past Monica to the mirror beside them. She stared at her reflection. "Yes, I will." She faced Monica once again. "But Bette won't die."

"Laura——"

"She won't." Laura tightened her jaw. "Bette is made of steel, I swear to God. The woman has more strength in her little finger than I have in my entire body."

Monica huffed out a laugh. "I very much doubt that. Your strength is palpable."

Laura frowned as concern for Monica's welfare grew once more. "Does Malcolm know you're helping me with Adam's play?"

"He has no idea we're associated. He knew you were working here and asked I advise you to cooperate with him." She smiled. "He stupidly expected me to intimidate you because of my supposed celebrity status. The man's an imbecile."

Laura smiled. "Not entirely. I was pretty intimidated when I first met you, for all of five seconds and I realized how lovely you are."

Monica smiled softly and stood. She clasped Laura's hands in hers and squeezed. "You must keep a low profile. Better still, do not leave the house while Adam is in Bristol. I will tell the manager you have taken ill. If Malcolm finds out where you are living, he will come after Adam as well. I cannot let that happen. He means too much to me for me to see his life endangered."

Laura's smile slipped. How could she not have considered before that Adam and Monica were more than costars? Did Adam open the doors of opportunity for her too? Had he slept with Monica as he had her?

Monica frowned. "When Malcolm was courting me, he kept the pretense of a gentleman. Little did I know the money he attained from keeping whores supported my acting. I thought he was a businessman. I thought he loved me and was happy to support me in my endeavors, whatever they might be."

"Until it was too late?"

"I loved him, Laura. I fell, and fell deeply."

Nausea rose bitter in her throat. Monica loved Malcolm? "How could you . . . how did you ever . . ."

Monica shook her head, her mouth twisting in disgust. "He wasn't the same then as he is now. He was considerate, charming, and instilled a belief in me I could achieve anything. Then once he had me . . ."

Laura's heart filled with anger. "Your reputation was on the line as well as your family's. God, the man is scum."

"Just like Adam's family, my parents have never condoned what I do. When I finally fled Malcolm, he was all too keen to tell them we had spent night after night together. My parents cast me out."

"Didn't you tell them he ran whores?"

She smiled wryly, her eyes cold. "They would never believe such a thing of such a well-dressed, well-educated gentleman."

Laura sniffed. "Malcolm is about as educated as me. How could they fall for his lies?"

"I did." Two spots of color darkened her cheeks. "We all did."

A few seconds ticked by in silence before Laura met Monica's gaze once more. "So Adam helped you?"

She gave a wry laugh. "Oh, he did not know about Malcolm or the fact I risked my entire happiness for such a man. He just knew I was going to leave the theater for lack of money and he would not let that happen."

"So, what did he do?" Laura stared. The notion of anyone, especially someone as beautiful and talented as Monica, wanting Malcolm repulsed her, but how could she judge her for risking everything for a moment's lovemaking? Heat warmed her cheeks.

"When I told Adam my parents cast me out and I had no choice but to give up acting and find a regularly paying job, he refused to let me walk away." Her eyes softened. "He shared his income with me. He gave me money to live in an apartment until I could earn enough to keep myself."

Trepidation and the whisper of stupidity rippled through Laura's body. "And now I'm the second woman to come into his life who was connected, and possibly ruined, by Malcolm. The second woman he wants to save."

"Yes." Monica's concerned gaze bore into hers. "He now knows through Malcolm we are connected, and if I know Adam, he'll be planning Malcolm's demise. We must find a way to change his mind before he does anything he will undoubtedly regret. We have to make him realize vengeance will end in bloodshed. Whether it be his, yours, or mine."

Laura resisted the shiver that ran up her spine. This couldn't go on. She and Bette had to leave Adam's home. She would not risk him being beaten or killed.

"I need to leave Bath and disappear." She pulled her hands from Monica's.

Monica touched her hand. "This is not your fault. Together, we will find a way to keep Adam safe and our lives as they are."

She pushed to her feet. "No, this isn't the life I should be living. I'm a whore with her own destiny, not Adam's project or Baxter's slave." She stared, traitorous tears burning her eyes. "And I'm not your friend. I need to go."

"Laura, wait."

She rushed for the door and yanked it open. What had she done? What had Adam exposed himself to by saving her and Bette from Malcolm that night? This wasn't who she was. Laura Robinson helped women and friends; she didn't make their lives worse. The walls closed in on her and her breathing turned harried.

"I have to go. I'm sorry." Remembering the note she had for Monica, she thrust it at her. "Here. A gentleman in the audience . . . I forgot. Take care of yourself."

She rushed into the corridor, her mind reeling. She would wait until Adam left for Bristol in the morning; then she and Bette would be gone upon his return.

Nausea swirled in Laura's stomach as Adam came down the stairs of his town house. Unbeknownst to him, this would be their final moment together. She shivered against a sense of foreboding that crept like icy fingers up her spine. Resisted the ache in her heart wanting to rush forward and embrace him. He reached the bottom stair and laid his suitcase at his feet. His gaze wandered over her face before he gently cupped her jaw.

"I will be back before you know it and then we can hit rehearsals full force." He hesitated. "If everything goes as planned with the investor, I hope I can at least persuade the Theater Royal here in Bath to take a risk with my play."

Laura exhaled a shaky breath. "I'm sure everything will work out perfectly."

He smiled. "You and I both know you are going to make this play fifty times better than it would be with someone else as Lucinda."

"I certainly could do no better with you and Monica as my tutors." She forced a smile, hating the way she deceived him.

What else could she do? If she told him what happened at the theater the night before, he wouldn't leave for Bristol but would undoubtedly go looking for Baxter.

"You must consider Monica and I as your allies." Adam's voice dragged her from her thoughts. "We want this for you as much as you do for yourself. You must turn to her whilst I am gone."

She pushed aside the hurt she felt when he referred to the two of them as allies. Did he not think them more than that? "I will."

"Monica sees so much potential in you."

Words battled on her tongue. She longed to ask him if every kiss he gave her, every embrace, every stroke of her skin meant more than a balm for his own satisfaction. He was a good man, but she did not need saving by him. She yearned for him to look at her as an equal. As a woman.

She stared into his eyes. "Why is Monica so generous with her time when she won't even be in this play? I long to trust you, her, and a million and one other people, but I won't lie to you. It's hard for Bette and I to do that after being deceived so many times."

His smile slipped. "You do not believe our caring for you is genuine."

Care? I don't want you to care! I want desire, love, respect. . . .
"No."

He stepped away from her, tilted his head back, and planted his hands on his hips.

Laura's heart picked up speed and her determination soared. Second by silent second, the romantic clouds drifted away, leaving behind the realistic, down-to-earth woman she was before she met him.

He dropped his chin. "Monica knows Baxter."

Laura stiffened. Was he about to tell her he intended to go after Baxter? "Do you know how?"

His jaw tightened and he looked to a spot past her shoulder.

"She would not tell me, but it does not take a genius to work out her relationship with a man like that."

Laura carefully studied him as pride swelled behind her ribcage. "Am I another project, Adam?"

"What?"

"I know how you helped make Monica what she is today. Isn't that what you're trying to do for me too?"

His jaw tightened. "How can you think that?"

"How can I not?"

He moved to touch her and then halted as if he'd changed his mind. He pushed his hand into his hair, his gaze confused. "Yes, I helped her, but this . . . us . . . is different."

"I've looked after myself for far too long to want or need anything from anyone. I think deep down you want me to stay because you think you can save me."

"Goddamn it, Laura. I did not *save* Monica. The woman was, and still is, as full of spunk and verve as you. I do not feel I saved her, and I am not trying to save you. I see your potential. Potential that should not be wasted because society will not give you a chance."

The question she really longed to ask . . . the issue that really bothered her stung on her tongue. Dented pride and hurt reeled inside. Their eyes locked and the atmosphere shifted.

His brown eyes darkened with passion and she fought the need to have him take her in his arms and hold her as he had yesterday afternoon.

It was clear from his talk of her *potential* that she couldn't dwell on their intimate moments. Why did fate have to be so cruel to have her dream of seeing more than ambition in his eyes when he looked at her?

"Monica and I never laid together, Laura." His voice was velvet soft. "Nothing of any intimacy has ever occurred between us."

She stared as unease rippled through her. He saw through her so easily. She'd become entirely incapable of hiding her thoughts and feelings from him. She lifted her shoulders. "It would not bother me. The decision to sleep with you was mine."

He gripped her waist. "Our lovemaking meant a lot to me. I do not want you to think what is happening here is about me swooping in to save anyone. Monica came into my path expecting nothing. I will not regret doing something to help her, and I will not regret this time with you either."

She studied him. Nothing but sincerity shone back at her from the depths of his eyes. How she longed to trust him, but that notion would never come to fruition. She'd been burned too many times to stride headlong into a potential disaster. Her attraction and passions for this man had already led to decisions beyond her usual control.

If she stayed longer, Lord only knew what would happen next. She would not allow Adam to mist her eyes and fool her heart.

She tilted her chin. "People matter to me, Adam. The theater will always come second to that. Always."

He smiled. "I would not have that change for me or anyone else. Just because I live and breathe the theater, that does not mean I expect the same from you. All I know is you are meant to be Lucinda, but you have to feel her too . . . in here."

He touched his hand to her breast and her body instantly heated. The connection between them was dangerous. He stepped closer and pressed his lips to her jaw and lower to her neck. Her center pulled and her nipples tightened.

"Adam, stop."

He pulled back and met her eyes. "I have never met anyone like you."

She cursed the instant desire that curled her toes. She'd been down this road before and it had become her personal nightmare. She stepped back and absently brought her hand to her stomach.

"Our time together is something I'll never forget." She drew in a strengthening breath. "But we mustn't lose sight of who we are. I didn't lie with you as an act of gratitude or expecting anything in return. I did it because I wanted to."

"As did I." His gaze hardened. "I had hoped you would have felt that. Known I was with you. Not Lucinda. Not the play. Not the theater. I did not expect to feel so strongly about you, but I should have known it was inevitable from the moment I laid eyes on you."

She pulled her shoulders back in an effort to heighten her resolve. She had to leave him. Leave Bath. For his sake, even more than hers. Baxter would not let her go easily. That much she knew.

He took her hand. "Say you will be here when I get back."

Tears burned the back of her eyes. Shame furled inside her stomach. "I'll be here when you get back."

Color darkened his cheeks and he smiled as he released her hand to pick up his case. "Then I will ask nothing more of you." He glanced toward the front door. "I must go."

His gaze wandered over her face and hair a final time before he turned and opened the door. He turned, his handsome face alight with fervor. "Our future is going to be amazing. Promise me you will think about that for the entirety I am in Bristol."

She nodded and forced a small smile. "I will."

He hesitated before nodding curtly and heading down the steps and into the gray morning. With her breath catching in her throat, Laura hurried forward. He waved down a passing hansom cab and, without looking back, climbed inside.

From the steps of her lover's home, she stood stock-still until the cab disappeared out of sight. Turning, Laura went back inside and closed the door, their conversation tumbling through her mind and conscience. It was for her protection and his that she had said she would be there when he returned.

Tears broke. What if his child grew inside her? What if she lost another blessed babe? She had no right to expect anything from him and needed to take care of herself, Bette . . . and whomever else came along, alone.

Chapter 16

Laura pushed away from the door and swiped at her cheeks as she hurried upstairs to dress. The walls were closing in on her, and her heart was nothing more than a traitorous problem residing in her chest. She needed to get some things to take with them if she and Bette were to leave today.

Her head ached with tension as she entered the guest bedroom and pulled open a dresser drawer. Where would they go? Bette traveling to London was an impossible notion considering the state of her health. Laura retrieved a shawl and wrapped it around her shoulders. Bristol was no longer an option because Adam would undoubtedly be there for the coming months.

That left the surrounding villages.

She grimaced as she tied her boots. She'd never considered country life before because of her embedded love of the city. Nothing but fields and animals day after day. This might have filled some people with peace, but it filled her with dread and an innate burden of isolation.

Putting her off more than anything was the fact she was in the country when she lost her baby. Traveling to see a lover who promised her the world—who promised farm life would suit her once she left the bustle of the city. What a fool she'd been to think men who came visiting Bath had any intention of giving a teenage whore a future.

It wasn't a broken promise that lingered in her blood—it was the miscarriage of her unborn child. A baby she'd known was made because the lovemaking felt wholly different than ever before. Tears smarted her eyes and she hastily blinked them away. The passion, hope, and love she'd harbored for her baby's father had given them the blessing of a child. It was fear the same sensations had pulsed through her under Adam's caresses and love that frightened her more than anything.

Inhaling a deep breath, she looked around the room. What other choice did she and Bette have but to flee? Yet, she couldn't ease the fear of what it would do to Bette's condition, traveling into town, let alone enduring an undoubtedly rough and bumpy ride by coach into Saltford or somewhere similar.

She left the room and headed toward the stairs. They had limited money and limited resources. Lord only knew how they'd manage past a fortnight without her earnings from the theater. The sense of finality that squeezed her heart when speaking with Adam earlier reappeared. Why did she have to fall for the man?

As she descended the stairs, she shivered.

Something was wrong. Here. In the house. A sense of impending doom cast its shadow around her.

She reached the bottom stair and Nurse's muffled voice filtered from the back room. Laura lifted her chin and shoved her negativity aside. No matter what, her life was settled with Bette. Without her, it tipped and dipped until she felt sick with dread. Doing something tangible would only silence the little voice inside her saying she was running scared from her life, while constantly living through others.

Another shiver ran up her spine and she glanced toward the back room.

She swallowed. Getting them away from Bath would be the best thing in the long run. Her feelings for Adam were just a symptom of wanting more—of wanting a real, bona-fide relationship one day. Undoubtedly, the break from whoring and having a taste of something better had caused her to lose her mind a little. Once she and Bette were packed up and on the road, reality would ground her once more.

Looking to the mirror, she pinned her hat into place with shaking fingers.

"Miss Laura, where are you?" Nurse's hurried footsteps clattered along the parquet flooring.

Laura froze as every instinct in her body screamed of danger. She spun around. "What is it? What's wrong?"

"It's Miss Windsor. I'm so sorry."

Panic ripped through Laura's blood on an icy-cold stream as she looked past Nurse along the hallway. "What do you mean, you're sorry? Has something happened?"

"She's dead, miss. I'm sorry."

Laura stared. *No. No. No!* "You're wrong. She can't be."

She brushed past Nurse, their shoulders knocking, causing the other woman to stumble backward. "Get Dr. Penders. Now. Run there as fast as you can."

A vile, metallic horror coated Laura's mouth as she rushed forward. *Don't do this to me, Bette. Don't you dare leave me.* Tears blurred her vision and she stumbled into the back room. "Bette. Oh, God. No."

Her beloved friend was slumped motionless in the wheelchair, her head tilted to the side, her mouth gaping lifelessly open, and her pallor that of an old woman. Tears burned and scalded Laura's eyes as she touched Bette's forehead and her cheek. She was warm, but so very still.

"Bette. Bette, please." She shook her shoulders and Bette's head lolled backward. "No, please."

Laura drew her friend into her arms and held her tight. "Come on, Bette. Talk to me. Let's sing, shall we? What shall we sing?" Tears ran like hot wax down Laura's cheeks, searing and burning. "Please sing with me. Please."

The minutes passed like hours while she waited, holding and rocking Bette, memories of their years together tumbling through her mind.

"Laura? It's Dr. Penders."

She gently eased Bette back into the chair and kissed her cheek. "It's all right, the doctor's here now. It will be all right."

Dr. Penders appeared in the doorway just as she pushed to her feet. Their eyes briefly met before the doctor strode to Bette and placed his fingers at her neck. Laura trembled, her heart splitting and cracking. She pushed her fist into her mouth to stop from screaming aloud as the doctor leaned his ear to Bette's mouth.

If she dies, it's my fault. Talking with Adam, fretting over the state of my stupid heart instead of looking after her.

She swiped at her tears. She had no right to cry. No right at all. She looked to Dr. Penders and inside screamed, *Tell me she's alive. Tell me!*

The kindly doctor shook his head, his eyes glazed with tears. "I'm sorry, Laura."

She sucked in a breath that scratched her throat, like the sharpened blade of a knife, and staggered forward. She fell to her knees in front of the woman who'd shared her life for so long.

Her heart split in two as she dropped her face into Bette's lap and her friend's skirts muffled the howl that ripped from deep inside Laura. How could she go on? Would Bette ever forgive her for meeting Adam? For falling in love and neglecting the only person she could ever count on?

"Bette, don't leave me. I'm sorry. I'm so sorry."

Adam grimaced. The coach journey from Bath to Bristol would have been an uneventful one if he had not been squashed between a woman of ample stature and her daughter, who clearly wanted to make herself known to him in ways that left little to the imagination. Once upon a time, her pretty blond curls and delicate porcelain features might have caught his interest. The expensive and flamboyantly rich color of her clothes even more so. Clearly, the young woman's parents were not short of a penny or two. His ambition would have made her a tempting prospect.

However, any philandering came to an abrupt stop the moment he set eyes on Laura. She inspired him to be more and want more. He smiled. Good God, she would give these two a run for their money and leave them quaking in her wake. Silliness and vanity were so low on Laura's list of priorities, it was laughable.

The coach drew to a stop at the bottom of Park Street and Adam levered himself out from where he was wedged. He came free with an almost audible pop. He touched a finger to his hat and smiled at mother and daughter in turn.

"Well, it was very nice to meet you, ladies. Enjoy your time in Bristol."

He stepped from the coach and succinctly slammed the door just as the mother made a lunge for his sleeve. Forcing a wide smile, Adam waved as the coach rolled away. He released his held breath. Undoubtedly a lucky escape.

Shaking his head, he lifted his overnight bag from the cobbled pavement and strode toward the hotel where he had booked a room for the night. It was also where he had arranged to meet Lady Annabel Harvard, otherwise known as his interested investor.

Adam tightened his jaw. He should not be there. He should have gone straight to the audition and then caught the first coach back to Bath. Had being in Laura's company not taught him anything? A person did not run from trouble—or take the easiest solution to the detriment of their soul. They kept their integrity and strode the right path for as long as it lasted. Yet, here he was, walking straight along the wrong one.

He should continue to take his script to every theater in town and scout the actors' studios and bars for an interested director or producer. He should not be entertaining this meeting. He should not be seeing Annabel again. If all was as innocent as he had told himself a thousand times since he left the house, he would have told Laura the investor's name. He had not. Which was as good as lying.

The bronze-colored canopy of the Royal Hotel came into view and Adam's footsteps slowed. Nothing untoward had happened thus far, and if he had his way, nothing would. He intended on making it clear to Annabel he would welcome her money as a bona-fide investor, nothing more.

"So why is your heart racing and your nerves jumping? You're a fool if you mess this up, Lacey. A bloody fool."

Drawing in a long breath through flared nostrils, he mounted the steps and moved into the hotel foyer. The Royal Hotel was lavish and expensive. A stay he could ill afford. It would've been wiser to save the money for the production of his play. Forcing the scowl from his face, Adam approached the desk clerk.

"Good afternoon. I have a room booked. Adam Lacey."

The clerk beamed, his eyes lighting like lamps. "Ah, Mr. Lacey. Lady Harvard has been eagerly awaiting your arrival."

Adam's stomach knotted and his shoulders tensed. What was

wrong with the woman to be broadcasting his arrival to all and sundry? He smiled tightly. "Has she indeed."

"Yes, sir. If you'd like to leave your luggage, Lady Harvard is in the lounge taking a glass of wine before dinner. Maybe you'd like to join her?"

"My room——"

"Will be ready as soon as you are, sir." The clerk held Adam's gaze, one eyebrow raised.

Adam slumped his shoulders. "Instruction received and understood. I will join her now."

The clerk gave a curt nod and gestured for a bellboy. Knowing it was a lost cause to delay the inevitable, Adam turned and strode toward the lounge at the other end of the foyer. He entered the room and was greeted by muted chatter and high-ended, high-pitched laughter. After a less than comfortable journey, a glass of wine might be just what the doctor ordered. He glanced around.

Annabel rose from her chair a few feet away. "There you are."

He pulled on a smile and approached her, taking her outstretched hands in his. When she offered him her cheek, he chastely kissed her and pulled back. "You look as immaculate as always."

She smiled demurely, moving a thick coil of blond hair to lie over her breast. "I'm so glad to see you again."

He nodded toward her seat. "Shall we? I could do with a drink. That journey from Bath never gets any easier. I think I'll take the train next time."

"Oh, it's wonderful. You really should." Annabel's eyes glittered with her usual childlike euphoria that had lords and gentlemen falling over themselves to be with her.

Adam turned away, lest he be drawn into the farcical innocence of a woman who scratched like a cat in bed, drawing blood and squealing as she came. The waiter caught sight of Adam's raised hand.

He bowed. "Yes, sir?"

"Another glass for Lady Harvard, please, and I'll have the same."

"Yes, sir."

The waiter left them and Adam faced Annabel. "So . . ."

She smiled. "So, indeed."

Irritation simmered. So she was going to make this as awkward as possible. That was fine. She could play it whichever way she wanted. He had zero intention of indulging her. This was a business meeting. No more, no less.

"Shall we talk about the play?"

"I was very surprised to hear from you, you know. Beyond surprised, if I am honest." Annabel shifted back in her seat and fixed him with a calculating smile he knew well. Negotiation. She wanted something, and the chances were she would not leave without it. She glanced around the bar. "I thought our parting conversation the last time we saw each other made things perfectly clear how you feel about me and my offer to help you."

He stared at her profile. "Nothing has changed, Annabel."

She snapped her head around. "Yet here you are sending me a message to meet you. How very strange." Her green eyes were cat-like as they ran languidly over him.

He tightened his jaw. "I will not lie. Asking you to meet me was not what I wanted to do, but I hoped you would take me seriously about something I believe will make you a lot of money."

Her sweetly satisfied smile vanished. "It is not money I want."

Taking a deep breath, Adam held her angry gaze. "I have found my Lucinda."

She stiffened and her eyes darkened. "What?"

"The heroine from my play. I have found the perfect actress to play her."

Annabel's gaze narrowed and her cheeks flushed. "Is she as equally beautiful on the outside as inside, as you describe her in the play?"

"Yes."

"Her name?"

Protectiveness poured into his veins as Laura's face, relaxed and flushed after their lovemaking, filled his mind. "Does it matter?"

Her eyes flashed with anger. "Who is she, Adam?"

"No one you would have heard of or know. She had no idea she could even act until I showed her she could."

She raised her eyebrows. "You showed her? What on earth does that mean? You tied the poor girl to some scenery and shouted a few lines at her?"

Her laughter caught like fire in his blood and when the waiter stopped beside them with a silver tray, Adam swiped his wine from atop it.

The waiter nodded. "Anything else, sir? Madam?"

Annabel took her glass and waved her hand in dismissal. "Not at the moment, thank you."

The waiter left them alone and Adam drained half his glass in a single gulp.

Annabel's gaze bore into him as she delicately raised her glass to her lips. She sipped and smiled. "And so it all becomes clear."

Adam frowned. "What does?"

"You want me to finance this girl's career. Am I right?"

"It would be better if you looked on it as an investment."

She huffed out a laugh. "You treat me like a bank and expect me to see anything you do as an investment."

"That is not the case at all."

"I do not care about money or profit or any of those things. I have money. I will always have money. What I do not have is a lover." She drew her gaze over his upper body. "A lover who can touch me and make me melt with just the soft lick of his tongue."

Self-hatred furled inside his stomach. He could not do this. Nothing was worth this. "Do you know something—"

"I will give you whatever money you need, my love. I will get the money for you today. But you will not get a penny unless you return to our previous arrangement."

Frustration burned like wildfire in Adam's chest and he shook his head. "The arrangement will not be reinstated. I hoped you would deliver on your words. You once spoke about your belief in my play and me. I hoped you would view an investment as a sound business decision. Nothing more, nothing less."

"I see." She slowly placed her glass on the table between them. "Then we have nothing else to discuss. I am not a charity. If you want something from me, you have to be willing to offer something in return."

"Annabel, for crying out loud." He squeezed his eyes shut and took a long breath. "Why will you not listen to me?"

He opened his eyes.

She elegantly rose from her seat and stood above him, her eyes dark with fury and her cheeks flushed. "It is not difficult. I want a lover and you want money. Now you have a decision to make. I am neither blind, nor stupid. I see the change in you. I spoke to Monica before I left. She told me an orange seller has caught your eye and you believe she is your Lucinda. Do you really expect me to believe this girl can act? Can star in a play you hope to take to the West End?"

"Why is that so hard to believe?"

"You are passionate. Ambitious granted, but ultimately passionate. Something about this woman has affected you enough that you are not seeing the whole picture. Now, I suggest you get this girl out of your system in any way you see fit and then come back to me when you are ready to be serious about what you want to do in regard to your future."

Adam glared. "I am serious now."

She laughed. "This girl is nothing more than a strumpet. Admit it."

He stood, his body trembling with suppressed anger. "She is Lucinda, Annabel. I know she is. With her in the starring role, the play will succeed. That much I can promise you."

"Then you have wasted my time by asking me to meet you. I thought you would have come to your senses and wanted to take your play forward. Instead, I learn the rumors are true and you have become fixated with a pauper girl. My God, even Monica and her uppity ways were preferable to that. At least she has a modicum of talent."

"How do you know Laura hasn't without at least meeting her?"

Annabel smiled. "Laura? That's her name? Laura who?"

Goddamn it. "Why is it important? Why don't you meet her when you return to Bath? Let her and I play a scene for you and then you will need no further convincing I am right in what I am saying. She is everything I have been looking for."

Her smile dissolved and two spots of color darkened her cheeks. "Get rid of her. Your eyes contain nothing but blind lust. With Monica it was different. You had seen what she could do and wanted her to continue to act. This is nothing more than a girl who has stirred your loins. My God, how could you be so foolish to think she did not target you?"

Adam glanced around the lounge. People talked and laughed, oblivious to the atmosphere between him and a woman who possibly held the future of his play in her hands. She was his final point of call. He could think of no one else from whom to beg, borrow, or steal.

He stepped toward her. "Annabel, please. Do this for me and I will never forget it. I promise you."

She stared at him for a long moment before she narrowed her eyes and shook her head. "How dare you think you have anything other than sex to offer me." The words were whispered from between her clenched teeth.

"All I'm asking—"

She jabbed her gloved hand into the air, cutting him off. "My money is mine to do with as I will. I saw your potential and supported you so you could keep acting. Now you think I will do that again, for one of your *friends,* for nothing but risk in return. How dare you."

"Laura is not a friend."

Her eyes flashed with knowing and her mouth twisted in contempt. "As I said. Lust, not the appetite for success, mars your common sense."

Rare heat warmed his cheeks. It was undoubtedly obvious how Laura affected him. How he wanted to hold her every minute of every day. Look into her eyes and feel the soft sensation of her skin against his lips. How the hell was he supposed to hide that from a woman who knew him so intimately?

Annabel's eyes widened with knowing. "My God, you have already slept with her, haven't you?"

"No." He clenched his jaw.

Her smile turned wolverine. "Oh, Adam, it is written all over your puppy-dog face. You are besotted." She lifted her purse and pulled out a key. "Here."

"What is this?"

"A spare key to my room. You know where I am when you have come to your senses and realize you have a decision to make. What is it you *really* want? A piece of strumpet on the side and a lowly role in a small play in a backstreet Bristol theater? Or do you wish to see you and a real actress starring in the West End? The future is entirely up to you." She took his hand, opened it, and curled his fingers around the key. "I will invest if you come back to me. You are supposed to take care of me." She leaned close to his ear. "You are supposed to take me where and when I want, fuck me like you mean it, and enjoy every damn second." She pulled back and smiled demurely. "The decision is yours."

"Annabel—"

"You know where I am." She whirled away and sashayed toward the lounge exit.

His heart raced as she disappeared through the gilded double doors. He slumped into his chair and picked up his glass. The liquid trembled within. He drained his glass and put it back on the table with a clatter. Damn Annabel. Damn his parents. Damn his entire situation. He glanced toward the doors once more.

The faint image of Annabel reflected in the glass of one; Laura in the other.

For the first time in his life, his heart was split between the stage and something—or someone—else. How was he to know which would last?

Chapter 17

Laura smoothed her trembling hands over the skirt of her black dress and glanced along the deserted street. As she stood in the doorway of Adam's home, the ache in her chest wouldn't abate, and her eyes were sore from crying. It was as though the whole world had gone into mourning since Bette's passing. The last remaining red and gold leaves had fallen from the trees across the street, leaving the branches bare, and the sun hadn't shone for days.

When footsteps sounded behind her, she drew upright and turned. Dr. Penders placed his hand gently at her elbow. "It appears Mr. Lacey has decided to stay longer in Bristol than originally intended. When you dictated that letter to me, you should've let him know where you're going. It's not fair the man has to scour the city looking for you upon his return."

She smiled wryly. "It's likely he'll not feel the need to look for me."

"I am reluctant to agree. He's done so much for you and Bette. It's inevitable he'll be hurt by your leaving."

"It's better this way." She lifted her chin. "Mr. Lacey has his life to get on with and I have mine."

"You're stubborn not to grab the chances the man is offering you." He frowned. "Don't you want more than the life you have now?"

Tears burned her eyes and Laura closed them. "Without Bette, I just want to get away from Bath and everything in it. The city was only my home because I shared it with her. There's nothing here for me anymore."

"How can you say that?"

She opened her eyes, her heart quivering under the concern in the doctor's gaze. "I'm not saying I haven't met some good people. I have. Like you and Mr. Lacey, but I don't want to stay in a place filled with memories of the bad, or even the good, if I'm to endure them alone. Everything will remind me of the dearest, kindest, and funniest woman in the world. I couldn't bear that." She struggled to keep her eyes on his as the thought of not seeing Adam or Bette again threatened to suck the air from her lungs.

"But Mr. Lacey—"

"Is a star of the stage, Doctor. His notions I might be a part of that are based on nothing but fantasy. Real life doesn't happen in the way of stories and scripts. You, more than anyone, should know that." Easing her arm from his grasp, she brushed past him into Adam's hallway and picked up her bag. "Now, let's go. I'm afraid I have many hours of struggle ahead and there's little point delaying them."

"And what of Mr. Lacey's delay? Don't you think something might have happened for him to be held up like this?"

Laura swallowed. *Please, God, don't let anything bad have happened to him.* "I hope and pray Bristol has opened its doors of opportunity and he's enjoying what it has to offer for a few days. I would've most likely left Bath much sooner than this had Bette not died. My intention was always to leave, but I'd hoped with Bette beside me."

"I see."

The doubt in the doctor's eyes forced Laura to look away along the street. "Plus, I refuse to lessen Mr. Lacey's good fortune by sending him a message of Bette's demise. Neither she nor I should be factors in his life. We barely know him."

Despite that I laid with him, and through our lovemaking my heart was truly stolen.

"I'm confident he'll make his way home when he's good and ready. I won't be the one to end his time in Bristol prematurely."

The doctor sighed. "I would be happier if you waited to see what he has to say. The man doesn't strike me as one who would torment a woman's aspirations . . . or feelings without genuine care on his part."

Pride warmed her cheeks. "My feelings have nothing to do with this. I'll always be grateful to him for confronting Malcolm Baxter and letting Bette and I come here, but that's where our association ends. Once Bette is buried on Tuesday, I'll leave Bath and find work elsewhere."

"What work? I can't bear the thought of you having to resort to what you did before, now you've worked yourself out of that world."

She stared as a knot tightened in her chest. The man looked weighted down with worry and it was all her doing. She clasped his hand and forced a smile. "That won't happen. I'll get a coach into the country and see where my luck lies. There's always work to be had at farms and the like. Everything will work out just as it's supposed to. Now I'm alone, I don't need as much money as I did before."

He shook his head, the worry in his eyes turning to frustration. "You're a city girl through and through. You belong here."

"I'm whatever I choose to be." She drew her hand from his and pulled back her shoulders.

He shook his head. "If it were up to me, you could stay with my wife and I until past the funeral, but unfortunately, Mrs. Penders rules the roost. She said until the funeral only."

Laura smiled. "And that is more than generous of her. A doctor's wife taking in two whores, one living and one dead? The woman deserves a medal. Come. Let's go. Mr. Lacey will no doubt be relieved to have his house to himself when he returns. Whatever has kept him in Bristol can only be good news."

She descended the steps to where Dr. Penders's carriage and footman waited, smiling her thanks to the footman when he took her case to store at the rear. Stepping aboard, Laura focused her concentration through the opposite window. The carriage tilted as Dr. Penders joined her. The door slammed and Laura winced.

Her constitution teetered on a knife's edge. One minute in control, the next she wanted to throw herself into the path of an oncoming train. Bette was gone. Adam was gone. The pain was twice what it should be. If only she hadn't allowed her barriers to weaken enough that Adam pushed through them and into her heart. Hadn't she and Bette sworn they'd never let a man close enough to mess with their minds, money, or emotions? Yet, she'd fallen headlong into Adam's arms as though she belonged there.

She let him touch her, kiss her, make love to her until she'd believed in his stupid, magical dreams of them making a play together.

Damn, stupid girl.

"Right, then." Dr. Penders's soft voice cut through her reverie as he settled on the opposite seat. "We'll speak to the funeral director and then head back home. I want you to try and get some sleep. I'll ask Cook to give you a light lunch and then you must try to relax. You have a hard few days ahead."

Laura smiled. "You're very kind to worry about me."

"I worry about all my patients, but you and Bette . . ." He shook his head. "She deserved a happier ending than this, and now I pray yours will make up for it."

"So do I." She turned to the window once more and the view blurred.

She prayed the next three days until Bette's funeral passed without incident or indictment. She needed to get away from Bath and Adam if she had any chance of surviving the loss of her dearest friend in the whole world.

Her friends were limited and her funds low. It would cost money to start again, as well as survive. The country was a foreign land where she knew no one or no place. Unless . . .

Laura's heart beat a little faster.

She knew of only one person with connections in the country. One person she'd helped by testifying in court the last year past. Testimony that unraveled her and Bette's livelihoods but ensured another's life entirely. Emily. Hadn't she said Laura could call on her help anytime, night or day? Surely a lady such as Emily Darson would know of someone wanting employment within the many estates surrounding the city?

Hope sparked and Laura clasped her hands tightly in her lap. All she needed was a place to start. The rest would be up to her.

The only question remaining was whether she was important enough for Adam to come looking for her before she fled the city and, thus, eradicated the chance of him finding her.

The spires of Bath Abbey passed the window and the haughty,

superior stature of a man in its courtyard reminded her of the
ever-present threat of Malcolm. If he wasn't already thinking of his
next approach toward her, he undoubtedly would within a day or two.
She narrowed her eyes as her fierce sense of survival erupted.

It was imperative she made her escape immediately after the
funeral.

Now she no longer had Adam's protection, she was as vulnerable
and exposed to Malcolm's anger as a waif on the street. Night
prowlers sniffed out waifs from the most unlikely of places.

Laura turned and stared at Dr. Penders's profile. Nothing was
more unlikely than a friendship between a whore and a doctor, yet it
had happened. She had no doubt things would get better, but she was
no safer from Malcolm than Monica was whilst she was in the city,
and Laura refused to risk giving him further reason to harass her
newest ally.

The carriage continued through the streets toward the funeral director's establishment. When it pulled to a stop outside, the doctor
alighted before helping her onto the street. The city was busy with
shoppers and businessmen hurrying to and fro. Life went on no matter what. She inhaled a deep breath and Bette's spirit willed her on.

"Laura?"

"Yes?"

Dr. Penders waved toward the door. "Shall we go in and get the
details finalized?"

She nodded. "Afterward, there's a friend I'd like to see before I
come to your home. Would you mind taking my case with you and
I'll come back to the house shortly?"

He frowned. "I really want you to rest, my dear."

"I will. I know just the person to help me find work in the country.
I can't believe I didn't think of her before."

Royal Crescent was Bath's most famous street and, no matter how
many times Laura saw the semicircle of architectural brilliance, it
never failed to take her breath away. Erected from Bath stone, the
houses were three stories high with servants' quarters at the top, with
the kitchens and cellars below street level. The houses shone in all
their butter-colored glory, the gorgeous sash windows glinting in the

late-afternoon sun. Only the very wealthy could afford to live in such an abode, but she refused to let the street's magnificence intimidate her.

Holding on to her resolve, she hurried along the pavement toward number twenty-four. Although conscious of the inferior state of her clothing, hat, and shoes, she kept her chin high, ignoring the condescending glances of the ladies walking arm in arm as they passed her.

She was on a mission and no one would stop her from completing it.

Reaching Emily's house, she marched up the small pathway and knocked on the door. A pretty young maid answered the door. "Can I help you?"

Laura smiled. "Is it possible I could speak with Emily Darson, please?"

The maid frowned, suspicion immediately darkening her eyes as she appraised Laura from head to toe. "May I ask who's calling?"

"Laura Robinson. Miss Darson will remember me from a year past."

"A year? I'm sorry, but she is very busy at the moment—"

Laura's smile dissolved. "Then I'll not press you further if she hasn't the time to see me, but I would very much appreciate you asking her all the same."

Their gazes locked.

After another few seconds, the maid cleared her throat. "If you could just wait here, Miss Robinson."

"Thank—"

The door closed, leaving Laura standing on the step. *Damn superior madam. Who does she think she is?* She turned her back to the door and studied the rich green grass of Victoria Park while she waited. On the maid's head be it if she didn't reopen the door, because Laura had no intention of moving until she heard from Emily she didn't wish to see her.

She hadn't survived by taking rebuffs and refusals.

A minute passed. Then two. Her patience stretched a little more with each passing second. At last, the door clicked open behind her and Laura turned.

"Laura? My goodness, it is you."

Laura grinned. Emily was even more beautiful than she remembered. "Emily."

Emily opened her arms and Laura stepped into them. She squeezed. "You look so well."

"I am." Emily pulled back and slipped her arm around Laura's waist, ushering her inside. "Come in. I am so glad to see you."

They stepped over the threshold and Emily addressed the maid. "You don't remember Laura, do you?"

The maid frowned as she stared at Laura.

Laura smiled. "I didn't remember you either. The circumstances under which we met were more than a little rushed."

"I'm so sorry, I don't . . . yes, I do!" The maid grinned. "You're the . . . the . . ."

Laura laughed. "Yes, I'm her."

Emily laughed. "Annie, would you be so kind as to bring some tea and cake into the drawing room?"

"Of course." Annie's cheeks colored pink. "It's good to see you again, Miss Robinson."

Laura smiled. "You too."

Annie turned and hurried toward the kitchen.

Emily squeezed Laura's waist. "Come. Let us sit. I want to hear all that you've been up to. How are you? How's Bette?"

Laura's brief moment of happiness shattered and her shoulders slumped as they entered Emily's luxurious drawing room. They sat on one of the plush settees. "It's because of Bette I'm here."

Her friend's smile wavered. "She's all right, isn't she?"

Tears smarted Laura's eyes to see such genuine affection in Emily's gaze.

She shook her head. "She's dead."

"Dead?" Emily whispered. "She can't be."

Laura swallowed the lump in her throat. "Pneumonia took her yesterday."

"Oh, no. I'm so sorry."

"I need your help. I want to leave Bath as soon as Bette is buried."

"Leave Bath? Why? If you need somewhere to stay, you are welcome——"

"I can't stay in the city." Laura shook her head. "It's too painful."

"Then what can I do?" Emily grasped her hand. "Do you need money?"

"I need work. If I go to the country, somewhere quiet where I can start again and nobody knows who I am or what I did before, I'll have a new beginning."

Emily slowly nodded. "I see. Then I'll contact my aunt. She knows lots of people with estates in Saltford and Colerne. We'll get you a position in one of the houses. Will that suit?"

Laura smiled. "That would be perfect."

"Then consider it done." Emily grinned and squeezed Laura's hand. "It really is good to see you."

It was early Tuesday morning when Adam paid the carriage driver and picked up his case from the cobbled walkway outside his home. He stared at its façade and trepidation rippled through him. He had been gone three days longer than anticipated and he longed to see Laura again. Self-hatred burned his throat and he swallowed hard. First, he would tell her the play had an investor—and then he would draw a very deep and very hot bath.

Climbing the steps, he took his key from his pocket and opened the front door. He tossed it onto a side table and shrugged off his coat. "Laura? Where are you? Is this any way to greet a man coming home from a longer than anticipated trip?"

The house remained eerily quiet.

His smile slipped and Adam frowned. Maybe she and Nurse had taken Bette for a stroll into town. He moved along the hallway into the drawing room. Although there wasn't a single cushion out of place, the scent of wilting flowers hung in the air. He shot his glance to the side table and then the windowsill where a vase of roses withered.

Foreboding stole through his gut. "Laura, where are you?"

He rushed into the hallway and took the stairs two at a time. He pushed open the door to the guest bedroom. Laura's bed was neatly made, the wardrobe doors open, revealing the absence of her small amount of clothes.

"You said you would not leave." He stormed across the landing to the room Bette had slept in. It was empty. "Goddamn it, Laura. You promised."

Slamming the door so hard it shook on its hinges, he ran downstairs and into the drawing room as though expecting, by some miracle, for Laura to reappear. An envelope propped on his writing bureau caught his eye. He raced over and ripped it open.

Adam,

Bette is dead. She died the afternoon you left for Bristol. I am grateful for everything you have done and, indeed, what you believed I could do, but I cannot stay here without her. I'm sorry.

I wish you all the best for both you and your play.

You are a remarkable man. I'll never forget you.

Best wishes,

Laura

He read and reread the unfamiliar handwriting. Who wrote this for her? Nurse? Regret pinched hot at his cheeks as he gripped the paper and ripped it into pieces. He tossed the shards in the air and stormed from the room. What the hell had he done? Why had he gone to Bristol? Why had he seen Annabel?

He snatched up his keys and left the house, slamming the door behind him.

Hell would freeze over before he would let Laura leave after what he had done to make the play happen sooner rather than later. He had done it for her as much as for himself.

Liar. Your actions are about you. About your own impatience for notoriety. Your own impatience to make your play come to life.

The last three days had nothing to do with Laura. It was only him who had succumbed to the easy route to ensure his dreams came to fruition. Laura would never have been so bloody weak. The woman would be honest and true to who she was. She would take each day as it came and cherish it, be thankful for it. Her perseverance through poverty and obstacles made shame course through his veins and pound at his temple. He had to find her. Had to return her to his home where she belonged, where she could grieve for Bette and know she still had a future without her beloved friend by her side.

He would never leave her again. He would be loyal and help her realize her potential.

Adam sprinted along the streets into town and made straight for the theater. If Laura had moved on, there was a small chance she would have handed in her notice to the theater manager—or at least her friend Tess might know where she was headed.

Upon entering the theater, he barged straight into the auditorium.

The play being shown was a farce, and the audience laughed and cheered along with the actress gracing the stage. Keeping his mind focused, Adam scanned the crowd for Tess and soon spotted her blond curls. He hurried up the aisle just as she finished a sale.

"Tess?"

She turned and her eyes widened. "Mr. Lacey. Are you all right?"

"I'm looking for Laura."

"Laura? She's gone."

Impatience made him curl his hands into fists. "I know. Where is she?"

Tess stepped back and Adam controlled his temper.

He forced a smile and pushed his hand through his hair. "I am sorry. I just need to see her as soon as possible."

Tess quirked an eyebrow, an all-knowing glint lighting her eyes. "You sure have a thing for her, don't you?"

Adam met her smile. "What can I say? She is a beautiful woman. Do you know where she is?"

Her smile dissolved and she shook her head. "No, she came in a couple of days ago to say she was leaving and to thank me for everything I did for her. She was cut to pieces about poor Bette. She was her nearest and dearest friend. Died, she did. These few days past."

"She did not say where she was going?"

She shook her head.

"Damn it." Adam squeezed his eyes shut, his mind whirling. She could be anywhere by now. On her way to Bristol. London. Anywhere.

"I wouldn't have thought she'd leave without seeing Bette buried properly."

He snapped his eyes open.

Tess lifted her shoulders. "God only knows what kind of funeral

Laura could afford for her, but I did see her talking in earnest with Miss Danes just before she left. Maybe she knows something."

Adam stared. "Miss Danes?"

Tess nodded. "They were talking in the foyer. I was a bit taken aback because Miss Danes put her arms around Laura, she was trembling so hard." She shook her head, her eyes glazing with tears. "I ain't never seen Laura tremble over nothing before. Strong as an ox, she is. She won't get over losing Bette easy, that's for sure."

His heart kicked painfully and Adam squeezed Tess's hand. "I will go find Miss Danes."

"Wait. There's something—"

He sprinted along the front of the stage toward a door leading into the corridor backstage. Pushing and shoving through the people gathered around, he headed for Monica's dressing room. He knocked and pushed the door open without waiting for her permission.

Stephanie, Monica's dresser, was packing boxes.

"Stephanie? Where is Monica?"

The girl spun around. Adam immediately stiffened. Tears shone wet on the woman's cheeks and her pallor was white.

"What is it? What is wrong?"

"She's not here."

He glanced around the room. Monica's dressing table was empty of makeup, hairdressings, everything. "Where is she? What has happened?"

"He came after her again. After all this time. He came after her and beat her in her home."

"What? Who did? Where is she?"

"At home. Recovering. I don't know what that Baxter animal wanted, but there was no way Monica was going to give it to him. The commotion caused her neighbor to come running from next door. The poor man near beat the door down, but Baxter scarpered before he could catch him."

"Baxter." Adam whispered the bastard's name from between his teeth and his vision tinged red at the edges. "Monica worked for him? In the past?"

Stephanie pursed her lips together.

Adam glared. "Stephanie, please. Tell me Monica's connection to Baxter. The man is a leech who deserves to be punished."

"She loved him."

He stiffened. "Loved him?"

She nodded. "It was a long time ago and she despises him now. I think he wanted something to do with Laura, but Monica refuses to tell me what caused him to come after her the way he did." Her voice cracked.

Adam pulled her into his arms and held her tightly as she sobbed. He stared blindly ahead, rage pouring into his blood. If Baxter had gotten to Monica, he would get to Laura, too, sooner or later. For the first time since he arrived back from Bristol, Adam prayed Laura had already fled the city.

He eased Stephanie back and held her at arm's length. "I will go and see Monica now. Do not worry. She will be all right."

"What if Baxter comes back? I've told her to leave. Get out of the city, but she won't hear of it."

He tightened his jaw. "The Monica I know would not run from anyone. Have no fear, I will put an end to this."

Releasing her, he turned and stormed back along the corridor and out of the theater.

Chapter 18

Adam flagged down a passing hansom cab and got in. Anger beat a pulse inside his head, hammering against his skull in a never-ending barrage of noise. How had Baxter become such a disruption? Adam had stumbled across a chance meeting with one of the most beautiful women to grace God's earth and was falling hopelessly in love with her, had a four-year friendship with another, yet this piece of scum unfathomably linked the two.

The carriage jolted across town, stopping and starting; the roads became busier as noon approached. Shouting salesmen and women, and the screaming of playing children mixed with the slamming of carriage doors and the pealing bells of the abbey. Adam dropped his head back against the seat and focused on regaining control of the rage bubbling inside, threatening to spill over.

He would find Baxter and get the man arrested once and for all. First, he needed to see Monica. See what the bastard had done to her and learn the parting words she had spoken with Laura. Baxter was the catalyst to them both being hurt. Adam curled his hands into fists on his thighs. The scum's control over them ended today.

The carriage turned onto the street where Monica lived in a modest three-bedroom house. Adam inhaled a deep breath. A house she was so proud to be paying for by her own means. It was ironic he had helped her obtain this home, yet very soon he would have no choice but to downsize to something much smaller.

It was a time for change. He could not go on like this. Laura's disappearance was like a punch to his damn heart. He was falling in love with her and had absolutely nothing to offer her as enticement to take a chance on him.

And once again, you are manacled to Annabel.

Closing his mind to the words reverberating in his head, Adam alighted the carriage and paid the driver. He had to focus and deal with one problem at a time. Right then, Monica took priority. He approached her front door and knocked.

The soft tap of footsteps came from the other side and Adam tensed, preparing for what he was about to see. Lord only knew what sort of state Baxter's beating had left her in.

"Who is it?"

He stared at the door as his anger hitched up a notch. He had never known Monica to check who called on her before opening the door. "It's Adam."

A second or two passed before a lock clanged back and a key turned.

The sight of Monica's abused face and glazed eyes stole the air from his lungs. Nausea rose bitter in his throat as he stepped inside, words momentarily failing him. A purple-gray bruise shone on her cheek, and an angry laceration showed scarlet above her eye.

She closed the door. "Do not ask me how this could have happened. Nothing you say will be any more than what I have already told myself."

He reached out and ran his thumb over her injured cheek and a single tear escaped her eye.

He brushed it away. "He will pay for this."

She covered his hand with hers and lowered it. "Come, let's take a seat in the parlor."

Adam's blood boiled with suppressed rage. Whilst he was in Bristol, an invisible demon had spread its wings over two people he cared about, leaving them bereaved or beaten in its wake. This was undoubtedly God's punishment for Adam selfishly pursuing his dreams over everything else. Well, now he understood His message loud and clear. Nothing was circumstantial. Everything happened for a reason.

They entered Monica's parlor and sat side by side on her upholstered settee. She winced and clutched her hand to her ribs as if she struggled to find a comfortable position.

"When did this happen?" He spoke the question from between gritted teeth.

"The day before yesterday."

"Have you seen a doctor?"

"There is no need."

"There is every need. Look at you."

She met his eyes and hers darkened with irritation. "I can look after myself. Baxter's a coward. A bully. He made a critical mistake coming to my home. The police will soon find him."

"They know he did this to you?"

"Yes, unfortunately for Malcolm, he came here so angry, so steered by frustration, he did not foresee I might have neighbors who care about me. I did not take his beating lying down. I fought back and made as much noise as possible. He only got away because my neighbor is twenty years his senior. If his son would have been home he wouldn't have been so lucky."

Adam stared as he balled his hands into fists. "Well, much credit to your neighbor. Is he all right? He was not hurt?"

She shook her head. "No, they grappled at the doorstep before Malcolm fled, but no punches were thrown. Thank goodness."

Adam nodded. "That is something, I suppose." He looked toward the window. "However, despite your neighbor's efforts to accost Baxter, there is no guarantee the police will follow this through. On the other hand, I will."

"Let the police take care of it, Adam. Malcolm's days are numbered. Do not let him number yours." They fell into momentary silence before Monica spoke again. "Have you spoken to Laura?"

His heart picked up speed. "Do you know where she is?"

"I have no idea where she is staying at the moment, but I know where she will be"—she glanced at a wall clock above the mantel—"in two hours."

Adam frowned, anticipation churning up a storm inside him. "Where?"

"The cemetery."

Of course. Bette. "Bette's funeral is at two?"

"Yes, I insisted Laura take some money from me, and I think a doctor friend of hers also helped so she could at least give her friend a decent burial. You should go to her."

He clenched his jaw. "I will."

The confirmation seemed to relax something within her and Monica shifted back against the settee and slumped against the cushions.

Adam frowned. "What did Baxter want? What did he say to you?"

She met his eyes, her gaze wary. "It does not matter."

"I know he asked after Laura. I will find out one way or another, so you might as well tell me."

"What happened in Bristol?"

Change of subject. Shame burned inside him, but Adam forced his eyes level with hers. "The part was given to another."

"I'm sorry."

"After what has happened here, I am glad. This is where I am needed. My time would be wasted in Bristol."

Monica nodded. "And what of an investor? Did you find one?"

The knowing look in her eyes was filled with accusation and he looked past her toward the window. "Yes."

"Were conditions attached?"

Adam pushed to his feet and approached the window. "Why don't you just spit out whatever it is you are really asking me? You know I went to see Annabel, don't you?"

"I guessed as much, yes."

He turned. "I did what had to be done."

"I see." She stared. "And do you feel better for it?"

Self-hatred furled inside him, but Adam held her gaze. "That is neither here nor there. I did what I did, and now my play will soon have a willing director. Annabel will see that happens and after the play is shown, I will not have to go down this godforsaken route again. My work will speak for itself."

"And you will tell Laura as much?"

He glared. "I do not need your judgment on this, Monica. I am doing enough of that myself. You know what my writing means to me. I have to get my play onstage if my life stands any chance of taking the turn I desire."

"If you truly believe that, you have nothing to fear from telling Laura, do you?"

He tilted his chin, knowing his defiance was weak and his gumption even more so. "Like I said, I have done what was necessary. Laura will understand."

Monica exhaled a heavy breath. "Then I wish you luck and hope you do the right thing. Laura's lovely, Adam. She is special. I would like to think I do not need to tell you that."

His heart was lead in his chest. "You do not."

"I pray this hunger for an investor does not ruin whatever might be going on between the two of you. Sometimes there are more important things in life than ambition. I would hate for you to jeopardize what could be the best thing that has ever happened to you for the sake of your career."

Their eyes locked and silent understanding hummed between them. They had become firm and honest friends, and he could not deny Monica's words were said with concern. He inhaled a long breath. "I need to go."

"Where?"

He stood. "There is something I need to do before I go to the cemetery."

She gave a satisfied nod and smiled. "Give Laura my love. I will be thinking of her."

He closed the space between them and kissed her gently on the cheek. "I will be back to check on you tomorrow. Get some rest."

Leaving the room, he strode through the hallway and out onto the street. He closed Monica's front door firmly and put on his hat. He drew in a shaky breath. He needed to find Baxter. The bastard did not deserve to roam free for another damn second. Scowling, Adam marched along the pathway toward Laura's old address.

His determined footsteps pounded the pavement, his mind void of anything except how good it would feel to have his hands around Baxter's neck. On and on he strode until the bustle of the town center lessened and the residences grew in number. He had no idea if his rationale would lead to wasted time, but as Baxter relentlessly pursued Laura, it was possible he did others in the alley too. Hopefully,

Adam would find him there or if not, someone would be able to tell him where else Baxter was likely to be found at this time of day.

Eventually, the richer residences gave way to less extravagant red-brick houses. Adam slipped into the alley where Laura once lived. The stench fueled his resolve, and the pitiful laundry hanging above him on lengths of rope reminded him again of a life Laura lived without complaint or fear. The passion to fill her life with laughter and love, abundance and applause, burned inside him. Determined, he stormed forward, his hands fisted at his sides.

The alley was empty but for some raggedly dressed children kicking stones back and forth to one another. He reached the door of Laura's house and knocked.

No sound came from within. Cursing, he was about to turn away when the material at the window twitched. Narrowing his eyes, he whirled back and rapped his knuckles against the door a second time.

"I mean you no harm, I just have a few questions I would like to ask. I am here about Malcolm Baxter. Do you know him? I am not asking for money, just information."

The door swung back on its hinges and Adam stared straight into the ugly and twisted face of Malcolm Baxter. "What the hell do you want?"

"I want you."

Baxter sneered. "Never took you for a nancy boy, Lacey. I thought you would want a female whore rather than me."

The rage that tore through Adam's blood rendered him incapable of thought or speech. He lunged forward and gripped Baxter's lapels. With an almighty roar, he yanked the son of a bitch off his feet and tossed him onto the cobbled street.

Baxter stumbled and cursed but did not lose his footing. He lifted his fists. "Come on, then. I'm ready for you this time. If you think you'll get a second chance of damn near strangling me, you can think again."

The children's cheers reverberated from the soot-coated walls around them. "Fight! Fight!"

Each time he inhaled, Adam's breath caught like broken glass in his throat. His mouth was coated with the bitter, arid taste of vengeance, and his vision was tinged crimson with fury. He took a moment to absorb the sight of scum lower than filth. This ended now.

He charged forward and slammed his fist straight into Baxter's nose. Bones snapped and blood flew.

"Jesus Christ!" Baxter hit the ground.

Adam ripped at Baxter's collar, raising his fist a second time. He caught him a beautiful blow to his scrawny, woman-beating jaw. The nose was for Monica; the jaw, Laura. The third would be for him. Smiling, Adam raised his fist again.

A police whistle pierced the air, sending the growing crowd of adolescents scuttling together in a huddle. The copper was built like a bear—big and broad and decidedly hairy. He dragged Adam off Baxter with a hand at the back of his jacket.

"Right, you're nicked, sunshine." He glared into Adam's face before his eyes widened with surprise. "Well, I never. Mr. Lacey? What in God's name do you think you're doing?" He released Adam's collar and looked at Baxter, who attempted to stem his bleeding nose with the sleeve of his jacket.

Adam clenched his jaw. "He had it coming. I want this man arrested for battery and assault."

The policeman scowled. "I think the man who gave the beating was you, Mr. Lacey, don't you?"

"In an effort to right a wrong, yes. This man beat my friend, sir. In her home."

The policeman's eyes darkened. "A woman?" He reached down and gripped Baxter by the arm and yanked him to his feet, heedless of the blood pouring from his nose. "Is this true?"

Adam's heart hammered as he glared. Baxter grunted and sniveled, coughed and spluttered something unintelligible that might have been admission or argument but was too garbled to understand. The policeman's face twisted with contempt and spun Baxter around, pushing his free arm, the one not held to his nose, up his back.

He looked at Adam. "I will take this *gentleman* in for the time being, Mr. Lacey, but the woman involved will have to come to the station and press charges for us to take this further. In the meantime, it will be my duty to retain Mr. Baxter at her majesty's pleasure for a day or two."

Adam nodded, satisfaction seeping like a balm into his stomach. "It is appreciated, sir. I will make sure the woman concerned comes to the station later today."

"Right you are. Come on, Baxter, there's a nice cell waiting for you."

Baxter huffed and cursed as he was frog marched away with blood dripping from his nose onto the stones.

It was not until the children patted Adam on his back and congratulated him on a job well done that he blinked from his stupor. He leaned down and picked up his hat. He brushed it off and put it on, shaking out his bruised fingers, clenching and unclenching the aching joints. With a wink to the kids, he marched from the alley. He had a funeral to attend.

Laura stood at the graveside and the vicar's words floated over her.

"Miss Windsor will be missed. A woman who knew hardship in life but will now find eternal peace in the Lord's open arms. . . ."

As she trembled with grief, Laura struggled to contain the need to scream and shout and throw herself over Bette's coffin and beg her friend to wake up, to come back to her so Laura could atone for the mistakes she'd made. No matter how hard she tried, she couldn't forgive herself that she'd lost focus of Bette's needs and dashed headlong into a love affair with a man she found too irresistibly exciting.

Tears slipped one after the other down her face, but Laura didn't move to wipe them away. Instead, she stood ramrod straight, her gaze trained on Bette's coffin. Dr. Penders stood to one side of her and a neighbor from the street where she and Bette lived on the other. A neighbor whom Bette had helped out more times than Laura could count on her fingers and toes. As she had everyone and anyone she could. Always protective and caring. God could only have taken Bette because He needed her elsewhere.

Behind her, the shuffle of feet and murmur of voices occasionally broke the subdued quiet. She had yet to speak to any other grievers but guessed they'd be people who'd heard of Bette's death through the grapevine and came to either pay their respects or hoped for some fare after the burial. Laura glared ahead, tears burning.

If it was the latter, they'd have a long wait coming. There were as many unfamiliar faces as there were familiar, so any strangers hoping for a free meal had wasted their time. She planned to leave for Saltford on the next available coach. There wouldn't be a wake. There wouldn't be a gathering at the doctor's for people who barely knew Bette, yet claimed they did well enough to mingle and offer condolences.

"And so we surrender Bette into your safekeeping, my Lord . . ."

Laura's heart lodged painfully in her throat as the undertakers stepped forward and slowly lowered the coffin into the ground. A sob hitched and she pressed her handkerchief hard against her mouth to stem another as inch by painful inch the coffin dropped lower. Dr. Penders's arm came firmly around her shoulders. Either holding her tightly for comfort or firmly to stop her from falling, she couldn't be sure. The single yellow rose she held trembled.

Her vision dipped and rose in sickening waves. Her legs shook and her heart broke. The coffin disappeared out of sight and panic roared up inside her.

No. No. Bette, don't go. I need you. Please.

She rushed from the doctor's embrace and dropped to her knees at the graveside. Her beloved friend was so far down in the ground. She would be cold and lonely. Bette hated the cold, hated to be alone for more than an hour or so. . . .

"Bette, I'm sorry. So, so sorry." Laura squeezed her eyes shut and just as she faltered and tipped to the side, two strong arms came around her and held her tight.

"I am here, Laura. I am here."

His voice enveloped her in a comforting cocoon.

"Adam." She sobbed against his chest, her fingers clutching his arms in desperation. "Oh, God. Bring her back. Please."

"It is all right. Everything will be all right." He rocked her as his breath whispered like kisses across her temple.

He made no move to lift her from the ground, and spoke no words telling her to pull herself together and stand. Instead, he came down onto the grass beside her and positioned her between his open legs, cradling her in his arms like a child. Her tears dried and her breathing steadied as the scent and strength of him seeped into her skin.

Moments passed. Awkward coughs and whispered words blew around them on a soft breeze, but still they stayed entwined in one another's arms. After what seemed like hours, the vicar left, and so did the doctor and other mourners until it was just her and Adam. Alone.

"How did you know I'd be here?" She ran her finger over the sleeve of his jacket.

"I saw Monica." He drew in a shaky breath. "She told me Bette would be buried here at two."

Laura pulled back and looked into his eyes. He brushed some fallen hair from her face and kissed the tip of her nose. Deep inside, a voice warned her to move away from him, to enforce the distance now, rather than have it thrust upon her later when it would undoubtedly hurt more. Yet, it was impossible.

"I'm glad you came."

"I am sorry I was not there for you."

"Monica said she'd come too."

He closed his eyes. "She could not."

Laura stared at his closed lids and her stomach tightened. Something had happened. "Adam? What is it?"

He opened his eyes and pulled her head down to his shoulder. "It does not matter. Let's just be here for Bette. Everything else can wait."

Unease prickled the hair at the back of her neck. "Tell me."

His heart gave harsh thumps. A heavy exhalation shuddered through him. "Baxter went to Monica's house."

A ball of red-hot fire ignited in her heart. "I see."

She pulled from his embrace and pushed to her feet. Stepping forward, she grabbed a handful of earth from the pile at the foot of Bette's grave. She stared down at her friend's coffin. The wood was dull and unvarnished, but the pewter name plate somehow glinted under the rays of the weak and hazy sunshine. It was no longer Bette in that box, merely her body. Her soul had risen, and Laura shivered as it breathed into her, strengthening her weakening spirit.

She tossed the soil onto the coffin. "I love you, Bette." She kissed the rose and threw it in too.

It landed perfectly across the name plate.

She turned.

Adam stood watching her. "I'm leaving, Adam. Today."

He frowned. "What? You cannot."

"I can."

"Where will you go?"

"It doesn't matter."

"It does to me."

"There's nothing in Bath for me anymore. I'm leaving, but first I need to see Monica."

With his eyes locked on hers, he took her hand. "It is over as far as Baxter's concerned. He has been arrested and with Monica's testimony, he will serve time."

"What did he do to her?"

His eyes darkened. "We will see her again before we leave, and then we can head out of the city at first light tomorrow."

"We? Adam, no. I'm going alone."

"Let me come with you. Monica can write if anything goes wrong with Baxter's arrest and we will return." His eyes grew bright. "Let's escape to London. We can be together. Become whatever we want there. Shed our old lives, our regrets, and start again."

Determined to hold on to her sensibility, Laura pulled back her shoulders. "How badly did he hurt her?"

Silence.

She'd already ensured one violent man paid for his abuse. She would not stand by and let Malcolm get away with hurting Monica. "Well?"

"Badly. I went after him, and he is now in police custody. Monica will need to press charges tomorrow. He will be in court by the end of the week. His control over you, her, and countless others is over." He kissed her forehead. "He is a pimp, a whoremaster, and a man who extorts money. Monica is well-liked and admired. There is nothing else we need to do."

"Are you certain she'll testify?"

"Yes."

"And if she doesn't?"

"Then I will find someone who will."

"She should know she isn't dealing with this alone. It will take more than the testimony of one woman. I know that from experience. I need to see her. Talk to her." She squeezed her eyes shut. "If I have to stay in Bath to see Malcolm pay for what he did to her and all the other women and families he's exploited, so be it. But when it's done . . ." She stared across the cemetery, away from the beguiling pull of his eyes. "I have enough money for a few nights somewhere before I find work."

The silence beat like minutes before he cleared his throat. His lips drew softly across her knuckles. She met his eyes and he smiled. "Come with me to London."

"No."

"If you aren't in Bath, there's nothing for me here either." His cheeks flushed and his jaw tightened. "We can go to London and seek our destiny."

"What about your play? What about Bristol?" She shook her head. "You have commitments you need to deliver upon. Did you find an investor willing to support you?"

His expression turned to stone before he stared toward Bette's grave. Laura frowned. "Adam?"

He faced her. "No."

"But—"

"There was no investor. It was a wasted trip. I never went for the audition either. It is not what I want anymore."

"I don't understand. You were gone longer than you thought. I assumed things went well, that you made progress." Afraid he might have missed the audition for her, Laura forced a smile. "I'm happy for your success. You must carry on regardless. Don't let Bette's passing—"

"Everything has changed. I do not want to be who I am anymore. You inspire me to be more, to do more. Let's get away from every-body and everything. We can do whatever we want." He kissed her hard on the mouth and she stumbled backward. He smiled and grasped her hands. "A beautiful young woman stared up at me in the Theater Royal not so long ago. That woman has taught me anything is possible. If you are willing to start over somewhere else, without Bette, let that somewhere be in London with me."

A yearning to believe what he suggested was possible thudded through her heart, making each second she looked at him harder to turn away. He pulled her tightly against him and his lips covered hers. Laura trembled in his arms; the spark between them exploded like a firework and singed her blood with passion and love. She clung to his muscular biceps and welcomed his tongue into her mouth.

They barely knew one another, but the depth of her emotion toward him was too much to ignore or disregard. What did she have to lose but her stupid heart? Wasn't it worth grabbing whatever the future held and seeing where it led them? At least for as long as it could possibly last? Their time together would end, of that she was certain. Yet, she needed something to hold dear—if only for a while.

Excitement pumped through her and she pulled back. "If Monica is strong enough to do this without us, then we'll go and live every day for Bette."

He ran his finger along her cheek. "She would not want any different for you. I know it. The look of happiness in her eyes the morning after we made love said it all." He smiled.

Laura grinned. "She enjoyed every moment of our discomfort."

He tucked her hand into the crook of his elbow. "Let's do this. For Bette."

She clasped his arm and together, they left the cemetery.

Chapter 19

Later that evening, Laura struggled to contain her anger as she stared at Monica's bruised and battered face. Her friend's beauty was marred, but more than that, her gaze burned with a new and bitter determination. Something Laura hadn't seen before. A seething rage had replaced the soft look of happiness.

She reached for her friend's hand as they sat side by side on Monica's settee. "So the police are certain your testimony will be enough?"

"Yes, they already have a long list of complaints from people brave enough to report Malcolm for overcharging their rent. I'm just grateful he didn't have that power over you too." Monica drew in a shaky breath. "These people have been forced from their homes but still maintained the gumption to let the police know of his activities. The officer said with my testimony added to what they already know, this should be enough for a judge to see Malcolm's nothing more than a leech to society."

Laura shook her head. "I cannot believe we both knew the man before we met, albeit in different ways."

Monica huffed out a laugh. "Like I said, the man's a leech. Slipping and sliding in and out of countless lives and hurting them all, from what I have learned over the years."

"It ends here."

Monica grinned. "Exactly."

Laura looked to their joined hands as her mind raced. If she left and Baxter walked away from court, then what? After everything she'd done to find her and Bette a place to live, getting Baxter's other whores alternative work, and letting them board with them from time to time would be for nothing? She glared at a spot on the carpet. Over her dead body.

She looked at Monica. "I can't leave. Not when Malcolm's fate is so uncertain."

Monica squeezed Laura's hand and glanced across at Adam sitting in an armchair opposite them. "I want you to go. Both of you. If needs be, I will write and ask you to come back. Time is too precious to wait when you have found something as wonderful as you both have."

Perpetual unease ran through Laura. She might've made the decision to enjoy her and Adam's time together for as long as possible, but passion was not a foundation—it was an irrational feeling. It didn't put bread on the table, a roof over one's head, or keep the wolf from the door. She tilted her chin. They had to focus on their problems and not their feelings. Working toward a better future took work. Hard work.

"You mustn't speak of Adam and I as a couple. A huge part of why we're going to London is for Adam's play. We'll try our utmost to find an interested investor, but if we fail, then—"

"You will have each other," Monica said succinctly. "Just leave Malcolm to me. You have no idea what I am capable of. I only have myself to take care of and I will be fine. We are strong enough to fight him. Hasn't this changed you, Laura? Hasn't it tripped something inside you? Made you want to do more now we are finally rid of him?"

The knot of excitement she'd felt when she learned of Baxter's arrest tightened once more in Laura's belly, and she smiled at the expectation in Monica's gaze. She laughed. "And here I was, thinking it was just me who felt like a phoenix rising from the ashes at the prospect of him being gone for good. I want to do so much. I feel as though it was him holding me back all this time."

Monica grinned. "We were meant to meet. I know it. We owe it to ourselves to make something good happen in our lives."

"Of course. But . . ." Laura's anticipation lessened from a roar to a quiet hum.

Resolutely avoiding looking at Adam, she rose to wander about the room, desperately fighting the self-doubt that battled inside her. Her monthly bleed was late and she had yet to say anything to him, or what to think about the miracle she carried—if she were to be pregnant again. What of the play? Her role as Lucinda?

Emotionally, she was in a far bigger mess than she'd ever thought possible. Worse, she was alone, without Bette's counsel.

"Laura?" Adam's voice cut through her thoughts.

She snapped her head around. "Yes?"

"What is it?"

She forced the scowl from her face. "Nothing."

He stood and came toward her. Concern further darkened his deep brown eyes. "If there's something else bothering you, you must tell me. I want you to be as happy about leaving as I am."

She glanced at Monica. Her eyes were bright, her mouth stretched into a confident smile. Would Laura ever have that same confidence? Would freedom and taking a risk make her as happy as Monica?

Aren't I equally as strong in my own way? She met Adam's steady gaze and drew in a long breath. "I am happy. We'll leave tomorrow." She turned to Monica. "Once we're settled, we'll let you know where we're staying. You're to write to us the minute anything changes with Baxter. We can be on the first coach back to Bath."

Monica nodded and carefully pushed to her feet, her obvious physical discomfort showing in a momentary grimace. She pushed her hand to her ribs. "Nothing will go wrong. I'll ensure it."

Concern for her friend continued to poke and prod at Laura as Monica came toward her and Adam, gesturing for their hands. "Everything happens for a reason." Monica smiled. "Even with the likes of Malcolm. He's joined in our history, but he won't be in our future. I want you to go to London and find your hearts' desires. Promise me."

Tears pricked at Laura's eyes and she blinked, turning to Adam. He stared at her as though she were a goddess. Insistent fear rippled through her, but she nodded and locked her eyes on his. "We will."

Adam sealed his letter to Annabel with a flourish and a huge sigh of relief. He leaned back and stared out at the street through his drawing-room window. Would he and Laura return to Bath in a week, a month, a year . . . ever? How his perspective and love of life had changed since meeting her! The fire of ambition that burned so ferociously inside him had somewhat mellowed, and now more than a passion for his career burned in his blood. He imagined a wedding, a family home, maybe even children with his lovely Laura when the time was right.

Smiling, he turned from the window and picked up the letter to Annabel. He stared at her name on the envelope. His words stated in no uncertain terms the deal they had struck in Bristol was no more. She could keep her money and her promises. He would find his own way with the woman he loved. Whatever challenges the future held, he was confident together, he and Laura could overcome them.

The scuffle of her feet on the ceiling above him broke through Adam's thoughts and he pushed to his feet. Leaving the drawing room, he entered the hallway and snatched his overcoat from a stand by the front door. He walked to the bottom of the stairs. "Laura?"

A second or two passed before she appeared at the top. Her pretty brow was furrowed and her cheeks flushed. "I'm almost packed. I assume you want to leave most things here for now? It doesn't make sense for us to make too many arrangements for your belongings. At least not yet. Until we know for certain London—"

"Is going to be fantastic." He grinned, her anxiety only making him love her more. "But you're right, when we leave, I'll lock up the house and decide what to do about everything in a week or two when our plans are clearer."

Her shoulders relaxed. "Good."

He raised his hand and flicked the letter to Annabel back and forth. "I just have a letter to put in the post box. Did you want anything while I am out?"

"No, I'm fine. I should be nearly done by the time you get back."

"I will be as quick as I can." He winked before turning and heading out the front door and onto the street.

As Adam made his way along the street to the main road, his mind reeled with anticipation of their future. Breaking from Annabel, for what he now knew was the final time, filled him with an inner peace that was only marred by the potential for her to make trouble for him and Laura later. He scowled. If and when that happened, he would deal with it. For now, he could not wait to get started on their journey across the country to London.

He estimated they should reach the big city the day after tomorrow. Adam smiled. Then their lives together could truly begin.

Despite her tired body and busy mind, the need for sleep eluded Laura as she stared wide-eyed at the chaos of London's streets. The carriage carrying her and Adam into their new life had taken them away from Bath two days before, and now the terrifying reality of what they were doing showed in all its soot-filled glory. The day had broken gloriously sunny as though God Himself was giving them permission to make their escape. Yet even in the pretty pink twilight, London's rich-to-poverty ratio was clear.

Grandly dressed ladies and gentlemen mixed with street urchins and beggars as though it were the natural order of things. Fancy hotels lit with lanterns and finery glowed like promised lands, when farther along the street, a gaudily dressed whore marked her corner. Laura didn't know whether to laugh or cry. Excitement mixed with trepidation; ambition with awe. She had no idea which emotion to cling to.

She dropped her gaze to her lap. Adam held her hand as though they were lovers. Where would they stay? How would they eat? Their attraction wasn't enough to sustain them. Their ambition was not enough to ensure their prosperity.

Laura lifted her chin. No, she wouldn't do this.

Bette was dead, but her spirit lingered. If their shared lives had taught her nothing else, Laura was certain of one thing—a person grasped whatever opportunities they could. Monica wasn't just willing to testify against Malcolm, but determined. Her steadfast glare and upright stature when she and Adam visited her had been inspiring.

Bette, Adam, Monica, Dr. Penders, even Baxter himself, had come into her life for a reason, and be damned if she'd ignore the lessons each of them taught her. Change was afoot in England. Women were standing taller and stronger than ever before.

Excitement churned inside. She desperately wanted to be a part of whatever that meant. Maybe her feelings for Adam were foolhardy. Maybe she sat with him now with little planned and led entirely by her heart rather than her head, but did that mean they would fail? No. Emotion lodged like a stone in her throat. Their time together might be limited, but by God, she'd enjoy it while it lasted.

Tears burned.

She had lain with a hundred men, maybe more. A gentleman would never marry such a woman, and when the smoke cleared from Adam's eyes, he would see her for what she was—a whore with little to show for her twenty-two years. Pain struck her heart afresh and she sucked in a breath. She couldn't bear the thought his desire for her was little more than his need to have her warm his bed.

Mentally shaking herself from her melancholy, Laura straightened her shoulders. Whatever he saw in her, the decision to leave Bath and come to London was a good one. It was a fresh start. A new beginning. After losing Bette, nothing felt more certain.

She stared at Adam's absurdly handsome profile. His delay in Bristol and his subsequent reluctance to talk about it weighed heavy on her mind and in her heart. There was definitely something he wasn't telling her, but who was she to demand it from him? She prayed to God he never asked her the details of her past. Some things a person had a right to take to their grave.

He turned suddenly and caught her staring. His face immediately broke with a wide smile, his eyes shining. "Could this day be any brighter?"

Her heart twisted and she couldn't fight her smile at his boyish excitement she was coming to adore. She released her held breath. "I hope it's a sign we're doing the right thing."

"It is." He squeezed her fingers. "We will find a place to bed and board for tonight, and no doubt the world will look even better in the morning."

Keeping her reservations to herself, Laura smiled and turned to the window once more. Adam's voice faded into the background as he instructed the driver where to drop them. London was clearly not as new a land to him as it was to her.

The carriage rumbled to a stop and she shook off her contemplation. Adam opened the door and helped her out onto the pavement. The shouts of the street vendors and the music of the buskers mixed with the laughter and shouting of inebriated workmen and hardworking flower sellers calling their wares.

She inhaled the smells of roasting chestnuts, soot, and rose water. It was Bath, but on a busier, more manic scale. Together or separately, who was to say she and Adam wouldn't conquer this place as they'd failed to do in Bath?

Adam took their cases from the driver and paid him before turning and taking her hand in his. "I know a tavern that offers a decent bed and breakfast. We will stay there until we find our feet. We can move on when we are ready."

Guilt formed a knot inside her. "I have very little money. I don't like the thought of you paying for everything."

He brushed his lips against her cheek. "This is temporary. All too soon, you will be working hard at my play and it will be me thanking you for making us richer than we could have dreamed."

His optimism shone like lanterns in his dark eyes, and the baby she suspected in her belly gave a phantom jerk, ensuring Laura remembered its presence. "I hope that's true. You must keep your mind open to changes."

He laughed. "I do. Always. Look at us. We are in London when three days ago we were in Bath."

She laughed. "Does nothing ever scare you? This city must be lined with people with dreams like ours. Where we will start?"

"It is a matter of when, not where. We will find the people to make our dreams come true. I can feel it right here." He dropped one of her hands and pushed his fist into his stomach. "Trust me."

She struggled to keep her smile in place. It had been a mighty long time since she trusted anyone but Bette—and now Bette was gone. "I'm trying to trust this entire circumstance. Can we afford two rooms?"

Silence descended and two spots of color darkened his cheeks. He grimaced. "I was hoping you would be happy with one."

Time stood still. *Of course he did. She was a whore after all.* Self-preservation simmered like fire in her blood. Her pride poked and prodded it alight. She glared. "I didn't come to London to resume a previous life. I came here to start a new one."

He frowned. "What do you mean?"

"I won't share a bed with you while you pay to feed and shelter me. That makes me the same woman I was before. I don't want your money for services rendered."

The previous excitement vanished from his gaze and turned to irritation. "You really think I am here in London with you, like this, with no plan or idea what to do next because I want *sex*?"

She flinched as he spat the word at her. "I just—"

"This is about so much more than that. So much more." He stared at her mouth before raising his eyes to hers. "I had hoped it was the same for you."

Shame seared her cheeks and she closed her eyes, her stiff shoulders slumping. "It is." She opened her eyes. "It is. I'm sorry."

They stood frozen as people passed. Her heart beat fast and fear rose. She didn't want to send away the only good thing she had to hold on to. How could she have leapt on him in such a way?

"Adam—"

He pushed his hand through his hair and smiled. "Come on. We are in London. We can do what we want, when we want." He lifted the cases. "If you do not want to share a bed with me, I will respect that. But, for me, the thought of waking up with you tomorrow . . ." He exhaled a shaky breath.

Laura's stomach knotted and her center pulled.

He cleared his throat. "We will pose as husband and wife, if it will make you feel better."

Pose. Act. Pretend. She pushed her negativity aside before it could fester once again. "All right. Why not? Life's one big adventure, after all." She gestured along the street. "Shall we?"

He flashed her a smile and turned.

Blinking back traitorous tears, she followed behind him. Her monthly bleed still hadn't arrived, and she was relying on a man whom she'd barely known six weeks for food, shelter, and love. She waited for Bette's laughter in her ear, or even her friend's whispered words telling her to grow a backbone. Anything. Nothing came but lonely silence.

They'd barely covered more than a few yards and Adam pushed open the door of a tavern. Laura looked at the sign swinging above the door before following him inside. The Golden Lion wasn't very golden. She squinted through the screen of cigarette smoke that drifted above their heads and almost to their shoes. With the air of a man used to being in such places, Adam strode toward the bar.

Pride rushed through her. To see Adam Lacey treading the boards in his finery, or even taking tea at his house in Bath, she would never have imagined the man could blend so easily into such surroundings.

She mentally admonished herself. He was an actor, wasn't he? A fact she'd do well to remember. She moved her hand to her stomach and quickly snatched it away, planting it on her hip instead.

Tilting her chin, she dragged on her most confident expression as Adam removed his hat and dipped his head to a woman as tall as she was wide standing at the end of the bar. They needed somewhere to stay for the night. Laura pulled back her shoulders. It was time to think with her damn head and pummel her stupid heart into submission.

"Good evening, madam." Adam smiled. "I wonder if you're the person in charge?"

She narrowed her eyes. "I am. Can I help you?"

He turned and waved Laura forward. Taking a deep breath, she moved to his side and smiled. If Adam thought she could act before, he hadn't seen anything. She dipped a slight curtsy. Experience had taught her a woman like this, who ran a tavern and bore a chip on her shoulder so heavy it made her lean to the side from the weight of it, would undoubtedly welcome some female civility. "How do you do, madam."

The woman straightened, interest sparking her eyes. "Good evening." She nodded before she glanced at Adam. "To you both. Is it a drink you're looking for? Food? A room?"

Adam smiled. "Two out of three, if possible. A glass of ale and a room for the time being."

Laura kept her eyes firmly on the lady's face, even as nerves and apprehension danced inside her belly. It had been a long time since she'd been homeless, and the feeling she'd been catapulted back to a time where she was once more reliant on others didn't sit well at all.

The woman rounded the bar and drew a leather-bound book from beneath the counter. With her eyes flitting from Adam to Laura, she flicked the pages before coming to an abrupt stop at a fourth page.

She glanced down and plucked a pencil from her hair. "I can offer you a double room, but you need to take it for a minimum of two nights."

"That is fine." Adam gave a curt nod. "If we can agree on a price satisfactory to us both, we will take it for a week."

The woman snapped her head up. Her eyes narrowed in suspicion once more. "A week? Ain't you just passing through? This ain't no fancy bed and breakfast, sir. This is a tavern."

"Indeed. And I suspect the price will reflect as much?"

Laura bit back a smile. Adam was clearly keeping his money back for more important things than bed and board. Why did the man have to continually enamor her by taking her by surprise? Did he already know she couldn't abide the waste of money on comforts and finery when survival was all that counted?

The woman shot them each another frown of distrust before she licked the end of her pencil and turned her attention to the ledger. "Mr. and Mrs. . . ."

Adam glanced at Laura. "Lacey, madam. Mr. and Mrs. Adam Lacey."

Laura closed her eyes as she tried and failed to stop the hurried pounding of her heart or ignore the way every fiber in her body came alive to hear him say such a thing even if there was no chance of it ever becoming a reality. A gentleman actor and a whore married? Who had ever heard of such a thing?

Chapter 20

London. Adam smiled and stared across the wide expanse of the River Thames. The magnificent Houses of Parliament glowed like a beacon under the purple-black of nightfall. His heart was fit to bursting. Laura stood so close the heat from her body seeped into his skin, and he fought the desire to embrace her, kiss her . . . damn well ravish her. His blood burned with unspent adrenaline, and his mind raced with possibility.

He had locked up his home and run away with a woman who stirred something so deep inside him, he dared not name it. London offered abundant opportunity, but if Laura had refused to come, he would have gone wherever she desired. He glanced at her from the corner of his eye. He would not tell her what was happening to him. Would not tell her how he could literally feel his old person disappearing like the shed skin of a snake. Not yet. It was too soon.

As hard as she tried to hide it, he sensed her distrust. She grieved for a friend who meant everything to her, and he feared she carried the misplaced belief it was her fault Baxter beat Monica. He had to convince his sweetheart just how wonderfully talented, intelligent, and beautiful she was.

He had never felt so whole. The blinders were gone from his eyes. The hollow in his heart had been filled. His stomach knotted. Somehow, he would find a way to tell Laura what happened in Bristol and they could make a fresh start, with honesty at the forefront from that moment forward.

He pushed away from the stone wall and Laura straightened. She tipped her head to look at him and Adam fell a little deeper in love as he looked into her eyes. His heart stopped. Beneath the lamplight, her eyes glowed like amethysts and her tears flickered like purple diamonds on her lashes. He brushed his thumbs under her eyes before drawing his hands lower to cup her jaw.

"Is it Bette?"

She nodded and another tear escaped. "Yes."

He dipped his head and caught the saltiness of her tear with the tip of his tongue before pressing his lips to her cheek. "Let me at least try to look after you as she did," he whispered. "Please."

She shook her head. "It's too soon for that. Bette was everything to me."

Would his selfishness never end? He pulled back. "You are right. I am sorry." He took her hand and put it in the crook of his elbow. "Let's go find somewhere quiet to eat. Are you hungry?"

She smiled softly. "A little."

"Then we will eat just a little."

He led her along the river bank toward Westminster Bridge. They crossed the dark waters toward a rank of two or three eateries that appeared welcoming. He chose one with a striped awning and blackened board scrawled with chalk, advertising hot pie and potatoes.

Laura slipped her hand from his arm as they entered. He instantly missed the weight of it. Inhaling a deep breath, Adam chose a table by the window that provided a good view of the street. He pulled out one of the two chairs for her.

"Why don't you sit down and I will speak to the man behind the counter. Would you like a hot potato? Maybe a pie?"

She looked past his shoulder toward the counter. "Anything is fine."

He stared at her a moment longer. So much unease graced her pretty features. Was she regretting their decision to come to London before their time there had even begun?

Leaving her alone, he ordered their food before returning to the table and taking a seat. She continued to gaze through the window as though she had no idea he was there.

Adam gently touched her arm. "You must talk to me about anything that is worrying you. If your thoughts are of Bette, then I will not badger you and leave you in peace to grieve, but if there is anything else?"

She faced him and her gaze swept slowly over his face. "I am miserable without Bette, but it feels right being here. In London. With you."

Relief pushed out the breath he had not known he had been holding. He smiled. "It feels good to hear you say that."

She smiled and reached for some cutlery and a napkin from a wooden box in the center of the table. "Ever since we arrived, I've been waiting for a bell as big as the one in the Elizabeth Tower to peal inside my head. Ring with its warning and tell me in no uncertain terms to return to Bath." She met his eyes. "It hasn't come."

"I am glad."

Her smile dissolved as she concentrated on placing her knife and fork side by side and her napkin across her lap just so. Adam reached for her hand. "I wish I had been there for you when Bette passed."

"There's nothing you could've done."

"I know, but—"

"No buts. You were busy in Bristol."

Adam waited for her to say more, but she remained silent. His heart beat fast. Did she already know what happened in Bristol? That he had been there under false pretenses and was more of a whore than she had been before she had taken the chance to better herself?

"Laura—"

"I'm scared, Adam." She took in a lengthy breath and faced him. "Scared of your certainty I'm Lucinda. Moreover, scared that I'm not. I'm scared why you look at me the way you do, but most of all, I'm scared we're in a city as big and dangerous as London when we barely know each other."

He reached for her hand and gratitude washed through him when she let him take it. He squeezed her fingers. "I have no more idea than you what will happen next, but we are here and we will try our damndest to woo a director or investor to get the play up and running. I believe in you. You are Lucinda. Please, Laura, trust me."

Trust you when you have not told her about Annabel, Bristol, or just how lowly a man you are?

He exhaled. "I think it is time I told you what happened in Bristol."

Her violet eyes shone in the semidarkness.

He swallowed the bitter taste of self-disgust that rose in his throat. "I lied to you, Laura."

She slowly pulled her hand from his and her shoulders stiffened. "About what?"

Shame seared hot at Adam's face as guilt twisted inside. He drew in a shaky breath. "There was an investor. A woman. A woman I have known for a while. A woman who has kept me in work these past twelve months."

She frowned. "Who?"

"Her name is Lady Annabel Harvard. She pursued me from Bristol to Bath after seeing me in a small play there."

"I don't understand. How has she kept you in work?"

"She is rich, lonely, and bored."

Her intelligent, beguiling eyes bored into his and his mouth drained dry as he waited for her response. Yet, pride lifted his chin. He might be a fool, but he was also a man trying his best to grasp his dreams by any means, rather than let them slip through his fingers.

Surely she would understand that? Surely she would not judge him as he judged himself?

The intensity of her study ensnared him the way every philanderer deserved to be caught—by the balls. She cleared her throat. "What is it you're trying to tell me?"

The rotund and jolly man who had taken his order appeared with their food and Laura looked to the table. The brim of her hat obscured her face and he had no way of knowing what she was thinking. There had been a strange lilt to her tone, and it confused him. He frowned.

"You folks just passing through, are ye?" The man put down two plates laden with food and straightened their cutlery.

Adam snapped his gaze to the proprietor and forced a smile. "Um, no. We have just recently arrived but plan to stay a while. London, after all, is the place of prosperity. Is it not?"

The man looked at him as though Adam had a bullring pierced through his septum. After a moment, the proprietor emitted a gravelly burst of laughter and slapped Adam hard on the shoulder. "Absolutely. No better place to make your fortune than the big city. From the country, are ye?"

"Bath, actually."

"Then you will be no stranger to people with thin air for dreams and hungry bellies that eat 'em. Enjoy your food."

The man waddled away and Adam stared after him. "Bloody fool. We will prove him wrong."

He turned.

Laura's pretty eyebrows were lifted in expectation, her gaze almost teasing. "What are you trying to tell me about Bristol?"

Own it, you fool. She likes you. She is in London with you, isn't she? He kept his eyes level with hers as a strange calmness swept over him. He had done what he had done, and life was too short to waste precious time in regret. He was here now and he would not return to Annabel. Ever.

"She used her influence to secure me parts in the last two plays I starred in. I was impatient. I could not wait for my break. I had my father sneering and spitting at my lack of success, and my mother mortified by her lowly actor son." He took a breath. "I stopped sleeping with Annabel the moment I laid eyes on you. As time went on, I sensed you slipping away from me. I didn't have very long to convince you to stay and play Lucinda. I panicked and, like a coward without backbone, I fled back to Annabel and asked her to invest in my play. She said yes."

Laura's expression was blank. Rather than her skin being lit bright red with anger as he had expected, it remained as pale as porcelain. The silence bore down on him as their pie and potatoes steamed between them. He sucked in a breath. "Won't you say something?"

Silence.

On and on she stared, until he thought his racing heart would burst clean out of his chest. The longer she stared, the more his misplaced pride gave way to irritation. He snatched up his fork and stabbed into his pie; the steam erupted in a gray plume between them. The next word uttered would be hers.

"So, in return for money, you had sex with her?" She picked up her knife and fork.

He lifted his chin. "Yes."

"Then you will again."

He gritted his teeth. "I will not."

She quirked her eyebrow, the first break in her almost wax-like expression. "How can you be so sure? No one can make a promise like that. We do what we have to do."

"It was over the minute I came back to Bath and saw you again." He tightened his jaw. "I will not sleep with another woman as long as you are with me. It is you, Laura. It is you I want in my bed and in my life."

She nodded slowly. "You want me in your bed."

"Yes."

"I see." She popped a cut of potato into her mouth and chewed. With each movement of her jaw, her eyes lit a little brighter.

He frowned. "What are you thinking?"

Her smile broke and she tipped her head back. Her laugh was loud, brash, and entirely infectious. It shriveled the tense atmosphere into oblivion. Her booming laughter was hearty in warmth and glorious amusement.

Adam smiled and stared at the creamy white column of her throat. "What is so funny?"

She slapped her hand to her chest. "You're more ambitious than I gave you credit for, Mr. Lacey. Where there's a will, there's a way, right? Bette would've absolutely come to love you."

He laughed. "You are not angry?"

She swiped at her eyes. "Angry? I have no hold on you. No claim. You're your own man, and don't you ever let anyone tell you differently. As for wanting me in your bed . . ."

His cock stirred as her laughter quieted and her eyes turned dark.

"Let's eat this delicious food Mr. Optimistic has served us and we'll see what's next on the menu, shall we?"

Laura had no idea if it was damnable how liberating Adam's moral failings were on her, but, by God, it was good to know he was equally as guilty of making foolhardy decisions. The thought he owed her any explanation was as flattering as it was ludicrous. Never in her life had a man given a damn what she thought of him—and now Adam cared. More than cared. He wanted her for the long-term as much as she did him.

Hand in hand, they laughed and kissed, stopped and stared into each other's eyes as they headed back to the tavern, as though it was to their honeymoon bed rather than a tryst for lovers posing as husband and wife.

Adam pushed open the pub door and Laura struggled to wipe the smile from her lips as they wove between the patrons toward the staircase at the back of the saloon. She followed him up the steps, reveling in the stares that followed them. This time there wasn't any turning her face to the wall. As far as anyone knew, they were husband and wife. She held her head high.

This was no secret tryst. Nothing immoral or illegal. At least not to them. He slipped the key into the lock and pushed open the bedroom door. He turned and swept a low bow, his arm directed toward the room beyond.

"After you, my lady."

She entered and turned to face him. Her heart pounded when he shoved the door closed and came toward her without finesse or decorum. She dropped her drawstring bag to the floor and he pushed her against the wall. Her breasts ached for him and her cunny throbbed. Had he read her mind that she wanted him to take her like this? Have her. Own her. Possess her.

Fear, frustration, grief, and passion whirled inside as though her heart was an engine rather than a muscle. She needed this. She needed Adam. She needed to act on the all-encompassing liberty he'd given her by admitting his mistakes: that he'd succumbed to paid sex in no different a situation than she had.

"Laura, Laura, Laura . . ." He whispered her name over her skin as he kissed her jaw, lower over the sensitive curve of her neck as he gripped her waist.

She clung to his biceps, her nails digging into the hardened muscles. He claimed her mouth once more and she shamelessly teased his tongue with hers, softly then hard with intent. A low growl came from deep within and he tugged at the buttons lining the front of her dress. She fumbled her hands into his jacket, desperate to rid him of that and the shirt beneath, desperate to get to hot, taut skin.

It was taking too long. Everything was cumbersome and in the way of what she needed. With her hands at his jaw, she eased him back and stared deep into his eyes. Unadulterated lust shone in their dark brown depths, frustration showed in the flush at his cheeks, and raw masculinity in the set line of his jaw.

Pressing a violent kiss to his lips, she pulled back and yanked at the buttons of her dress. As it slid over her shoulders, his gaze never left hers. He kicked off his boots and tore off his jacket. Piece by piece, their clothing strewn around the room, their eyes flitted over every inch of skin the other revealed.

At last only her chemise remained and she moved to lift it.

"Wait."

Adam's command halted her and the material slipped from her fingers and flowed back down her legs. She trembled and her harried breaths rasped against her chest. He walked toward her completely naked. Her gaze shot unashamedly to his cock and her body flushed hot from her scalp to her toes. Memories of their single time together crashed and burned inside her heart and mind. She ached for him to push his entire length inside her over and over.

"Adam . . ."

He came so close not a whisper of air passed between them. He gently kissed her before lifting her roughly into his arms. She wrapped her arms about his neck as he carried her to the bed and laid her down. Laura trembled as her control diminished and Adam's took over. Domination and determination shone in his eyes. The joy of a man wanting to make love to her with strength and passion, rather than with payment and degradation, filled Laura with hope for a happier future.

She sensed he was laid as bare as she as liberty emanated from deep inside him too. This was Adam. *Her* Adam. He lay down beside her. There was no act or pretense; this was raw, open, and beautiful.

He shimmied down her body. Second by unbearable second, he glided her chemise up to her waist and drew her drawers down her legs and over her feet. Slowly, carefully, he eased her legs apart, and Laura swallowed to feel his warm breath blow against her wetness.

Anticipation hurried her breathing, and her breasts rose and fell from the blessed torture. His lips and tongue followed his breath. She squeezed her eyes shut. Wave after wave of sexual yearning rolled through every pore, every cell of her blood as he tasted, teased, and licked her into a frenzy. She writhed beneath him, eventually reaching blindly forward to grip her fingers into his hair. Wantonly, she raised her hips, wanting more.

Did he have any idea what it meant that he knew what she'd done time and again with strangers, yet he still wanted his mouth on her? Love for him burned like fire around her heart.

"Adam, quickly. I'm so close."

Another taste, another gentle circling of his tongue and she opened her eyes as his breath left her. He crawled up the bed, covering her body with his. Broad, hard, and irresistible, he stared into her eyes as he nestled between her open legs.

His cock brushed against her pubic hair and clitoris before he pushed deep inside. Pleasure sighed from her lips to have him fill her at last. Together they moved, thrust for thrust, riding the wave, their eyes locked, their bodies growing slick with perspiration. On and on, their joined breathing became the only sound filling the room. Higher and higher he took her; deeper and deeper he burrowed into her heart.

As he picked up speed, Laura surrendered to the crash she sensed coming and raised her legs to lock them around his waist. She took him as deep as she could and together, the world came alive around them.

The lights, the noise, their joined shouts belonged not in the rented room of a tavern, but on love's grand stage. With a final cry . . . Laura came home.

Chapter 21

When Adam slipped his hand in hers outside The Adelphi, Laura exhaled a happy sigh. The play had been magnificent, the costumes and scenery even more so. Words had failed her throughout the production, despite Adam's whispered observations and frequent encouraging squeezes of her hand.

Now he pulled her into his arms and she stared at his handsome, smiling face. She laughed. "Look at you."

His smile widened. "What?"

"You look positively elated. Anyone would think you have a soft spot for the theater."

"Very droll, Miss Robinson. Very droll." He pressed his lips to hers for a moment before pulling back. "Well? What do you think? Could we not provide as equally good a performance?"

"Of course . . ." She grimaced as self-doubt twisted inside her. "Sometime during nineteen ten maybe."

He frowned. "Why would you say that? You can do everything those actresses did and more."

She eased from his arms and looped her hand into the crook of his elbow. They walked. "I can't imagine how I'll ever be as good as those actresses. They were marvelous. All of them. Even the ones playing the smaller roles."

He stopped. "We have been here five days. You have to start believing you can act. Soon there will be far too many people only too willing to tell you otherwise. You have to have immeasurable self-belief to succeed in this business."

She sighed. "I know all my lines, all my actions, yet—"

"Yet, nothing. You are phenomenal."

Laura stared deep into his eyes. They shone with hope and excitement. She longed to believe what he was saying, but things like this—dreams of the biggest spectrum—just didn't happen to the likes of her. "We've barely stepped out of our room all week and rehearsing isn't enough. Believe me, there's nowhere else I want to be than working with you, eating with you . . . making love with you." She smiled. "But we have to be realistic."

His gaze wandered over her face and lingered at her lips.

Apprehension caused her heart to pick up speed. She needed to tell him about the baby she was now certain she carried. By her calculations, she'd entered her second menstrual cycle, which meant her playing the role of Lucinda was impossible since she'd be showing in just a few weeks. She swallowed. "Maybe you should at least consider someone else for Lucinda."

He frowned. "Why would I? It is you I want. It was always you."

"Things change and things happen. I can't read. It's taking so much longer for me to learn the lines than someone who could pick up that script and not struggle with every letter. I'm not saying I don't want to do it, I just want you to . . . have a reserve in mind."

He smiled. "Always thinking of others, aren't you? Well, I am sorry, on this occasion only you will do." He briefly kissed her lips.

Heat warmed her cheeks. "And how are we for money? Surely our funds are getting low? Maybe we should start thinking about seeking other work until—"

"There is no need."

The tenderness in her breasts seemed to heighten, and the intolerance of her morning tea came back and rose bitter in her throat. "There's every need. I'm not saying I'm losing faith in the play, but—"

"With the boards beneath your feet and the light on your hair . . ." He fingered a curl at the side of her cheek. "My words on your tongue, all this doubt will disappear."

Her stomach knotted with further anxiety, despite the intoxication of his endless enthusiasm. "Please don't make me feel I'm the only one worrying what we'll do tomorrow or next week. Living with Bette, eking out a living for this past year, hasn't been a pleasant place to be. I don't want things to get worse than they were before she died. I owe it to her to get out and grab a better future."

"You are."

"I might not be doing what I did before, but I'm still not earning a wage. A moral wage."

"But you will." He brought his finger to her chin. "You will be outstanding. Trust me. Please."

She swallowed and looked away into the distance. The alluring shade of his deep dark eyes was more than she could stand. She had to be stronger than this. She had to make him understand her need for independence. In the months to come, she would have a baby to care for, another mouth to feed, and it would be negligent to run headlong into a fantasy with the man of her dreams—no matter how powerful the temptation.

"I love the way you are, but it's too much, too soon." She forced her gaze to his. "The circumstances of my life have stripped any optimism away and left just enough for me to believe better things come to those who work hard and pave the way. I'll wait for the break, but in the meantime, I need to earn my own money."

His ensuing silence bore down on her until Laura didn't know what else to do but lift onto her tiptoes and kiss him long and hard. Immediately, her body caught alight in the flame of her attraction. His deep sincerity to provide her with hope, ambition, possibility, and love was so beautiful, yet entirely too dangerous to rely upon. God, how she wished Bette were there to help guide her along this treacherous path.

Tears burned and she squeezed her eyes tighter and kissed him deeper. She'd already lost Bette. She'd escaped danger by Adam ensuring Baxter's arrest. She couldn't lose Adam . . . and never their baby.

They parted and she squeezed his hands in determination. "If we find work, we can put some money aside so we have resources to fall back on while we find an investor or director. Please. I'm not used to relying on others this way."

His jaw tightened. "I am not others. I will look after you."

Foreboding skittered up her spine and her innate fortitude whispered through her. She shook her head. "That's not enough. I'm sorry."

A cruel pain slashed across her heart and she pulled her hands from his to hold them tightly around the strings of her bag. "It's been Bette and me forever. You can't expect my way of thinking to change overnight. I need to know I have money of my own. I need to work."

Their eyes locked as people brushed past, separating around them. A human boulder that had taken root in the middle of a busy thoroughfare. The buildings pressed in and the night sky came lower until Laura's pulse beat relentlessly at her temple.

He pulled back his shoulders before offering her his arm. "Let's walk."

She hesitated before exhaling and returning her hand into the crook of his elbow. As they continued forward, the tension grew. Her old persona rose up and burned hot behind her ribcage. She fought the need to yank him to a stop and demand he listen to her, tell him she didn't need his care. Her independence was paramount.

Tears clogged her throat. They were so very different.

The silence grew and she focused on soaking up every moment of London's atmosphere. She inhaled its scent, strained her ears to its sounds, and opened her eyes wide to its sights. Who was to say how long this would last? Who was to say their differences wouldn't soon part them when their dream shattered into a million pieces and they were startled wide awake?

Adam cleared his throat. "Now I know how you truly feel, I can tell you my good news."

She glanced at him. "What?"

"I have found a director who loves my play. He wants to see us both for a test run of a scene or two tomorrow."

Laura halted and stared at his set profile. Words danced on her tongue and her heart soared with hope. She opened her mouth and closed it. Opened it again, only to snap it closed a second time.

He turned, his smile wide. "If you are not doing anything, of course."

"Why would you . . . why did you let me say all those things?" She made to lunge for him.

Laughing, he caught her by the waist and swung her around, heedless to the stares of the passersby or the leering calls of a group of young boys leaning against a wall behind them.

"Because I care about you. I want you to share every worry, concern, or hesitation you have. Always."

She stared at him. "When have you had time to see anyone? We've been working so hard."

"A couple of days ago when you took an afternoon nap, I wandered to a pub not far from Drury Lane where I used to go when I worked in London. I asked around and they gave me this director's name who is trying, as we are, to break in to the industry. He has money, but no one willing to take a risk with him."

"And he said yes?"

He grinned. "He said yes."

Laura's heart beat hard. "Are you telling the truth? You're not grasping at anything to stop me from pursuing a job? I couldn't bear it if you felt the need to do that, Adam. This is who I am."

"I admit I want to provide so you do nothing all day but act, but I would not lie. I did not say anything before because it is important to me I know how you feel"—he pressed a hand to her chest—"in here."

Laura blinked against her tears as her impending pregnancy preyed once more on her mind. "Oh, Adam. You shouldn't have put me through that."

"I should. We have to be honest with each other." He smiled. "This is it. I have got a good feeling about this man. He read my entire play in two days. Felt he knew Lucinda without even seeing you. I am confident you will speak one line and he will be putty in our hands."

A frisson of trepidation simmered inside. Sooner or later, she'd have no choice but to thrust inevitable disappointment on him. "He wants to see us tomorrow?"

He grinned. "Tomorrow."

She shook her head. "I don't know what to say."

"You say, 'Adam, get me back to our room quick. Ravish me and make me cry out your name, or so help me God, I will not attend that meeting tomorrow.'"

Laura forced a smile and lifted her eyebrow. "That is not what I had in mind at all to say."

He lifted his shoulders. "I understand. Say not another word. Your wishes are my command."

"Adam Lacey, you are incorrigible."

"And I'm a damn stallion in bed, I know." He grasped her hand.

He took off as if fire were at his feet and Laura had no choice but to follow—all the while resisting the need to swipe at the tears of apprehension that refused to cease.

Adam banged his fist against the director's front door for the third time in as many minutes. Where the hell was he? Humiliation threatened as Laura's skirts shuffled behind him.

"Adam, he's not here. We'll have to go."

"The hell we will." He banged on the door again. "Open up, Conrad. I demand to see you. It has been a week since our missed appointment. You will not do this."

His heart raced and his gut churned. They had been duped. His words stolen. Anger wound his stomach tight and pain shot like an arrow through his head from temple to temple. Intellectually, he knew the man would not remember every line, every action, but damn if the scoundrel would forget the essence of his beloved play. How would he sleep at night knowing his play might appear onstage one day, another claiming its originality?

He raised his fist once more, but Laura grasped his wrist. "Adam, no. Let's just leave. He's gone."

"I can't. I can't leave without seeing his face." He moved to bang on the door again when a window opened above them. He looked up.

A woman peered over the sill, her face etched with tiredness and her eyes seemingly ringed red from crying. "Who are you? What is it you want?"

Adam stepped back from the door to get a clearer view of her. "I am looking for Mr. Conrad."

"He's not here. Now, stop banging on my door and go away." She moved back to shut the window.

"Wait!" Adam shouted. "Are you his wife?"

"Yes, I'm his wife, but the last two days I wish I weren't. As it's my godforsaken husband you're after, I'm afraid there's nothing I can say to you but join the bloody queue."

Adam frowned. "Where is he? I have been trying to see him since yesterday."

"Well, you're banging on the wrong door, for a start. He'll be off across the Atlantic by now with his young piece of strumpet in tow, no doubt."

Adam's mouth drained dry. For the love of God. "America? He's gone to America?"

"So I've been told. Turned up at the dock under the cover of darkness. Skulking about like the cad he is with his jumped-up floozy teetering on her fancy heels behind him. More fool you for thinking you could deal with a man like my husband, sir. I married the son of a bitch by force, not love."

The window slammed shut.

Adam stood frozen to the cobblestones. His mind reeled with what-ifs and maybes. His heart burned with so much frustration, it was a fireball of anger. What was he supposed to do now? What would Laura think of his incompetence and yet another strike of failure? How was he to trust that Conrad would not breathe a word of the play to anyone else? Thank God, he'd at least managed to get the script back when he'd seen Conrad days ago and it sat in his room at the tavern and not halfway across the Atlantic.

"Adam?"

He released a shaky breath and turned.

Laura's violet eyes were wide with concern. "What do we do now?"

He opened his arms and she stepped into them, her crown fitting perfectly beneath his chin. He closed his eyes and drew strength from her slender curves pressed against him. "This is nothing more than a setback. I refuse to believe the man's enthusiasm was not genuine."

"Are you even confident he was a real director?"

He frowned and eased her from his embrace. He had entirely disappointed her, and the notion she had lost all belief in him cut deep. "Of course. Clearly, this is a case of a man thinking with his cock rather than his common sense." He forced a smile. "We are all guilty of that from time to time."

Two spots of color leaped to her cheeks and she looked past his shoulder. "Yes, I know that more than most."

God, I am such an idiot. Mentally slapping his head, Adam

cupped her jaw in his hands. "What you did before we met has no consequence. It is gone. It is in the past. Just as what I did with Annabel is in the past. This just means Conrad was not the right man for our play. We will find someone else."

She lifted her face from his hands and stepped back. The determination he was getting to know so well seeped into her gaze. "Fine. Then you go find a director while I look for work elsewhere. I've given you a week since we last talked about this. I won't let you keep paying our way on your own. You have yet to tell me how much money is left. I won't let you convince me black is white anymore."

Insecurity and failure wound a tight, painful knot in his gut. His father's voice yelling Adam would never amount to anything, never be able to provide for a woman or child, rose and spilled like bitter poison through his veins.

He raised his hands in reluctant surrender. "Fine. We will get work elsewhere, but at least tell me you are not giving up on this . . . on us."

"Of course not." Her shoulders relaxed and a glimmer of a smile played at her mouth. "It will make me feel better to know we're working for the success of the play equally. Tell me you understand."

Adam pursed his lips as he fought the overbearing need to demand she stay at their room where she could spend every minute rehearsing and building on all the amazing achievements she had made thus far. He tipped his head back and looked to the graying sky as the London smog rolled in from the Thames.

"Of course I understand. I do not want to stop you from doing what you want, whenever you want. That is exactly what I ran away from years ago." He dropped his chin and met her eyes. "It is just . . ."

She grasped his hand. "What?"

"You are starting to read, Laura. You are acting. You are grieving for a friend so beloved, she was all that mattered to you. Yet here you are, willing to do work God knows where until my play sees the light of day."

She smiled. "And? I'm a martyr for a good charity case. Always have been."

He shook his head. "I am not a charity case, and there is nothing funny about any of this."

"Bette's first rule was, life without laughter isn't an option. The woman lived by that and kept us fed, warm, and safe for years. It's about time you learned Bette's way of thinking too."

He stared at her beautiful face. "You are an amazing woman, Miss Robinson."

She smiled and pressed her lips to his. "From tomorrow, I'll find work and do whatever it takes to keep a roof over our heads. You'll scour the theaters night and day until you find your play a home. Do we have a deal?"

The excitement in her eyes and the lingering taste of her lips on his should have been enough to push him on, but Adam could not ignore the self-hatred burning inside him like a wildfire. Wasn't he relying on her as he had his parents? Wasn't he sending her out into the lion's lair of London like a lamb to the slaughter? The woman had more gumption and courage in her little finger than most men of his class or creed. He was a fool to think she needed his protection. She could undoubtedly survive these streets alone.

Determination gathered momentum and he gripped her waist, lifting her from the ground.

She gasped. "What are you doing?"

"One week, two at the most, and I will have a director and an investor. More than anything, more than the play even, I will be a man worthy of you."

She grinned, her eyes shining with tears. "Amen to that."

He brought her lower, still gripped firmly in his embrace, and covered her mouth with his. *I am in love for the first time in my life. I cannot lose her.*

Chapter 22

The man's spit landed barely two inches from Laura's hand. Yellow-green, it stuck to the coffee shop's flagstone floor like putrid glue. Her anger simmered perilously in the pit of her stomach. The dangerous thoughts she'd been fighting for days gathered strength.

Clenching her jaw, she slapped her cloth onto the man's oral filth and wiped it up, dashing it back into the bucket of soapy water beside her. She dunked the cloth with gusto and wrung it as she would have the filthy sod's neck, given half a chance. Slapping the cloth down on the floor again, she wiped over the stone and the ones surrounding it before pushing to her feet.

The floor gleamed—if for only a minute or two before the shop's patrons thumped their work-worn and muddied boots all over it again. Two weeks. Two arduous weeks, she'd been on her hands and knees scrubbing and cleaning, washing and wiping. She picked up the bucket and marched through to the back door leading to a small, dank yard. She'd yet to see even a single shaft of light penetrate the space in the days she'd worked as a cleaner-cum-general lackey.

Opening the rickety wooden gate leading onto the cobbled alleyway beyond, Laura hefted the bucket and sloshed the water into the gutter. She narrowed her eyes and followed the water's path as it flowed away to join the rest of London's soil.

Hour by hour, her heart hardened. Every hour she and Adam went on without an investor in his play, she cared less and less about her dream of starring onstage. She swallowed against the stab of pain that ripped sharply in her chest. She had to tell Adam her pregnancy suspicions. Would he welcome the news? Of course not. His ambitions started and ended in the theater. She was still his Lucinda.

Laura glared at the empty bucket. Enough was enough. She didn't need to be cleaning like this to keep her and Adam fed and sheltered. There were other ways that would pay per hour what she could earn in this place in a week.

The bitter tang of temptation coated her mouth and she savored its flavor. She closed her eyes and Adam's face appeared. Animated and admiring, his eyes shone as he stared, his mouth stretched wide with a confident smile. How would he look at her if he found out she'd succumbed once more to the trade she knew so well? Would he understand she did it for him? For them?

Money would give them the freedom to stay in London and keep knocking on theater doors until someone gave Adam's work a chance. He'd understand in time. He'd see it made sense. There was no emotion in such a vocation. He knew her to be a good, kind, and honest woman. He knew the same of Bette.

"I don't pay you to stand around all day, Lady Muck."

The sharp, shrill voice of the lady proprietor snapped Laura's eyes open and she turned. The woman stood in the yard watching her; her eyes were cold and her fists rested at her hips.

Laura glared. "I was just emptying my bucket."

The woman lifted her eyebrow. "That ain't the tone to take with someone paying your wages neither. Now stop milling around and get back inside. There are plenty out there who'd give their back teeth for your job, you know. Come on. There are dishes needing a washing."

She turned on her heel and lumbered back inside. Laura stood stock-still, staring at the now-empty doorway. Second by second, her cheeks grew hot and her body trembled. No more. Laura strode inside the shop. The proprietor was all smiles and good humor with the two gentlemen ordering coffee and buns from the other side of the counter.

Laura stood at the end of the long wooden barrier, her fingers gripping its curved edge as though she intended to break it clean off. Money exchanged hands and the men took their fare to a table at the window. The woman she currently had the dirty job of answering to tipped their paid coins into the cash box. Slapping her hands together, she turned and stopped when her eyes met Laura's.

"What are you doing standing there like the day is for your leisure? You lost your way to the kitchen or somethin'?"

Laura narrowed her eyes. "I want what I'm due and then I'll be on my way."

"What?"

"I said, I want what I'm—"

"I heard what you said." The woman came forward and stopped inches from Laura, her eyes alight with anger. She pointed her finger in Laura's face. "Now, you listen here. You don't work for me and get away with throwing your weight around. I pay you well enough. If you've got a complaint, then maybe you'd like to talk to my old man about it. He ain't quite as amicable as me."

Struggling to control the suppressed rage scalding and burning her tongue, waiting for release in a torrent of ugly words, Laura tilted her chin. "I thought there was no need to speak to anyone but you. Aren't you in charge of staff and everything else in here?" She glanced toward the doorway leading to the family rooms upstairs, where the mystery husband hid for most of the day. Not that Laura blamed him—considering the alternative was sharing breathing space with his gorgeous, partially toothed wife. She faced her current pain in the ass once more. "But if I need to speak to the boss, I will."

The woman glared and jabbed a thumb into her ample bosom. "I'm the boss."

Laura smiled and held out her palm. "Then I'll have what I'm due and be out of here . . . if it's not too much bother."

Their gazes locked in silent battle and Laura took immense pleasure in every passing second. God, it felt good to be back in control of her life. Bette laughed uproariously in her ear and Laura trembled with the need to laugh right along with her. Why hadn't she done what needed to be done to pave her and Adam's way in a little comfort before now?

Her confidence swayed on a knife's edge and she slammed it back into place. No. He need not know. She was doing what she needed to do to support him in his dream. To support her dream.

"Fine. You take your money and get out of here." The woman marched to the cash box and extracted a couple of notes and five or six coins. "Here." She slapped the money into Laura's outstretched hand. "Now get."

Taking her time, Laura nonchalantly perused the money before clasping her fingers tightly closed around it. "Thank you. I'll wish you good day."

Feeling the woman's eyes burning holes in her back, Laura strolled to the door and out into the cold. The bright December sun bathed the litter-strewn streets in the best light it had seen for the past few days. She grinned and drew in a long breath. Just one day. For just one day, she'd do what she had to and earn enough money to give them decent food and shelter for the next couple of weeks.

Her smile faltered and she fought it back into place. By then Adam would have found someone who believed in him as much as she did and be none the wiser. Tilting her chin, she tightened the strings on her drawstring bag and strode forward. If she was going to do this, she needed to find out where the men with money "shopped." She might be succumbing to laying with a man for money once more, but she'd be damned if she'd do it with a man who didn't treat her with some modicum of respect.

With her mind made up, she mentally quashed the niggling in her conscience and turned left along the street that would lead to the West End. From what she'd learned from Adam and Monica, people had money there. Money to spend. Money for pleasure.

"You've got experience, then, have you?" The house's madam quirked an eyebrow, her blue eyes intense with amusement and interest.

Laura kept her gaze level with the madam's as she lounged on the settee in the sedate and classily decorated back room of one of London's many whorehouses. Laura guessed the woman to be older than her by six or seven years, but her beauty would have outshone someone much younger. The madam's casual confidence and quiet sophistication had Laura doubting why she'd come.

Fighting her wavering confidence, she straightened her shoulders. "Yes, ma'am. I worked in Bath since I was fifteen."

"And you say you want to work just for today?" The madam's appraisal traveled from the tip of Laura's hat, over her best coat, to the shoes on her feet. "That is not usual in any century. I'm intrigued."

"I was told to come and see you. Take my chances you might allow it, ma'am."

She lifted her eyebrow. "Told by whom? And stop calling me ma'am. It's Mrs. Fleet."

"A barmaid at The Horseshoe and another girl working at the West End, Mrs. Fleet. They spoke very highly of you. Said you were fair and took care of anyone who came here looking for work."

"I see." Her gaze languidly traveled the length of Laura's body once more. "Well, when they said anyone, that's not necessarily the case. I make judgments as to whether or not I like the girl first. Then I decide what I will and won't allow."

Laura nodded. "I wouldn't expect any more than that."

The madam's eyes narrowed. "Are you fussy about the client you'll service?"

Laura stiffened. "What do you mean?"

She smiled. "It's all right, darling. I'm not asking you to share your undoubtedly pretty cunny with a vagrant. The company who use my house are all of a certain class."

"I've been told that too." Laura tightened her grasp on her bag as the thought she might have made a mistake by coming there skittered along her nerve endings.

"Glad to hear it." The room lapsed into silence as Mrs. Fleet redeemed her study.

Laura's mouth drained dry under the woman's scrutiny as she focused on standing perfectly still. She'd spent the last twenty-four hours scouring the town asking questions in order to discover the local houses and where men of money frequented. She surmised Mrs. Fleet's establishment as the best of a bad situation, and she'd be damned if she'd leave after finding the courage to step inside.

Mrs. Fleet rose from the settee, her sapphire blue satin dress glinting beneath the sun's rays penetrating the window. "I am kind and generous to the girls who come through here." She rounded her desk and flipped through a large ledger. "I don't ask their names or backgrounds until I am of the mind I want them to stay." She looked up. "It is usual for me to have them request an appointment upon recommendation from another of my girls. If I take to them, I'll decide whether or not they can have a room. This situation is entirely different." She smiled softly. "Yet, your confidence impresses me, not to mention the color of your extraordinary eyes."

Adrenaline hummed through her and Laura offered a small smile. "I'm good, Mrs. Fleet. That much I can promise you."

The other woman studied her through narrowed lids. "Can I ask why you only want to work today?"

Something about this woman spoke to Laura on a level she couldn't name. Her intelligent blue eyes and soft lilt of her voice offered reason and concern. Laura cleared her throat. "I came here from Bath a few weeks ago, having given up the trade. My plans in the city have yet to come as I'd like and my money's running out. I'd like the opportunity to earn quickly and honestly. Then be on my way."

A moment passed before Mrs. Fleet spoke. "What if my clients take a fancy to you. Then what? I can hardly tell them you have disappeared into the night. What are these plans you hold so dear?"

Laura held her gaze. "I'd rather not say."

Mrs. Fleet smiled. "Then you'll have to give me a little more guarantee than one day of spectacular performance. I don't like disappointing the men who pay good money for my girls." She came around the desk and stopped a foot away from Laura. She tipped her head to the side and openly studied her. "You're very pretty. Your eyes are exquisite and your bosom generous. I think I would have three or four clients who would happily pay for your time."

Laura swallowed, cursing the heat that rose at her cheeks. Three or four. It had been so long. So very, very long. "That sounds perfect." The words were like pebbles on her tongue.

"There's something about you I like very much." After another moment of silent contemplation of Laura's face and person, Mrs. Fleet whirled away, her luxurious skirts brushing audibly across the carpet. "I'll give you your single day. I appreciate a woman trying to get out of this business and make her way, and would never deem myself her Maker by insisting she stay working if it isn't her wish." She returned to the desk and her ledger. "However, if you return to me wanting work again, you will give me longer than a day. Are we agreed?"

Laura slowly exhaled in an effort not to show her relief. She nodded, "Yes."

"Good." Mrs. Fleet smiled, her blue eyes soft. "The next thing you need to know is I run a clean house. I expect every client to use protection. If they refuse, they leave. Do you understand? Under no circumstances are you to break this rule. If you have trouble, you make enough noise that either myself or another girl will come running."

Her fondness and respect for this woman escalated and Laura smiled. "I understand perfectly."

Mrs. Fleet nodded, her kindly eyes shining. "Good. Then let me show you to your room. I believe your first client will be arriving in half an hour."

Laura stepped back and Mrs. Fleet led the way from the room. Laura inhaled a shaky breath as her old persona—before Adam—crept slowly over her shoulders and settled there like a well-worn blanket. Her heartbeat quickened and her hands were clammy, but she kept her head held high as they cut across the lobby to a huge wooden staircase.

Ignoring the curious stares of the other girls standing or sitting around the lobby and landing, Laura followed Mrs. Fleet to a closed door. She flashed Laura a friendly smile before opening the door and gesturing her inside with a wave of her hand.

"Make yourself comfortable. You'll like this man. He's gentle and unassuming. Wear the pink corset. There are black stockings in the top drawer." She nodded toward Laura's bosom. "And if you make the most of those assets, he'll be out of here before you know it."

Praying the trembling in her legs wasn't visible, Laura nodded. "Consider him taken care of."

Mrs. Fleet grinned. "Good girl. I'll see you shortly."

Laura didn't release her held breath until the door firmly closed behind the formidable Mrs. Fleet.

Chapter 23

Adam let himself into their room above the tavern. Laura was sitting at the small dressing table, pinning a flower into her hair and humming softly. He stared. Dressed in nothing but her chemise, her coffee-colored nipples were shadowed beneath the material.

His libido stirred.

God, he hadn't seen her looking so relaxed or flushed for days. Weeks. Since before Bette died. He closed the door and at its click, she turned. Her mouth curved in a wide smile.

"You're back." She rose and came toward him. "I'm so glad to see you."

Satisfaction warmed his heart and he smiled. "Well, don't you look happy?" He pressed a firm kiss to her mouth, before pulling back. His gaze drifted over her hair to the flower. It wasn't a flower at all but a sprig of lavender. He touched his fingers to it. "What's all this? You look beautiful."

She laughed and a faint blush stained her cheeks. "Oh, a gypsy woman gave it to me. Said it would bring me luck."

"Well, let's hope she is right." He pulled her tightly against him and the feel of her breasts made his impatience to have her all the more potent. "I might have to show you just how beautiful you look, rather than just saying it."

"Well, aren't you the charmer?" She pressed a brief kiss to his lips and moved to leave his arms. He grasped her tighter.

"You're going nowhere when you look so radiant. Something's changed about you. You look more . . . I don't know, confident. I like it."

A whisper of something he could not decipher flashed in her eyes and her smile faltered.

She laughed. "Don't be silly. I'm the same as I was yesterday and the day before. Now, where would you like to eat tonight? It's time you let me pay for something. My treat."

Adam tried and failed to drag his eyes from her hypnotic gleam. He laughed. "My God, woman. Do you really expect me to go anywhere without making love to you first?"

"Adam . . ."

He pulled her close once more and she stiffened. He dropped his mouth to the curve of her neck in a bid to relax her. It was impossible she didn't know what she meant to him. Just the smell of her—the sight of her—and the knowledge she was entirely his scrubbed away the stain of yet another disappointing day. Pride surged through him when her skin trembled beneath his lips. Was she equally as helpless to their attraction as he?

"You are so beautiful." He whispered the words against her collarbone and moved his lips across her shoulder.

Her fingers raked into his hair. "Adam . . ."

"Mmm?"

"We should go out. Take some supper."

"We will. After." His erection pulsed against the constraint of his trousers and he reached for her breast. He slid his thumb across her nipple and it hardened into a pebble.

"Adam, please. Not now." Her exhalation lifted the hair at his temple.

He smiled against the satiny softness of her jaw as he raised his head to look into her eyes, his hand still softly kneading her magnificent bosom. "We have time. We will always have time."

The skin at her neck flushed pink as she swallowed. "I've been waiting for you. I want to go out and enjoy the evening. Please."

What is wrong? Doesn't she feel my need for her? "Darling, please. Let me make love to you. Right here. Right now." He dipped his mouth to hers.

She gripped his upper arms and pushed him back. "I said no."

Her sharp tone and the severity of her shove threw icy-cold water on Adam's desire, shriveling his penis and ego in one fell swoop. He stared at her. Her violet eyes were alight with determination and her cheeks dark red.

He stepped back. The animosity emanating from her was such a contradiction to her earlier state, confusion hit him on a wave of unwelcome rejection. Dented pride wound tight like a fist in his chest and he planted his hands on his hips. "What is it? What have I done?"

The skin at her neck shifted as she swallowed. "Nothing. You weren't listening to me." She approached the wardrobe in the corner of the room. "I just want to get out of here for a while. I'm hungry."

His sexual frustration became anger. "I do not believe you."

Her shoulders tensed as she stood before the open wardrobe doors, her back ramrod straight.

Unease rolled through him. Why wasn't she turning around? Demanding he not speak to her in such a tone and awaiting an apology?

Her turned back brought guilt crashing down upon his shoulders. "Laura, I am sorry. It is just you looked so damn content when I came in and then—"

"And then I rejected sex from you." She snatched a dress from the wardrobe, the hanger clattering to the floor. She whirled around. "And you turned into an animal, foaming at the mouth." She stormed across the room and tossed the dress onto the bed. "What is it with men? Why do they seem to think women want sex all the damn time? Just because we're smiling or happy." She laughed. "No, even when we're damn miserable, men surmise sex is the answer to cheer us."

Adam frowned. What the hell was going on here?

She grabbed her petticoats and God only knew what else from every corner of the tiny room.

"Will you talk to me?" He glared. "What have I done?"

"I've already told you. I'm hun—"

"This is not about food."

Silence.

The tension between them coated everything in distaste. Keeping her face turned, she pushed one leg and then the other into a petticoat and yanked it onto her waist. Her face glowed red in the candlelight, and the sprig of lavender quivered in her hair. She was beyond angry. She was livid.

He had not seen her like this since the night they had first spoken outside the theater when he had insisted on walking her home. Well, be damned if she thought for one second he would let her storm off into the night like she had then.

"Has someone said something to you? Upset you?" He marched to the bed and curled his hand around the bedpost. "What has happened?"

She snatched her crinoline from the floor, steadfastly ignoring him.

Enough was enough. He strode toward her. "Talk to me." He yanked the crinoline from her hand and tossed it behind him. "I will not let you shut me out. I will not be treated in the same damn, dismissive manner I endured from my parents. Now, tell me what has put you in such a sanctimonious frame of mind?"

She froze for a brief moment before slowly lifting her eyes to his. "Sanctimonious?"

Damnation. She glowered at him as though she might swipe his face clean off with a single slap of her hand.

He raised his hands in surrender. "Fine. Angry then. I do not know."

She fisted her hands on her hips, her breasts rising and falling with each agitated breath. "I'm not yours, Adam. You don't own me and I don't owe you anything. I'll do what I want, when I want."

A horrible sense of foreboding seeped into his blood. "Of course, I do not own you. Why would you say that? Me kissing your neck, touching your breast has made you feel that way? That I think I have ownership of you?"

"I told you I wanted to work."

"What?" Confusion rolled through him as he grappled to understand what she wanted, what he needed to give her to bring the light back to her eyes. "You are working. The coffee shop—"

"Was like earning money scrubbing up an animal's filth for a penny a day." Her eyes blazed with anger. "I left that hideous place. I told the woman in charge exactly what she could do with her job."

So it was not the job. He frowned. "And that is fine. If you hated it there so much, I would not want—"

"There you go again." She shook her head and huffed out a laugh. "What *you* want. What about what *I* want? What about that?"

The longer he stared at her livid violet eyes, the quicker realization dawned. Was this about his failure to find an investor? His shoulders slumped as his heart grew heavy. What right did he have to expect her to wait with no end in sight? She had been patient, undemanding, and kept her word to support him. She was worldly wise and intelligent. She deserved so much more than he was currently able to give her.

She glared. "As I thought, you have absolutely nothing to say to defend yourself. You're the same as the rest of them."

"Laura . . ."

"What, Adam? What are you going to say now that will have me falling headfirst into bed with you?"

No words formed as he stared into her eyes. Anger and frustration emanated from her, stripping him of anything to say. Christ, had he lost her? Nausea whirled and clenched in his gut. Shame and self-hatred that he had not felt for weeks settled like lead behind his breastbone.

"Is this about your insistence I find someone else to play Lucinda?"

"The play has nothing to do with this."

He shook his head. "I cannot expect you to continue to believe in me after weeks of failing to find an investor. I have no right." He wiped his hand over his face. "I practically accosted you in Bath, asked you to wait for me while I went to Bristol . . ." She tilted her chin in response and he halted. "Is that what this is about? My sleeping with Annabel? I thought you were at peace with that."

Laura stared. *Tell him. He told you about Annabel and you're both still here together. Everything will be all right. You have no hold on him; he has no hold on you. He'll understand. He has to.*

Inhaling a calming breath, her anger abated as she crossed the room. Sitting on the bed beside him, she took his clenched fist in her trembling hands. "I don't want the burden of what I did today on my shoulders. I refuse to let it bring me down or make me feel guilty."

"What you did today? A burden?" His smile was tentative, his brow still creased in confusion. "Tell me. I do not want you to worry about anything."

Laura swallowed hard, before taking a deep breath. "Well, I . . ." The admission stuck like broken glass in her throat, and the intense confusion in his eyes stretched her nerves to breaking. "It really is no different than what happened with Annabel. I really just did the same thing."

His smile dissolved as he slowly pulled his hand from hers. "What do you mean you have done the same thing?"

The tension in the room turned icy cold. The laughter from the bar downstairs drifted under the door, loud and mocking. The room darkened as though twilight had fallen without warning.

Her mouth drained dry. He wouldn't do this. He wouldn't make her feel like the villain of the piece. He was no better. His actions no different. Her body traitorously shook, belying her shame. "I worked today. I worked and earned more money than I would have in a month at that coffeehouse."

He stared, the lines on his forehead deepening as his color rose. "You worked?"

She nodded.

Second by second, her nausea grew and her hands turned clammy.

His realization came immediately and with sickening clarity. His dark eyes turned almost black and his jaw to a hardened line. He rose and the bed shifted beneath her as Laura's world tipped on its axis. He stood, looking down at her as though he didn't quite know who she was.

"You worked." The words slipped from his tongue as a statement rather than a question. He spun away and fisted his hand into his hair. "Oh, God, you *worked.*"

She swallowed once more. "Adam, listen to me. It was one day. It doesn't matter. We've now got enough money—"

He whirled around and Laura sucked in a breath to see his face so contorted and mottled red in anger.

He yanked his hand from his hair. "Of course, it matters. Don't you see? Don't you see what this means?"

Pride and self-defense bolted her from the bed and she stopped inches away from him. Eye-to-eye. Toe-to-toe. She was her own woman and always would be. Her stomach quivered, but she held firm. "It means nothing. We now have the means to stay in London longer. We can continue to look for an investor. Together. We will go to the theaters. We will——"

He glared. "For how long? A week? A month? And what happens then? You *work* again?"

Anger twisted inside and it took all of her self-control not to raise her hand to his face. Why couldn't he see she did it for him? For them? Tears threatened and she blinked. "I won't apologize for what I did. It was my decision and it had nothing to do with you."

His eyes widened as he stared. "Nothing . . . you think you sleeping with another man has nothing to do with me? It has *everything* to do with me."

Her temper burst. "Why? Because I'm here with you, you think that makes you responsible for me? I never asked that of you. I wouldn't expect that from anyone. I don't even *want* that from you or anybody else, for that matter."

"What *do* you want, Laura? That is the real question here. If I cannot be the man who provides for you, looks after you, what is it we are doing here?"

Her heart ached and the tears she fought blurred her vision. How had this happened? They had been foolish to let their relationship tip into the personal. She should've resisted his kiss, his excitement, his aspirations and weak, weak love. She swiped at her cheeks and brushed past him in a bid to breathe.

"I never wanted you to feel you had to look after me." She faced him as fear bounced around in her stomach and distress seeped icy cold into her veins. "I never wanted that. I've been alone too long to start taking orders and expectations from you or anyone else."

He shook his head. "I do not believe this. I thought . . . Goddamn it, I love you."

Her heart stopped. Her body trembled. "What?"

He came toward her and cupped her jaw in his hands. His deep, dark eyes gleamed with unshed tears. "I said I love you, but if you cannot let me look after you and be the man I need to be for you, it will never work between us."

You're losing him. He loves you. He loves you, and you're pushing him away. She reached for him but couldn't bring herself to beg him to stay or even understand. Her hand dropped to her side, trembling with the force of her self-worth. "Adam, listen to me——"

"I have my ambitions . . ." He shook his head and closed his eyes. "But more than anything, I have my pride. I swore I would never have a wife, a family, none of those things." He slipped his hands from her face and a tear slid over his stubbled cheek. "I should have damn well listened to my instinct and never let things get this far between us."

Panic furled in a painful ball behind her heart. "What does that mean?"

He opened his eyes and searched her face. "I am sorry. I cannot be the man you want."

He whirled away and snatched his hat from the hook behind the door. With a final glance at her, he yanked open the door and disappeared into the corridor.

Frozen with shock and paralyzed with heartbreak, Laura sank onto the bed.

"Don't leave me, Adam." Her whispered plea was full of regret for the loss of his love. For something she'd never dare think she'd have.

Chapter 24

Laura clutched Monica's letter as she stared at the façade of the Theater Royal, Bath. No part of her wanted to step inside. No part of her wanted to be in this position. She'd waited for Adam to return to the London tavern for two nights before she'd accepted his abandonment. Two days following that, she'd received a message from Monica saying she needed Laura's testimony to ensure Baxter's incarceration. Once again, she was back to losing everything in return for testimony against a scumbag.

She narrowed her eyes. Well, that was fine. She'd do what she had to a thousand times over if it meant Baxter didn't beat another whore or extort money from another starving family.

Her original plan of living and working in the country lost its appeal the moment Adam left her in London. Excluding Bette, he was the only other person she'd met who believed she could be more than a whore, waitress, or washer-woman. If she couldn't have Adam as her lover, she wouldn't waste the unique and wondrous feeling of possibility he'd inspired in her. She would try to aspire to a different dream than the theater and everlasting love come true. There had to be more Bath could offer her.

She ran her hand over her burgeoning belly. There had to be another way.

The sense of failure and loss would abate soon enough. Right now, she wanted nothing more than to help Monica after her friend had been so willing to help her. Strength in the female race was unparalleled.

Back to the city where Bette was buried and Baxter awaited trial,

Laura had gotten through the heartbreak of one and the harassment of the other. Why keep running only to be left alone? She had her baby. That was what mattered from then on. Soon, the pain of loving Adam Lacey would be nothing more than a dim memory.

She exhaled a shaky breath. *Please, God, let this agony fade. . . .*

"Laura?"

She started and turned. Tess came toward her. "My God, it is you." She wrapped her arms around Laura. "It's so good to see you."

Forcing a smile, Laura hugged her friend. "You too. How are you?"

Tess pulled back and clasped Laura's hands at arm's length. "I'm good. The last I heard, you'd run off to London with Mr. Lacey." She grinned. "I can't think of anything more romantic." She turned Laura's left hand over and stared. "Darn. Hasn't the man put a ring on your finger yet?"

Pain struck Laura's heart afresh, but she laughed. "I don't think so. Adam Lacey marrying the likes of me? Didn't I tell you to get those stars out of your eyes, Tess Cambridge?"

Her friend laughed and looped her arm through Laura's. "Well, you can at least come inside and tell me what happened in the big city."

"Inside?"

Tess tilted her head toward the theater. "Aren't you here for your job back?"

A spark of hope ignited in Laura's stomach. To get her old job back would provide reason for her to be in the theater every day, if nothing else. Maybe they wouldn't mind her waddling a few hours a day through the aisles to earn some money. Would it matter that an orange seller carried a babe?

She glanced toward the theater doors. "Do you think they'd give me a job here when I left without as much as a backward glance? I can't imagine they'll take—"

"'Course they will. One word from Miss Danes and you'll be back working before you know it."

"Is Monica in a play here now, then? I've only been gone a few weeks and when I saw her last . . ."

Tess scowled. "Baxter had given her a going over. I know." Her face softened. "It will take more than that to keep a lady like Miss Danes down. Her face is healed up. Baxter's in prison awaiting trial. She's happy, Laura. Come on. Let's go inside and you can tell me all about you and Mr. Lacey. Where is he, by the way?"

Laura swallowed as she and Tess mounted the steps and entered the theater lobby. "In London, I assume. I haven't seen him for a few days."

"What?" Tess ground to a halt. "He didn't leave you there?"

"He had every right. I let him down, Tess." Regret burned hot at her cheeks, but Laura's sense of pride burned brighter. "I'm not who he thought I was. I'm just Laura. I'm not sure he ever understood that."

Tess frowned. "What do you mean?"

"Come on." Laura tugged on her hand. "I need to see Monica, even if I can't get my old job back."

They passed through the auditorium and entered the door taking them backstage. The usual hustle and bustle greeted them, and Laura emitted a satisfied sigh. The smells and sights of mingling actors, stagehands, makeup, and scenery filled her senses and sent tiny darts of inexplicable comfort over the surface of her skin. She smiled and waved hello to a dresser who recognized her. God, it felt so good to be back in the theater, no matter how short-lived her stay might well be.

Tess touched her elbow. "Maybe it would be best if I left you and Miss Danes to get reacquainted. She doesn't know me like she does you. She'll wonder what I'm doing there."

"Don't be daft. Monica——"

"Is a wonderful lady, but it wouldn't feel right being in her room without a message. Go on. You go." Tess squeezed Laura's arm. "You go and say hello and, in the meantime, I'll go and see the manager and try to lay some groundwork for getting your job back. Come and find me when you're done, all right?"

Smiling, Laura nodded and laughed when Tess pulled a funny face and hurried away. Inhaling a strengthening breath, Laura pushed on toward Monica's dressing room. She paused outside. Sudden nerves assaulted her. Monica was Adam's friend, not hers. What if Monica had written for her help with the understanding Laura and Adam were still together? What if she had no wish to befriend her now Adam had gone? Laura straightened her spine. All that mattered was her testimony—personal emotion was no longer significant.

She forced her nerves into submission, raised her hand, and knocked.

"Come in." Monica's happy greeting came from the other side of the door.

Laura pushed open the door and stepped inside. "Hello, Monica."

Monica spun around from the full-length mirror where Stephanie was helping her into an enormous bustle. "Oh, my Lord, Laura! It's so good to see you." She opened her arms. "Come."

Relief pushed the breath from Laura's lungs and they embraced. "You look so much better than when I last saw you." Laura smiled over her shoulder. "I'm so happy to see you looking so well."

Monica stepped back, her hand still clasping Laura's. "I feel so liberated. Knowing Baxter is where he belongs has a funny way of putting some color into a girl's cheeks. Now we've just got to make sure he stays there." Stephanie tied the bustle into place and walked to the wardrobe. Monica's eyes softened as she looked at her trusted friend. "Stephanie has been a godsend. I don't know how I would've gotten through the last few weeks without her."

Guilt infused Laura. She and Adam had left so soon after Monica's attack. Maybe they'd made more bad decisions than good when they were together. Love blinded even the most jaded of eyes.

"I'm sorry we left the way we did."

Monica waved her hand. "Don't you dare feel sorry for leaving. I wanted nothing more than for Adam to pursue his dreams." She gave a sheepish grin. "I wanted even more so for the two of you to grasp the opportunity for some romance. God knows we could do with a bit of that around here."

"Maybe."

"What do you mean *maybe*?" Her face fell. "Are you . . . where's Adam?"

Laura slowly pulled her hand from Monica's and stepped back when Stephanie approached carrying a gown of the most precious cream-colored satin. "He's in London as far as I know."

Monica looked from her to Stephanie and back again. "In London?

But why? Why would he not return with you? Doesn't he care Baxter could be freed?"

Stephanie helped Monica into the dress, giving Laura some time to catch the unexpected sob that escaped her. She concentrated on breathing past another stab of loss that jabbed cruelly into her chest. The dress rustled and swished, making conversation impossible, as Stephanie raised it up the length of Monica's body.

Tears pricked Laura's eyes like needles as she looked at her beautiful and unlikely friend. "You look stunning."

Monica stared at her expectantly. "Where's Adam?"

Laura glanced toward the door, considering whether or not to make an escape. "He's—"

"Oh my word. Did he find an investor? When all this nonsense with Baxter is dealt with, you can sort out his house. He'll start earning his own money." Monica's eyes turned bright with undisguised excitement. "Has someone agreed to fund his play? Oh, my God. Produce it?"

Laura's tears broke. She covered her face with her hands. "I'm sorry. It's none of those things, and I've no idea where he is."

The silence that followed pressed down on Laura's chest until she thought she might scream with the need to halt its accusatory power. A sense of heartrending loss built and built, growing heavier and heavier.

"Oh, Laura. Please don't cry. Everything will be all right."

When Monica and Stephanie came forward and embraced her, Laura's tears flowed as they hadn't since the night Adam left. The loss of Bette and Adam—even the feeling of independence she thought she yearned for so much, and now had—pinched and twisted inside her.

They led her to a chair and Laura sat. Their softly spoken protestations and words of comfort came around her in an invisible blanket of female comradeship. So grateful for Monica and Stephanie's support, but missing Bette's even more so, Laura struggled to maintain a semblance of dignity. Lifting her head, she accepted the handkerchief Stephanie pressed into her hand and wiped her face. "I'm so sorry. I thought I could do this. I thought I could come back here, move on, but . . ."

"Tell us what happened." Monica wiped a thumb over her cheek. "Whatever it is, we can mend it. You belong here. The theater is your home. If you will give me the chance, I will prove it to you."

Laura frowned. "What do you mean?"

"Your acting, Laura. It is what you should be doing."

"My acting."

"Yes."

She took a deep breath. "Acting is no longer an option. I just want my old job of selling treats back. If you could help me with that, I'd appreciate it."

Monica shot her a stern look. "Adam first. Then we'll talk about what happens next. What happened in London? Where is he?"

With her last tear spent, Laura pulled back her shoulders and looked Stephanie and then Monica straight in the eye. "I don't know."

"You don't know?"

"No, but I know why he disappeared." She looked at each woman in turn before emitting a sigh. "Mrs. Fleet was one of the nicest madams I've ever met. . . ."

The unfamiliar noises around him told Adam he needed to open his eyes. Drag his heavy lids wide open and face the consequences of his alcoholic binge. He would . . . if his eyelids would only cooperate. *Has someone soldered them shut?*

"Sir?" Soft floral perfume drifted by. "Sir, are you awake? It's time for you to leave."

Mustering every ounce of his depleted energy, Adam finally managed to crack open his eyes to slits. The sight of the woman leaning over him brought them wide open. He scrambled away and upward, banging his shoulder blades against the cushioned headboard.

"Who are you?"

The woman was most likely younger than him by a year or two, but still astoundingly attractive and dressed in some of the finest clothes on the market. She smiled, revealing white and attended teeth.

"I'm Mrs. Fleet, sir. The owner of the house. Your money's run out. It's time for you to leave."

Adam stared. "My money? You mean . . . oh, Christ." He dropped his head back. "This is a whorehouse?"

Her kindly smile vanished and she rose slowly from the bed and wandered to its foot. She curled her lace-mittened hands around the iron footboard. "I'd prefer you didn't speak of my establishment in such a derogatory tone. Especially as you've languished in all it has to offer for the last forty-eight hours."

Nausea rose bitter in his throat. "I have been here for two days? Oh, my God. I have to get out of here."

He whipped back the covers and dragged his naked ass from the bed, heedless to the madam watching. The ache in his head gripped like a vise around his brain, and his stomach quivered with sickness. Two days? He struggled to a bureau where his clothes lay neatly folded. He fought his unsteady legs into his trousers.

"Who laundered my clothes?" He glanced at Mrs. Fleet. "Surely that is not a normal aspect of your service."

She smiled softly. "Not usual, but you paid well, sir. There's only so much sex a brokenhearted man can take. I took the payment and put it to good use with other services while you slept."

Adam stood upright. More money he had wasted. Pride burned hot at his cheeks as his last conversation with Laura came hurtling back to him. "I am not brokenhearted."

She gave a dry laugh. "Oh, sir. There's no shame in coming here to distract you from pining for a girl you can't have. You aren't the first, and you certainly won't be the last. It makes you more a gentleman than the men who choose to vent their anger violently on unsuspecting sisters, friends, and whores."

Adam stared. Could he really sink any lower? A whorehouse. He had never stepped foot inside one before now. "I did not come here pining. I have no idea why I am here." He snatched his jacket from the chair beside him.

"I do."

The knowing tone of her voice tightened his jaw. "How can you?"

"You spoke of a woman named Laura."

He stiffened. "When?"

She smiled. "Many times."

Adam pursed his lips and turned away from her to look for his shoes. It would be advisable just to keep his big mouth shut and get the hell out of there as soon as possible. Did Laura know he was there?

"You asked if she's been here."

He spun around. "I did?"

She strolled to the other side of the bed, her pretty head held high as the skirt of her dress brushed the carpet. Retrieving his shoes from beneath the bed, she held them out to him. "Here."

After a moment's hesitation, Adam marched toward her and grabbed the shoes. He tugged, but she held fast, looking at him intently, all humor gone from her gaze. "Can you remember what one of my girls told you?"

Irritation hummed inside and he yanked on the shoes.

She released them and raised her hands in surrender. "I don't mean to rouse your temper, sir. I think it's important you remember what you were told. Whoever Laura is, she's quite clearly important to you."

"She is." He sat on the bed to put on his shoes. "Too important to discuss here. I was drunk, and it seems I was saying far too much to you or any of the women working here."

"Do you want to know if she's been here or not?"

Adam stilled, his fingers frozen on the laces of his shoes. Did he want to know if it was here Laura had lain with a man for money? Money she felt they needed and he could not provide? Sickness furled in his stomach as he gave a final yank on the laces. He stood and pulled back his shoulders as though bracing for a violent blow.

He quirked an eyebrow in a gesture of nonchalance. "Why not?"

She planted her hands on her hips, her face stern. "If it's the woman I think you were asking after, she came here a few days ago. She was confident on the outside, but her eyes gave her away. I've seen it a hundred times before. She spent the time here for someone she wanted to help . . . maybe even someone she loved."

A barrage of emotions tumbled and twisted inside. Heat pinched at his cheeks, and frustration curled his hands into fists. "She doesn't love me."

She frowned. "Oh?"

His heart kicked painfully. "When I told her I loved her, there was no declaration on her part." He shrugged into his jacket, pride rising up and pushing painfully at his heart. "You are right to some extent. If she was here, she came out of desperation. Desperation brought on by my actions, not hers."

She studied him for a long moment before inhaling a long breath. "So, what happens next? You leave her to the wolves? Let her go it alone to find somewhere else to work?"

"That is none of your business."

She glared. "Any girl who comes here becomes my business whether they like it or not. Now, Mr. Lacey, will you go after her and tell her how you feel and that you acknowledge what it must have taken to do what she did for you? Or will you act like a typical man and pretend it never happened?"

Adam clenched his jaw. How many hours had he wasted here? How would he find Laura now? He was a blind fool to not respect her. To not see her for the proud, self-sufficient woman she was. A woman used to making her own decisions. A woman who had fought and survived far worse challenges than he had ever endured.

"Well?" Mrs. Fleet stared. "Yes or no? Will you go after her?"

His love for Laura surged through him, making Adam tremble with its ferocity. He prayed to God he had not lost the brightest spotlight to ever shine on his life. "I will find her, Mrs. Fleet. Do not worry about that. I will find her and I will do everything I can to convince her to forgive me." Adrenaline overtook the banging in his head and lit a fire deep inside. He made for the door and pulled it open. "I am going to find her and ask her to be my wife. No . . . my life."

She winked and her pretty face lit with a wide smile. "Well, go on, then. What are you waiting for?"

Chapter 25

Laura stood in position as the theater curtain lowered, her heart racing and her hands clammy. Her fifth performance without a single blip or stutter over her lines. She owed everything to Monica and her help in getting her a small part in the play currently showing at Theater Royal. Never in her wildest dreams did she think this day would ever come. She was an actress. An actress with a small but perfect role. If only for a week or two. A short-lived but fantastical dream come true—not dissimilar to her and Adam . . .

Tears threatened. God, to have the curtain lift and see Bette sitting in the front row, her huge smile lighting up the auditorium. Adam lingered, as he always did, at the periphery of Laura's mind and she steadfastly pushed him away. There was little point in dwelling on what could've been when she had a baby to take care of. Her child meant more to her than a lost love ever could.

She forced a smile and cheered along with the rest of the cast as they exited the stage and made for their different dressing rooms. It had been two long weeks since she'd last seen Adam and her heart still ached for him. She'd kept busy with rehearsals and sharing quiet evenings with Monica in her parlor whilst she stayed with her. Yet, the gaping hole in her heart still remained.

The regrets in her life were several, but she'd never regret her time with Adam or the conception of his child. She pressed a hand to her precious cargo as she entered the dressing room she shared with two other actresses. Thankful the room was empty, her mind filled with the options she had open to her once her pregnancy started to show. She'd yet to even tell Monica, for fear she'd disappoint her. How long could she work when the baby would only grow bigger and stronger? Laura smiled. She'd worry about that when the time came.

She ducked behind the screen to change. Purposefully focused, she undressed. Her burgeoning hormones played constant havoc with her determination to forget Adam and accept she would soon be a mother alone with her babe. Not that her solitary state bothered her.

A pull deep in her belly told her the baby disagreed.

Stripped down to her costume chemise, Laura lifted it over her head and turned to the floor-length mirror behind her. She smiled softly to see the beginnings of a soft curve at the base of her belly. It would be barely noticeable to anyone else, but to her it was real and as precious as a million diamonds. Her baby was secure. Her second child had already grown so much further than her first.

The dressing-room door clicked open and Laura snatched her robe from atop the screen. She slipped it on and stepped out, concentrating on tying the sash at her waist.

"How did you do, Katie? Wasn't it fabulous?"

Silence.

"Katie?" She looked up and the breath left her lungs on an audible breath. "Adam."

"Hello, Laura."

Her mouth drained dry as her heart picked up speed. With trembling hands, she gave the sash a final tug and lifted her chin. He would not see her pain—or joy—at seeing him. She swallowed. "You're back."

"I am." His gaze bored into hers.

The moment stretched.

He stood in the same spot and made no move toward her, his set expression telling her nothing of why he was there or what he wanted to say. For want of something to do, she swept to her dressing table and sat, grateful for the support beneath her. Two weeks. He'd been gone two weeks, but to see him again, to see his handsome face and dark brown eyes, gripped the loss of him tighter around her heart.

Her hand trembled as she reached for a cloth and cream. She dipped the cloth into the substance. "How are you?"

His footsteps faded as he strolled to the door. Laura's heart pounded. Was he leaving? Her body screamed with the urge to stand

and run after him. She stared into the mirror at his reflection. The sound of the key turning as he locked them alone inside the room brought a rush of relief from her open mouth.

Snatching her eyes from his turned back, she lifted the cloth to her cheek and slowly swept at her makeup. Never before had she been so conscious of another human being. She sensed his approach and every nerve in her body tingled with heightened awareness. He stopped directly behind her.

The cloth slipped from her hand. She met his eyes in the mirror; they were dark, his jaw set. "I could not find you, Laura. I scoured the streets. I looked through and around London like a madman. . . . I thought I would lose my mind."

She stiffened. "I lost mine when you walked out on me, Adam. I've never felt so alone."

"I am so sorry. I could not think. I could not breathe when you told me what you did. . . . what you felt you had to do." He shook his head and squeezed his eyes shut. "I have missed you so much."

She flicked out her tongue to wet her lips. "I missed you too."

His gaze left hers and ran over her hair, then lower to her neck and shoulders. "I made the biggest mistake of my life by leaving you the way I did." He ran his finger gently over the exposed curve of her neck and she shivered involuntarily. "I was so afraid I would never see you again."

The deep and sincere growl of his voice lifted the hair at her crown, and traitorous longing heated her skin. She closed her eyes, trying to regain her equilibrium. She had to know what this meant. Was he back? What about London? The theater? She opened her eyes and forced herself to straighten her spine against the desire weakening her body.

"I did what I did, Adam. I don't regret it." She swallowed against the painful lump stuck fast in her throat. "Nothing's changed. I can't let you take care of me."

"Do you love me?"

Her heart stuttered and she gripped the side of her seat. "What does it matter? We are who we are, and we're too different."

"Answer the question." It was a raw, masculine demand.

She held his gaze, tears burning. "Yes."

The silent tension hummed between them and she counted the seconds, waiting for him to walk to the door a second time. Who was to say he hadn't confessed his love to her in London as a way of cutting her stupid heart after what he deemed to be her infidelity?

His voice sliced the silence. "Would you stand? Please."

She stared at the stiff set of his features, lower to the tense plane of his shoulders, drawn in a perfect line across the base of his neck. "Nothing's ch—"

"*I have* changed. Please. Will you stand and face me? I need to see you. I need to look straight into your eyes."

Inhaling a long and shaky breath, she released her grip on her seat and stood. Slowly, with as much dignity as she could muster, she turned and stood directly in front of him.

His gaze focused on her mouth as he spoke. "I love you. I love you more than I have ever loved anything or anyone." He lifted his eyes to hers. "If you can find it in your heart to forgive me for walking away from you, I promise I will love you for the rest of your life." He smiled, a glint of the old Adam, the man she loved, sparked devilishly in his eyes. "Even if you are an independent and maddening woman at times."

She fought the smile that tugged at her lips. "I'm not sure that will ever change."

"I do not care."

Hope burned in her stomach and mixed with the fear of losing him a second time. "You have to be certain. I can't . . . I won't go through the last two weeks again. Not ever."

He closed his eyes. "I was wrong. I made a mistake. Please, Laura. I cannot live without you." His eyes snapped open. "You are my everything."

Her heart twisted and her resistance broke. "I love you, Adam. I love you so much."

The power of her admission teamed with the strength of her surrender, pushed every ounce of regret, loneliness, and pessimism from her body. She felt lighter and happier than ever before.

He inched closer and dipped his head, his lips meeting hers. The passion and heat she had tampered down and ignored for the previous two weeks rose up and enveloped her soul in forgiveness.

Their mouths took and their tongues tangled in a ferocious battle of ownership, love, and fear.

He tugged her robe open, revealing her naked breasts to the cool air of the room. She gasped when he roughly gripped her bosom, pain and pleasure ripping through her senses, leaving her wide open to his desires.

She grappled with his jacket, sliding it over his shoulders and releasing it. It fell to the floor behind him. Her fingers clawed with desperation at the buttons on his shirt. His mouth left hers to feed over her neck, lower to her collarbone, sucking and nipping her sensitized skin until desire tugged high between her legs.

At last, his chest was bare and she scored her fingers over his heated flesh, and relished the hard and truly masculine power of his chest and iron-hard stomach muscles.

"Adam." His name whispered from her lips.

He dropped lower and lifted her breast to tease and suck at her nipple. Tremors flicked through her core like they only ever had with him. Calling to him. Begging him to caress her there, to bring her to the blessed liberty of an orgasm given in love and trust.

She reached for his trousers and felt the hardness of his desire through the material. With her robe pooled at her feet, his fingers slid over her waist and hip, ever closer to the place she longed for him to explore. She snapped open his trouser buttons and grappled the material over his hips and down the length of his muscled thighs.

She gripped his penis and massaged him as he massaged her. Sensations built and rolled through every inch of her body, escalating her want of him.

"I have to have you, Laura." He growled against her ear. "Now."

Backward they stumbled until the wall against her back stopped them. Her breaths came in harried desperation as he continued to massage her into a frenzy of lust.

"Adam, please. Please. Now."

Bang, bang.

A dual knock at the door.

They froze. Suspended in time. Breaths slowing to audible rasps, bodies slicked with perspiration, and hearts beating fast.

"Miss Robinson?"

Victor.

Heat rushed to her face. Neither she nor Adam removed their hands from each other's most intimate place.

"Yes?" Her voice sounded relatively calm despite the way her heart thundered.

"Is Mr. Lacey with you?" She snapped her gaze to Adam and slowly they released the other. "Yes."

"Ah, good." He rattled the doorknob.

Silence.

Laura looked at Adam. His eyes danced with amusement and he wiggled his eyebrows. She brought her hand to her mouth in an effort to stem the bubble of laughter threatening to erupt.

Victor cleared his throat. "Well, when you've finished . . . whatever it is you're doing, I'd like to see both of you in my office."

Laura grimaced, her eyes still locked on Adam's. "Of course."

"And, Adam?" Victor's voice drifted from the other side of the door.

Adam's smile vanished with comic rapidity. "Yes?"

Laura sniggered and dropped her head to his chest.

"That play of yours? You were right. Miss Robinson can act and act well." The soft shuffle of Victor's retreating footsteps receded to silence.

Slowly, half-numbed with shock, Laura lifted her head. "My God, does he mean to—"

Adam grinned. "Indeed, he does, my love. I think we've just found a director for my play."

He brought his mouth down on hers and gripped her waist. The baby. She couldn't be in his play. Not now. Not ever. Second by second, her body re-ignited and she pulled him closer. Now. She had to tell him now. His fingers drifted across her belly . . . and he froze.

He pulled back.

Her heart beat almost out of her chest; heat rose like a flame to her cheeks. Laura swallowed. *He knows.* She held his questioning stare—a stare tinged with pleasure, yet clear in its apprehension.

She swallowed. "It's yours, Adam. You have to believe me."

Tears glazed his eyes. "You are pregnant?"

She nodded. "Since the very first time we made love."

"But that was months ago. Why didn't you—"

"I wasn't sure and then you left before I could explain."

A tear slipped over his lower lid. "Oh, my God."

Sickness rolled in her stomach. "You do believe it's yours? I wouldn't—"

"A baby." He pulled her to him and kissed her hard. "A baby. My baby. Our baby."

Laughing, Laura snuggled against him and took unprecedented joy in the feel of a man holding her up and making her feel she'd never have to face anything alone ever again.

CPSIA information can be obtained at www.ICGtesting.com
Printed in the USA
BVOW04s0231250614

357284BV00001B/14/P